THE TRAP

"In this terrifying and inventive adventure, Fukuda turns the vampire novel inside out . . . With an exciting premise fuelled by an underlying paranoia, fear of discovery, and social claustrophobia, this thriller lives up to its potential while laying groundwork for future books." *Publishers Weekly*

"A fresh take on the vampire story . . . a cracking read, very grisly and compelling." *The Bookseller*

"Bona-fide creepy." *Booklist*

"Readers will devour this book, be greedy for more and scared to put it down. This is one for all the people who said vampire novels were overdone and unoriginal. That may have been true, but now there is THE HUNT." *Bookbabblers*

"From page one, Fukuda draws the reader into a fast-paced, suspenseful narrative of suspicious coincidences, unanswered questions, and building action . . . In addition to fans of vampire fiction, this book will appeal to readers who enjoy survivalist stories, action and adventure." *Voya*

"Fast-paced . . . quick and suspenseful . . . Fukuda creates a character in terrifying danger and draws his readers along for the ride." *Bookbitz*

"The sheer terror of the goings on will have you hooked to the very last page." *Flipside*

"THE HUNT was an excellent dystopian novel and a fantastic read that I Cannot. Stop. Thinking. About. I dare you to immerse yourself in the world of THE HUNT, where no one is safe and there's everything to play for." *Narratively Speaking*

"A really fresh take on the genre." *Bart's Bookshelf*

"I was on tenterhooks, page after page, fearing the worst ..." *Bookzone for Boys*

"The book ends with a cliffhanger that left me craving a sequel, eager to discover more about this strange and unsettling new world." *The Irish Times*

"Excellent YA dystopian of a grim future . . . great characters, great plot." *Booksmonthly.co.uk*

"THE HUNT is undeniably enjoyable, due to breathless setpieces and an intriguingly amoral tone." *SFX*

"A compelling new thriller." *Bliss*

"I was hooked from the start, and I kept reading well into the night to finish this. All the way up to the ending, this book was fast-paced and wonderfully written, and then it went out with a bang!" *Books of Amber*

"For too long vampires have been the pop stars of the literary world, bright, beautiful and desirable. With THE HUNT, Andrew Fukuda takes them back to their bloody roots as hungry, monstrous beings." *Teen Librarian*

Also by Andrew Fukuda

The Hunt
The Prey

THE TRAP

ANDREW FUKUDA

SIMON AND SCHUSTER

First published in the USA in 2013 by St Martin's Press,
175 Fifth Avenue, New York, NY 10010.

First published in Great Britain in 2013 by Simon and Schuster UK Ltd.
A CBS COMPANY

This paperback edition published 2014

Simon & Schuster UK Ltd
1st Floor
222 Gray's Inn Road
London
WC1X 8HB

This book is a work of fiction. Names, characters,
places and incidents are either the product of the author's imagination
or are used fictitiously. Any resemblance to actual people living or dead,
events or locales is entirely coincidental.

A CIP catalogue record for this book
is available from the British Library.

PB ISBN: 978-0-85707-548-2
E-BOOK ISBN: 978-0-85707-549-9

1 3 5 7 9 10 8 6 4 2

Printed and bound by CPI Group (UK) Ltd, Croydon CR0 4YY.

www.simonandschuster.co.uk
www.simonandschuster.com.au

For Jim and Mike

Our torments also may, in length of time,
Become our elements, these piercing fires
As soft as now severe . . .

—John Milton, *Paradise Lost*

One

THE TRAIN ARRIVES in the dead of day.
The sun, perched high in the sky, scorches the desert a blinding white. Only the black filament of the train's moving shadow taints this baked wasteland. The train slows, its line of cars rattling like the links of a metal chain dragged. None of the occupants on the train—and there are many, and they are tense, and they are standing with taut backs and frightened eyes—make a sound.

A tiny black dot circles high in the blue sky. It is a hawk, gazing curiously at the rippling shadow of the train beneath. The hawk squawks in surprise as the train suddenly dips into an opening in the ground. Like a snake, swiftly into a hole, disappearing. Gone as if it were never even there.

About ten miles away, on the other side of a range of low-slung hills, lies a gigantic disc-shaped building spanning several city blocks. It lies silent as a tombstone, circled almost completely by a thin rampart. A tall, slim obelisk rises from the building's dead center. The windowed tip of this obelisk glimmers brightly under the sun like a lit candle. The obelisk is otherwise, as with the entire building, the color of the desert. Nothing moves on, in, or around the building. Not at this time of day.

The hawk observes this building with a steely, unblinking stare. Then, with a sudden squawk, it flaps its wings and flies away.

Two

WE PLUNGE INTO the tunnel. Its opening gapes wide like a diseased mouth that eagerly swallows us whole. Our world of stark white and cobalt skies, in a sudden blink of an eye, is erased with pure black. A hot wind, dank and moist as a tongue, hurls through the bars of our caged car, gusts through our clothes and hair, our clenched hands, our crouched, shaking bodies.

Under us, sparks of light shoot out from the shrieking, braking wheels of the train. As one, we're flung forward onto the metal mesh floor. Fear hums off our piled bodies in droves. A small hand, clammy with fear, clutches mine. "Not the Palace, not the Palace, not the . . ." she murmurs. One of the younger girls.

Yesterday, after Sissy and I recovered from the turning (the hellish fever broken, our discombobulated bodies knit back together), we told the girls what we suspected about our destination. Not the Civilization, the idyllic city they'd been told by the Mission elders was filled with millions of *humans* populating its streets and filling its stadiums and theaters and parks and restaurants and cafés and schools and amusement parks.

But the Palace. Where the Ruler reigns. Where, it is said, the only humans are those imprisoned in the catacombs like cattle in pens. Their individual fates hostage to the whims of the Ruler's voracious appetite.

For a few minutes, the train drifts along the tunnel before lurching to a stop. Nobody moves, as if motion alone will cause the next unwanted chain of events to begin.

"Everyone stay still," Sissy whispers next to me. "Stay very, very still." For three days and nights on the rattling train, exposed to wind and sunlight, motion has been our constant companion. This stillness, this blackness, it is a world too suddenly and starkly reversed.

A loud metallic click rings from the train car door. And for the first time in days, the door begins to slide open. The girls nearest to it, screaming, recoil from the opening.

But I leap toward the door, grab hold of one of the bars. I lean back, digging in my heels, and attempt to halt its progress. I sense somebody else next to me, also pulling back on the door. It's Sissy. For days, we've tried, futilely, to pry it open. But now, in this dark tunnel that can only portend one thing, we're trying to close it. But again our efforts are futile. Even as we grunt, our feet scrabbling for position, the door slides open, clicks into place. In the darkness, I hear similar clicks clacking along the length of the train. The doors of each train car are now opened and locked into place.

A wave of cold fear washes over us. Nobody moves.

"What now?" a trembling voice asks from the darkness.

"Nobody move!" Sissy shouts, loud enough to be heard down the length of the train. "Everyone stay where you are!" I feel the strands of her hair brushing against my arm. She's swiveling her head, trying to get a visual on something, anything. But we see nothing. We might as well be hanging suspended in a black void. And that's why Sissy warned us not to disembark. We might be stepping off into a steep slope or even a sheer drop.

A loud hiss suddenly explodes from the front car, jolting all of us. A pungent odor of steam and smoke spreads down the tunnel, drifting through the bars of the cars like sodden ash.

And then, only silence.

We huddle closer together, anticipating the sound none of us want to hear.

"David," Sissy says. "Toss out one of the cans of food." He does. In the darkness, we hear the can land with a metallic rattle against a floor of some kind. It bounces twice before rolling to a stop.

"Everyone stay on the train!" Sissy shouts. "Gene and I are going out to investigate." Then she drops through the opening and onto the dark floor of the tunnel. I follow her. The ground is pebbly, it rattles under our feet. My eyes are getting used to the darkness, and when I look back at the train I can see the girls. The whites of their eyes gleaming slightly, hoping for assurance. But we have none to give them.

"Do you see anything?" Epap whispers. "Sissy?"

"Hold on."

But he doesn't. He drops out of the train car, clattering pebbles as he lands. He approaches us, arms spread in front. "Only one thing to do, Sissy. Head back the way we came. All of us, we follow the train tracks back outside."

But Sissy shakes her head. "The entrance to the tunnel must have closed after us. Otherwise light would be pouring in; we'd be able to see more in here." She's right. There's not even a distant dot of light behind us.

Epap speaks, his voice fraught with fear. "Doesn't matter. We need to start moving. Any moment now, duskers might—"

A loud metallic clang suddenly crashes overhead. Everyone jolts. A few girls scream out.

And then there is light.

Three

THE LIGHT STREAMS out from a large glass shaft that rises from floor to ceiling near the last train car. I take a closer look: the soft light emanates not so much from the shaft itself as from a glass elevator now descending inside the shaft. Like a falling curtain of light, the elevator illuminates the craggy walls of the tight tunnel. The single elevated platform, seemingly hewn out of the same rock, stretches along only one side of the train, and it is up onto this platform that Sissy, Epap, and I now hoist ourselves. We pause, then turn to the sound of footsteps running toward us. It's David, and his hand slides into Sissy's.

The glass elevator reaches the bottom. For a brief moment, its internal light flickers. Then the doors slide open.

Nobody moves. A crackling sound suddenly fills the air, like static over the school PA system. *"Attention. Any passenger on the train must enter the elevator. You have one minute."* The earsplittingly loud voice—electronic and robotic—blares through the tunnel, its words echoing down its length.

David turns to Sissy. "What happens after one minute?" he asks, his voice trembling. "What happens, Sissy?"

She doesn't answer, only swivels her head, her eyes nervously scanning the walls. She tenses. There is a row of doors set into the far wall. Her eyes flick back to the elevator, narrowing.

Through the bars of the train cars, the girls' eyes are wide with fear and panic. As one, they start exiting their train cars, first a trickle, then a flood of bodies pouring out.

"Fifty seconds."

Sissy grabs David's hand. "This way," she says to Epap and me. "C'mon, hurry." We start running toward the elevator glowing with white light.

The girls are stumbling on the pebbles of the tunnel floor. In their haste, and with their lotus feet, they fall and topple over one another. They are crying out now, their fear reaching breaking point.

"To the elevator!" I shout to them, swinging my arms urgently. "Hurry, everyone!" Epap breaks away from us, races to the edge of the platform, starts pulling up a few girls. But there are too many of them and too little time. I grab him, try to push him toward the elevator. He resists.

"There's no time, Epap!" I shout.

"Forty seconds."

Epap's jawline ridges out. He lifts up one more girl, then lets me pull him away. The girls on the platform are doing their best to run, but their lotus feet can only plod along so fast. Sissy, Epap, David, and I are the first to reach the elevator.

"Thirty seconds."

For a brief moment, we can only stare into the elevator's interior. Our hearts sink. It's tiny inside, able to accommodate five at the most if we squeeze tight. It was never meant to transport a whole *village* of girls. We tumble inside. There's nothing. No button, no control, no switch. The walls are smooth unbroken panes of glass. I quickly examine the outside. Same thing: no controls at all.

"Twenty seconds."

Sissy's forehead is scrunched into deep grooves of concentration. Then they smooth out, decision reached. "There's still room for one more!" she shouts. "You all stay here; I'll be right back!" And then she runs off and disappears into the darkness.

"No, Sissy!" I shout. "There's no time!"

Out of nowhere, a girl suddenly stumbles out of the darkness. It's Cassie, the girl with freckles who's proven to be a leader among the girls. Epap shouts at her, urging her to hurry. She throws herself headlong into the elevator, her mouth distorted in a silent scream. And that's it. There's no more room inside. We're shoulder to shoulder.

"Ten seconds."

"Sissy!" I scream. "Sissy, get back here!"

No response. No sight of her. More girls are blundering toward the spread of light now, falling, shuffling, yelling. Then I see Sissy. She's at the platform, bent over, trying to help more girls up. But in their panic, they're grasping, clutching at her, and though she's yelling at them, they're refusing to let go. Five, six, seven of them are grabbing at her arms, her legs, and Sissy can't extricate herself. She's in trouble.

"Five seconds."

I'm sprinting out for Sissy, knocking over a few of the girls on the platform. Behind me, Epap is shouting at David, ordering him to stay put. I seize Sissy's shoulder, pull backward. But there are too many girls clinging to her.

An electronic series of pings sounds from the row of doors on the far wall. Even from where we stand, on the other end of the platform, the sound jars us. Whatever is going to happen next, it's starting. Now. For the briefest of moments the girls' hold on Sissy grows slack as they turn to the sound. I quickly slink my arms under Sissy's armpits and heave backward. I feel the snap of grips broken, and then we're crashing onto the platform floor.

On the other end of the platform, the metal doors slam open. Black shadows pour out with frightening speed. Glistening fangs, gleaming claws. Wet, wild, desirous eyes. They move in a swift blur of movement. The girls nearest to the doors are killed before they can even scream. All I hear is the wet splat of fluid against walls draped in darkness. More shadows glide out of the opened doors, swim across the walls and floor. Then the screaming starts.

Now it's Sissy pulling me up by the back of my shirt. Before I've even found my footing, she's dragging me to the elevator. The screams sharpen and rise behind us, but we know better than to turn and look. We run around clumps of girls panic-plodding toward the elevator, their faces frozen in the garish elevator light.

"Sissy! Gene!" Epap shouts. *"It's closing!"* He's standing in the doorway of the elevator, his back against one sliding door, his arms and legs pushing against the other. But it's a losing battle. His arms are crooking and folding with the pressure of the closing doors. Inside, David is searching frantically for a control switch I already know does not exist.

The screams reach fever pitch. Knowing better, I glance back. In the wide cone of light, I see girls pouring out of the train cars in blind panic now, stumbling and falling to the ground. A few are frozen in place, cowering in the corners of the train cars, arms wrapped tightly around one another, their hands white-knuckled on the bars.

Meters from the elevator, Sissy dives first, sliding between the closing doors and into the elevator. I follow a second later, banging my shin and scraping my back as I slide under Epap through the narrowing gap. Epap, screaming with pain, can't extricate himself; he's too tightly bunched into a fetal position, his ankles pressed up almost against his head. Sissy, off the floor, wraps her arms around his legs even as I grab hold of his shoulders. We give each other a quick nod, then lunge backward. Epap pops inward, ankles and wrists twisting in ungainly angles.

The elevator doors slam shut.

Outside, girls smack against the elevator like birds into windows. Their hands slap against the glass with staccato panic. Their faces smush against the glass, pleading, begging, distorting as they're pressed flat.

"We have to do something," David whimpers. "We can't just leave them."

But we say nothing. Because there's nothing we can do. There's no way to open the doors, no way to squeeze in one more person even if we could. More girls smack against the glass on two sides, then all around, encircling us. Cassie squeezes her fingers into the gap between the closed doors in an effort to pry them open. We don't bother stopping her. Soon enough, she gives up. She places her palms against the glass, head shaking, crying softly to herself. More bodies press up against the glass, flattening those already there.

And then the elevator starts moving. Slowly up the glass shaft.

A cry of panic sounds.

Epap puts his arm around Cassie. "You can't do anything for them. You tried—" His voice stops.

I see the duskers. To my surprisie, despite the mass bloodshed and cacophony in the tunnel, it's only a handful of them. I'd expected more. Their faces are blood splashed, eyes delirious with this unexpected arrival of culinary paradise. Judging from their drab uniforms, these duskers are nothing more than low-rank crew consigned to work the graveyard daytime shift. They came only to unload the train. Now they'll have a tale to tell for the ages. But it's not over for them. Not yet. Shielding their eyes against the light streaming from the elevator, they bound toward the girls pressing against the glass shaft.

"Close your eyes, David," Sissy says, and he does, burrowing his head into the crook of her arm. Vicious thumps rock the elevator, signifying the duskers' arrival. Screams erupt around us, screeching, pleading, seemingly loud enough to crack the glass. David cups his ears with shaky, pale hands.

The elevator rises. Blood splatters on the outside of the shaft like buckets splashing their contents. No matter how high we rise, the blood follows us, the screams surge up at us. Epap puts his arm around Cassie's quaking shoulders.

Until all is silent. Blood flicks up like the dotted splatters of a paintbrush. Spread beneath us, on the platform, inside the train cars, is the specter of gruesome atrocities. The elevator rises and the arc of light thankfully withdraws from the scene of violence beneath. Darkness blankets the carnage below.

A dusker leaps up at the elevator, its pale body slapping stickily onto the outside of the glass shaft. Its face, only inches from mine, regards us coolly. Then its hold, compromised by the slick blood, slips, and the dusker slides down.

We stare up, praying for an exit. The black ceiling looms ever closer. And only when it seems like we are going to bump up against it does it suddenly slide open to expose an even darker blackness. The elevator ascends into it. And once again, we are swallowed by darkness.

Four

NOTHING HAPPENS FOR five minutes.
Long enough for the air inside the sealed elevator to grow stale. And
for claustrophobia to set in.

"What happens next?" Cassie whimpers. "What should we do?"

Nobody answers.

Then we start moving, sideways, a slow trundle that quickly picks
up speed. We must be on some kind of track, but it's hard to tell in
the darkness. We come to a stop again, then start moving, in a different direction this time. The elevator dips and turns, the constant
changes in directions and speeds disorienting. After a couple of minutes, we suddenly stop.

We wait with bated breath.

Searing light floods our vision. We clamp our eyes shut, then
almost immediately pry them back open, desperate to see. The elevator sits in the center of an enclosed space, large as an auditorium.
Tracks coil around us in a tangle of crisscrossing and encircling
loops.

David starts kicking at the door in panic.

"Don't," Sissy says softly, her hand on his shoulder. "It's not
helping."

We wait for five minutes. Breathing shallowly, trying to conserve the diminishing air.

"Sissy," David murmurs. "I can't breathe."

"Try to stay calm," she says. "There's air enough for all of us." She brushes his hair back, slick with sweat.

"We're going to die in here," he says.

"No, we're not. Sissy's right," I say. "We just need to stay calm. The light is meant to annihilate duskers, not humans. Any dusker somehow able to steal into this elevator would be dead by now."

David turns quiet, his expression pensive.

"We can be hopeful," I say. "There wouldn't be all this light to kill duskers here unless there are humans at the end of this ride."

David puts his hand on the elevator door. "How much longer until we start moving again?"

"Any time now—"

The lights blink out. Just like that, we're submerged in darkness. The elevator starts moving again, picking up speed, descending.

And then we're slowing down. A thin vertical line of light suddenly pierces through the darkness, widening into a column as we draw closer to it. And finally we're right up against this light, then merging into it, blinded by its brilliance, the brightness flooding the interior of the elevator. A series of loud electronic beeps jolts us. The elevator doors suddenly open. And just as quickly, they begin to close.

"Hurry!" Sissy says, pushing us all through the brightly lit opening. We tumble out of the elevator, falling to the ground.

It's the smell that hits us first. A stench of unwashed hair, ripe armpits, the effulgence of raw sewage. A fluorescent ceiling light glares down on us.

The elevator door clicks shut behind us.

Silhouettes emerge out of the brightness in front of us, bony and angular. Their voices are male and young.

"There are *five* of them!"

"No way. Not five. There's no way—"

"Count them yourself!"

"We've never had more than three at a time!"

"—doesn't make sense—"

I stumble toward the voices, the silhouettes.

"Look at this one," a young, boyish voice sounds from the dark. "Kind of old, don't you think? Must be almost twenty. Positively ancient."

I blink, coaxing vision into my eyes. Faces merge into view, young and uncouth, sneering. "Where are we?" I demand.

"Where are we?" A rough, caustic voice, mimicking. The group of boys starts walking away.

"Wait," Epap says.

They ignore him, keep shuffling down the corridor.

Epap grabs the nearest one by the shoulder. "Where are we?"

The boy regards Epap coldly, then whirls his arms around dramatically. A smile touches his lips, but his eyes remain icy. "This is the *Civilization*! Where all your precious dreams come true!" The smile twists into a sneer as he turns to a group of boys standing nearby. "That's what they always ask. *Is this the Civilization?* Without fail. *Please*."

The boys break out in cruel, mocking laughter.

"Brother?" says Cassie.

And just like that, the laughter stops. One of the taller boys steps forward. He's all bones and sharp angles. His cheekbones jut out.

"Is that you?" she asks. "Matthew, is that really you?"

His lips tremble. "Cassie?" The name comes out hoarse, as if long unspoken.

The other boys move away. Quickly, as if they know what's going to happen next and want no part of it.

Cassie takes a tentative step toward Matthew. Her eyes are shaking in their sockets, glistening over. "You're so tall now." She reaches up, is about to touch his face, then withdraws her hand. "And skinny. How long has it been? Since you were . . . sent here?"

"One year." Softer and with sadness, he continues. "Three months, twenty-three days."

"Where's Timmy?"

His eyes cast downward.

Cassie's lips wobble as tears pool in her eyes.

Matthew rubs her arm. "Come with me. I'll get you some clothes to change into." He looks at the rest of us. Maybe it's the change in light, but a softness touches his face. "Bring your friends, too."

Five

 I T IS A world of metal and garish light. With only narrow, low-ceilinged corridors to maneuver within. Every corridor we walk down is identical to the previous: metal and light, metal and light. On each side of us, recessed into the walls, are enclaves, rows of them stacked three high in perfect alignment and spaced apart with mathematical precision. Each is the size of a large coffin, steel plated and embedded deep into the wall.

But it's the other humans we gape at the most.

They mill around aimlessly, or gather in small groups of three or four. All young, mostly boys. Pale, gaunt, emaciated, often staring off vacantly at the walls. They blink as we pass, gazing back at us with neither hostility nor warm hospitality. Just mild curiosity bordering on indifference, as if the arrival of newcomers is commonplace. Occasionally, Cassie would gasp with surprise, her face paling at the sight of yet another familiar face from the past. But none call out to her or acknowledge her. They only avert their stares quickly.

Matthew leads us to the end of one corridor. Inside an enclave are stacks of clothing. All the same drab garb worn by everyone else, brown and bland, mildewy. I slip into the clothes quickly and approach Matthew as the girls get dressed.

"My name's Gene."

He regards me with narrow eyes.

I point to the boys. "And that's Epap—"

"No names," Matthew says curtly.

"What?"

"We don't have names down here."

"But you're named Matthew."

He shakes his head. "That's . . . from before." He purses his lips. "Listen, we just don't do names here."

"Why not? You all—"

"We all disappear. Inevitably and suddenly. So there's no sense in giving names. No sense in forming bonds." He turns his back to me, starts walking away.

I take his elbow. Gently, but with insistence, I stop him. He flinches but does not snatch his arm away. "They take you for food, don't they?" I say, remembering what Krugman had told me about this place. "Randomly, you never know when you might get taken."

Matthew doesn't say anything, but he gives the slightest nod.

"Tell me how," I whisper. "How do they take you?"

He resists at first. Only after the girls join us, Cassie standing closest to him, does he speak, mechanically, with only the slightest tremble in his voice.

About once a week (at least they think it is a week; there is no way to measure the passage of days and nights in these underground catacombs), an alarm goes off. You have one minute, he tells us, to climb into one of the enclaves in the wall. Only one person per unit. Then a glass window will snap down, sealing you inside. That is a good thing. Because it protects you. The lights go out—the only time they ever do—and the darkness is morbid and terrifying. And then *they* come down into the catacombs to gawk at the hepers. The Ruler and his retinue. Up and down the corridors, looking and staring, drooling and shaking. The Ruler will inevitably point to a particular heper. If it's you, you're as good as dead. Because within the next hour your enclave will be retracted into the walls, then

17

whisked away on some transportation system. From bed to coffin, just like that.

"To where?" David asks.

Matthew's lips stretch into a sad, horrific smile. "The kitchen."

"You know this for sure?"

The smile droops. "No. Some think you end up in the Ruler's private chambers. But nobody's ever come back to say, so it's all conjecture." He spits on the ground. "Empty, useless conjecture. 'Cause you're dead, either way."

Cassie speaks, her voice strained and tense. "Girls are taken first, right, Matthew?" She gazes down the corridor. "Because girls are the choicest of morsels. That's why there are so few here. We're the first to get chosen."

Matthew doesn't reply for a moment. "Not necessarily," he says, but his voice lacks conviction. "The Ruler likes to spread out the girls. Save them for special occasions. You might not get selected for a while." He says all this with his eyes staring down at his feet.

We're quiet for a minute.

"Just make sure," Matthew says, "when the siren sounds you get into one of these enclaves. Immediately. Drop whatever you're doing. The glass separations will come down sixty seconds later whether you're ready or not. If you're not, you'll be stuck out in the corridors. Completely unprotected and vulnerable. And when *they* come down . . ."

"What happens?" Cassie asks.

Matthew pauses. "That's when the rest of us roll toward the wall, shut our eyes, clamp hands over our ears."

We stare down the brightly lit corridor at the rows of recessed enclaves on each side. Arms and legs dangle out from a few.

"And this siren," I say. "You said it goes off about once a week."

He nods. "Thereabouts. You guys are lucky. The siren just went off yesterday, so you're safe for a few days yet."

David sits down halfway into one of the enclaves, his face drained of color. "It never ends, does it?" he says quietly. A flash of anger crosses his face. "We should have listened to Gene. We should have headed east when we had the chance. Going back to the Mission was naïve and stupid. And what did it accomplish? The whole village was wiped out anyway. We did nothing. Even the girls who escaped with us by train—they're now dead. So we saved Cassie. So what? We lost Jacob, and probably Ben, to save one girl?"

"David!" Sissy says. "Stop."

"No, it's true," he says, his eyes glistening with tears. "We wouldn't be here if we'd only listened to Gene." He looks up at Sissy. "We'd be free, all six of us, journeying east. Not stuck in this place. Not sitting here like food on a platter ready to be served up for *their* consumption." His lips tremble, and as he closes his eyes two tears slide down his cheek.

Sissy sits next to him, puts her arm around his shoulders. She doesn't say anything. Because David is right, and she knows this.

"I'm sorry," he says. "I shouldn't have said that."

"We'll find a way out of here," Sissy says. She nudges his face. "Hey, chin up. We're survivors, remember? We'll find a way out of here."

He doesn't answer, only stares at the steel floor.

I look at Matthew. "You've been here over a year now. Tell me the weak spots. We can find a way out of here."

Matthew opens his mouth to say something, stops. His face ripples with ambiguous emotion.

"Can we backtrack our way to the train?" I say. "Down the elevator, back to the platform? Not now, of course, but later when the station is empty?" An idea lights in my mind. "Then we could all board it, trigger the train controls, set the train in motion, escape out of here?"

"That might work," Epap says, catching on, his excitement growing. "Back to the Mission. It'll be safe. The duskers there would have been destroyed by the sun days ago. Then we could set off on foot eastward. Yeah, that really might work." He looks excitedly at Matthew. "Is that possible?"

All Matthew does is stare back. And then he starts giggling with a shrill laugh, his body jiggling up and down like it's the funniest thing he's ever heard. The sound of his laughter sends chills down my back. And still laughing, he walks away, leaving us to stare and wonder. And then to realize.

There is no escape.

Six

FOR THE NEXT hour we're left to explore on our own. But it's all the same dreary, monotonous repetition: brightly lit narrow corridors, glaring light reflecting off the floor and walls. Only the recessed, shadowed enclaves offer a break from this garish sameness. The boys in the catacombs, their eyes vacant and dark, stare ghoulishly at us, but when we meet their gaze they flick their eyes away. They walk away from our questions, ignore our greetings.

We discover two large spaces—both about the size of a large lecture hall—at opposite points of the catacombs. One space is the dining room, although that's too fancy a term. It is really little more than a feeding area for animals. Troughs run from one end of the room to the other, filled with slop-like porridge. The boys (and a sprinkling of girls) mill into the room, and eat quickly with their hands, cupping the food into their mouths. Another trough is filled with water, and it is there we head first. The water is brackish and lukewarm, with a metallic tinge to it. Other boys—giving us little more than a curious look—slip in and out of the dining hall, spending only about a minute at most. I realize this is how they dine: in small doses and quickly, only enough to quell hunger pangs.

Nauseating as that realization is, nothing prepares my stomach for what awaits in the other large room. We smell it long before we reach it. It's the communal restroom, but again, that's too grandiose a term. It's really just an open cesspool of raw sewage. We stand at the cusp, none of us daring to go in.

A young boy walks out, shows only faint surprise on seeing us. "Don't urinate or defecate anywhere but here. We don't have many rules down here, but this is one of the few ironclad regulations. Do your business in here and nowhere else. Or else." He walks away, hitching up his pants.

Eventually, we'll have to walk in, bear with the smells and sights inside. But not now. We walk away, the stink of sewage following us down this empty corridor. Farther away, where the smell fades (it never entirely dissipates), we gather around one of the recessed enclaves.

"This is bad," David says. "What are we going to do, Sissy?"

Sissy doesn't answer. She examines the top edge of the enclave, pokes her finger into a thin groove. "I feel glass. This is where the glass door comes down." After a second, she climbs into the enclave itself, starts banging on the back wall. A hollow echo sounds back. She bites her lower lip, deep in thought.

"What is it?" Epap asks.

"It's empty space behind this wall. Remember what Matthew told us? There's a whole transportation grid back there. Probably a network of tracks or rails to shuttle these enclaves back and forth." She climbs back out with a look of disgust. "Feels like a coffin in there."

We slump against the walls, preferring to sit on the floor rather than inside the enclaves. Although we've been in the catacombs for only about an hour, I already feel the fingers of claustrophobia entombing me. The bright light unrelenting, the smells unbearable, the air morose and bleak. We will, eventually, have to eat the slop from the trough, use the bathroom. Fall into a routine like everyone else here. And eventually, the alarm will sound and we will join the

22

mad rush to find an empty enclave. This same dreary existence, repeated in indistinguishable cycles until, inevitably, one day, enclosed within an enclave, we will be shuttled away. Into their kitchen, into the Ruler's Suite, into his mouth, passing in half-digested chunks through his organs.

An unwanted thought flits through my head, one that catches me by surprise: life in the Mission, governed by Krugman and his predecessors, now seems in comparison not so unconscionable. I shudder at the thought.

A determination sets in my bones. I look at Sissy and David and Epap. "We're going to get out of here."

"How?" David asks.

"I don't know. But one thing I do know: we'll escape or die trying. Because I'm not going to . . . simply waste away in this horrid place." I put my hand on David's, pat it hard. "I promise you, David. We're not going to become like these people here. Because their existence . . . it's not living. It's not even surviving. It's . . ." I shake my head. "It's not for me. It's not for us. I think I speak for all of us: I'd rather be dead tomorrow than alive for a year in here."

Sissy's eyes, withdrawn for the past hour, spark. I place my other hand over hers, and she grips it back tightly.

"Matthew told us the siren went off yesterday. That gives us six days to find a way out of here. Six days. That's plenty of time. And we'll spend every minute of that time examining every nook and cranny of this place. We use all our wiles and cunning and smarts. We'll find a way out."

"But Matthew said—" David starts to say.

"Matthew isn't us. Matthew hasn't survived a mass Heper Hunt, hasn't escaped a horde of thousands. We have. Matthew hasn't survived a journey down the Nede River, a plummet down a waterfall. We have. Matthew hasn't survived swarms of duskers in the mountains. Matthew didn't just survive mass carnage in the station below." I grip Sissy's hand tighter, grab David's arm tightly now.

"But we have. We are awesome together. We are formidable. I really believe that. There's something about the four of us together. The duskers—thousands of them, armies of them, armadas of them—have *never* defeated us. At the dome, on the riverbanks, in the mountains. Not once. We've stared them down each and every time."

Next to me, Epap is nodding. "Gene's right. We'll leave nothing unturned in this place. And we stay together over the next six days. Let's not separate at all."

The smallest smile breaks across David's face. "Okay."

"Then let's do this," I say. "Let's start exploring and studying the structure, talk to people. Because I have a feeling that six days is going to fly by—"

And that's when I'm cut off.

By the sound of a siren.

Seven

FOR A FEW seconds, we're frozen in place. We're not the only ones; everyone around us is stunned. Then mayhem ensues. Bodies running, jostling. Bumping, knocking against one another. David is elbowed to the ground.

I grab a young boy flying past me. "What's going on?" I yell, my voice barely audible over the blaring siren.

He pulls his arm away. "What do you think?" he shouts.

"The siren went off yesterday! We've got six more days!"

But he doesn't reply, only sprints down the corridor, head frantically swiveling from side to side, looking for a vacant enclave.

I climb into the nearest one. Crouched in the back is a terrified boy. He suddenly delivers a violent kick to my head.

"What the hell!"

"Get out!" he yells.

"There's plenty of room for two, even three of us!"

"Only one to an enclave. Otherwise the enclave is automatically taken! Now get out!"

I feel a hand on my back, tugging me out. It's Epap. "C'mon, if he's right, we've got to move. We've got to find an empty enclave for each of us." He stares down at Cassie, at her lotus feet. "You take this enclave!" he shouts, directing her to an empty enclave on the bottom row. "Don't let anyone pull you out," he says as she dives in. "Kick and punch if you have to!"

She nods frantically, pressing against the back wall.

And then we're sprinting down the corridor, the four of us. Bodies are flying everywhere, in opposite directions, colliding, bumping, cursing. It's obvious that the siren has caught everyone by surprise and out of position.

Screams, shouts. Boys aggressively fighting over empty enclaves. Blood spilling, the cracks of noses fracturing, eyes blackening. We run past these scuffles, knowing better than to waste time. Here and there, we sprint past a girl staggering on her lotus feet, tears streaming down, lips quivering in terror.

Seconds pass, ten, twenty, thirty. Fewer and fewer people are running along the corridors. Mostly smaller boys, those pushed out or pulled out by older, stronger boys, their eyes darting from side to side in growing distress. Ahead of us, a burly boy pulls out a skinny girl from an enclave, subduing her with a vicious kick to the rib cage. She doesn't even try to regain the enclave but takes off down the corridor in search of an unoccupied space, as fast as her plodding lotus feet carry her, anyway. She leaps into an enclave, and seconds later a skinny, tiny boy is kicked out. He sprints off, doubled over with pain, fighting back tears.

We turn a bend, race down another stretch. There. An empty enclave on the top row. We grab David, order him in there. When he protests—and he does so vehemently—Epap grabs him by the scruff of his neck, barks something at him, then roughly shoves him farther inside. And then we're sprinting again, trying to find another unoccupied spot. I glance back, see David's face pop out from the opening, his expression full of fear.

By now, the corridor is empty of stragglers. It's just the three of us. Whenever I glance into a passing enclave, a scowling, terrified face stares back, arms and legs ready to ward off any attempt to supplant.

The lights start to blink quickly. On, off, on, off; then faster, *on-*

off-on-off. We stop, panic stalling us. The lights strobe manically, in rhythm with our frantically beating hearts.

"They're all occupied!" Epap shouts, sweat pouring down his face. "There's nowhere to go!"

We need to go where there's less people! are the words in my mind, but before I verbalize them I'm grabbing Sissy and Epap, pulling them roughly. Back the way we came. Back toward the smell of raw sewage.

They don't question me, only match me stride for stride. We break into a panic-fueled, mad sprint. We turn around a bend, gun down yet another corridor, force our legs to pound faster. The smell of sewage grows more pungent.

"You look left!" I shout at Sissy and Epap without breaking stride. "I'll look right!"

And almost immediately I see an empty enclave. Epap is closest to me and I grab him by the shoulders and, before he has a chance to react, throw him roughly into it. He shouts in protest, then crashes against the metal sides of the enclave.

I don't stop, only continue to sprint faster, Sissy next to me, neither of us bothering to even glance back. We're too far away now—Epap has no choice but to stay where he is.

And then, just as we reach the end of one corridor and start bounding down another, the siren stops screeching. It's quiet. I hear only blood rushing in my ears and the rapid thumping of my heart.

A loud series of electronic beeps suddenly sounds from every enclave. From the top edge of each unit, a glass window starts to descend. The enclaves are about to be sealed off.

"C'mon!" Sissy shouts, pulling me by the arms.

The glass windows continue to fall, teasingly slow.

Then Sissy is grabbing me by the neck and thrusting me into an enclave on the bottom row. It's empty. But I catch myself before I tumble in. Spinning and dropping to the ground on my back, I hurl her over me. She goes flying into the enclave with a shout of surprise. Her hand shoots out, grabs me by the wrist.

"Get in!" she shouts.

"No!" I yell, trying to pull away from her. But her grip is tight as a steel trap. "Only one per enclave!"

"Never mind! *Get in!*"

I kick at her forearm with enough strength to break her wrist. I hear a cry of pain; then her grip loosens just enough. I fall backward with the unexpected release, and tumble across the corridor. My back smacks against glass on the adjacent wall. I feel it grate against my back as it descends.

I spin around. With barely a second to spare, I throw my body under the falling glass. I'm only just able to slide my body through the narrowing gap before it completely seals me in. I roll around, expecting to feel a kick or punch. But wonder of wonders, the enclave is empty. Trapped inside now, my chest heaves up and down with exhaustion, my breath condensing on the glass. As if with a will of their own, my arms and legs flap against the sides and back of the enclave, banging hollowly on metal, adrenaline still racing through my system. The ceiling looms right above my head, like the lid of a coffin. Too close, too near, too suffocating.

Across the corridor, Sissy is gazing at me, her head turned to the side, breathing hard. She lifts her arm, places her hand flat against the glass, whitening her palm. I do the same. For a moment, our eyes lock. *We made it, we made it.*

And then the lights go out, and everything goes dark and black.

Eight

THEY COME AN hour later, gray phantoms gliding in the brine of darkness. Mercuric light spills out of their flashlights, giving them optimal vision. The dozen or so duskers stand before each enclave, shining their flashlights on the occupant before moving on.

Turn around.

Let us see your face.

When they reach Sissy's enclave and peer inside, they perk up. I see the sudden infusion of energy in their silhouettes, a perky enlivening. Even from behind the glass wall, I can hear the cracking of their necks. Judging from their regal, highly decorated uniforms, these men must be the highest echelon of the Palace.

Then they turn around, walk toward my enclave. Their faces are orbs of sickly paleness.

Turn around.

Let us see your face.

Fingernails rap on the glass, insistently. *Tap tap tap.* I reluctantly lift my head to them.

They stare at me without speaking, and recognition flows into their eyes. For I know what I am to them: the heper boy who lived his whole life in their midst, who pulled the wool over their eyes by brazenly masquerading as one of them for almost two decades. The very one who then escaped from right under their noses during the Heper Hunt.

One face floats out of the darkness until it is almost pressed up against the glass. It is the Ruler. He's smaller and more diminutive than his carefully crafted public image. Saliva drools from the corners of his mouth, twin lines that converge at his chin before dripping down in a glutinous ooze. His tongue snakes out, licks his thin lower lip.

Another face emerges. A man. I've seen him before. Not too long ago, in fact, but I can't quite place him. He's burly and tall, with mountain-range shoulders, so different from the other observers with their oversized uniforms and twig-thin arms. His eyes stare hard at me, circled by a pair of rimless round glasses.

The Ruler whispers to his retinue. A second later, they glide away as one. They apparently have no further need to inspect other enclaves. They've found what they were looking for.

I stare across the corridor, trying to locate Sissy in the darkness. I see nothing.

"Sissy! Can you hear me?" I press my ear against the glass. I hear her muted, faraway response but can't make out a single word. I yell back, but her reply is again muffled. Eventually, we both give up, resigning ourselves to our isolation.

Three minutes later I jolt up, banging my head on the enclave ceiling. I remember the broad-shouldered man. I'd bumped into him at the Heper Institute only a few weeks ago, the night before the start of the Heper Hunt. During the Gala. The man had cornered me in an otherwise empty restroom at the Heper Institute. He had asked me questions about the Heper Hunt, made a few odd suggestions regarding it, and I'd dismissed him as a paparazzi hack. But then he told me—and I remember his exact words—something odd as he exited: *Things are not as they appear.*

A skein of fear shoots through me, cocooned inside a metal coffin, deep in the darkness of the earth. What is that man doing here? Who is he?

Things are not as they appear.

And I suddenly recall something else he'd uttered as he exited the restroom, words spoken with an almost flippant casualness but which now echo off the walls of the metal enclave. Cryptic words about Ashley June.

You need to watch out. She's not who you think she is.

Nine

ASHLEY JUNE

ASHLEY JUNE PILLAGED the village all night. For the first hour, it was sheer delirium: a rampage through heper-ladled streets, a frenzied romp of a hunt with hundreds of other duskers. The hepers—almost all girls—tried to flee, but their strides were oddly plodding and ungraceful. The duskers picked them off as easily as dandelions in a field. Some heper girls tried to hide, just as futilely, under beds and inside wardrobes. They were eaten right where they cowered in an explosion of splintering wood. For hours, the snap of jaws and the rattle of teeth cracked the night skies. Afterward, when there were no more hepers to eat, the duskers licked up dots of blood splattered on walls, wooden floors, the cobblestone paths.

They ran their tongues over the village like a ravenous pack of wolves licking a bone clean.

Still, the night was not without its disappointments. A large number of hepers slipped through their clutches, escaping on a train. More than a few dozen duskers made a dash for that runaway train, ramming through the bottleneck at the bridge, and managed to cling on to the ribbed cages of the train. The smarter ones U-turned, headed right back into the heper village. They knew the train was picking up speed and that the hepers were, in any case, unreachable behind impenetrable steel bars. There were more hepers in the village ripe for the picking.

Afterward, the duskers' bodies sated, their tongues licking blood-stained lips, they dozed upside down from street lamps and roof-tops. Or they ranged toward the fortress wall, drinking from whisky bottles discovered in the dining hall, where narrow slit windows served as near-perfect, almost custom-made sleepholds. They stared into the night sky, and their bloated, engorged bodies quivered with satisfaction. They knew for a fact that no matter how many years lay ahead of them, they had experienced the apex of their lives. Nothing could ever top this. Perhaps that is why they were so careless—they had nothing ahead of them anymore. Filled and sa-tiated, they drifted into a deep, bottomless sleep, forgetful that they were outside, that they were facing east.

But Ashley June did not sleep. She was haunted by her encoun-ter with Gene. She had hoped to meet him in the mountains, but in her most honest moments she had suspected him dead already. A victim at the hands and fangs of a hunter, or perhaps of the Nede River. And yet there he was, standing in the middle of an empty street in the village square. As if by mutual arrangement, a midnight tryst.

She had felt two emotions. Most keen was an urge to protect him, to shield, to embrace. She approached him slowly, and how her lungs wanted to scream out. She had expected, with the turning, some dilution or diminishment in her feelings for him. But they rumbled deep as ever, amplifying along her jaw and collarbone and spine.

But she felt something else, too. She wanted to devour him. To taste his flesh on her tongue, the warmth of his blood filling her, his body broken down and digested and fused seamlessly with hers, merging with her muscles and bones and eyes and hair and mole-cules and atoms. To feel him saturate her as he passed through her and, in passing into death, into her very being.

The inherent conflict between these two feelings overwhelmed her, stopping her in her tracks. Until a third feeling plowed right through her, dismantling everything. Jealousy. She saw the girl standing next to Gene and noted all too easily the intimate, natural bond between them. Jealousy raged in Ashley June, springing her into action. She found a target and it was not Gene.

Ashley June sucked down the girl's blood. Virginal and hot and pure, it flowed down Ashley June's throat like lava. For a short spell, she forgot Gene. But only for a few seconds. Another hunter moved in, eyeing him. A surge of protectiveness swept over Ashley June, and she made quick work of the interloper. But then Gene was gone. She chased after him as he fled down the meadows, toward the train station. She ran not to hunt but to protect him. She raced to the front of the pack, broadsided many hunters, sent them tumbling away. But there were too many and she was quickly overwhelmed.

But Gene got away. She saw him crouched inside the train as the distance stretched between them. And then the train was across the bridge, gaining speed. But no matter. She stared at the train tracks disappearing into the folds of the mountain. They would lead her to him. She would find him again.

Resolve energized her, rendering sleep impossible. While everyone else—after every heper had been devoured, every spot of blood licked up, every bone chewed and sucked on—fell into a sedated slumber, she roamed the streets, the buildings, the fortress wall. The night was hers alone. She was a solitary pale dot moving under a canopy of a billion stars.

Stars. She remembered the night (it was not so long ago, yet how far away it seemed) when it was her with whom he held hands, the skin of their palms touching. They lay (so bizarre a body contortion to her now) on the rooftop of the Heper Institute under the sprinkling of those bright, celestial dots, unaffected by the moon's full brightness. The muted sounds of the Gala beneath them lifted harmlessly into the night. Gene had whispered to her, and a weird slip of laughter escaped his lips as she scratched her wrists.

Gene was careless that way, less disciplined than her. Or was it *because his heperness was more native than hers, a life force that could be tamped down only with vigilant, deliberate effort? Either way, it was she who succumbed first, and that fact still surprised her.*

Through the hours of the night, she roamed alone the streets of the village. She walked aimlessly, but at one point she caught a scent. Only a whiff, but it froze her.

It smelled of Gene.

Not quite. Even with the scent so faint, she knew immediately it was a few degrees off. The way the scent of family members could be so similar yet slightly different along the edges. Between siblings. Mothers and daughters. Fathers and sons.

She followed the wispy trail, losing it when a breeze blew. She waited; she was patient—she had time. And after the breeze died, she found the scent again. The frailest tendril. It led her away from the center of the village and toward an outcast building that sat alone at the lip of the forest. The building resembled a cinder block for its lack of windows and aesthetics. She stood before the closed door, sniffing. The door, like the building itself, had been spared from violence. No heper had taken refuge in this outcast building during the night, and so no hunter had pillaged and gutted the inside.

It was a laboratory. The almost-Gene scent bloomed thicker inside, months of accumulated smells. They pulsed off test tubes and vials and flasks and goggles, off the workbench tops and stools and the hammock in the corner. She closed her eyes in concentration, her nostrils flaring. The almost-Gene scent had the pungency of someone related to Gene, older, male. Gene's father, perhaps?

Since turning, her enhanced olfactory senses never ceased to amaze her; but she was about to be marveled all the more. Because this scent—it now ruptured a distant memory. She had smelled this odor long ago, when she was only a child, when she was a heper, when she wasn't even conscious of smelling it, much less storing it in her memory. The scent had burrowed into the irretrievable depths of her brain and only now, with her empowered sense of smell, did she recall it.

This almost-*Gene smell was the smell of the doctor.*

The one who had performed that awful surgery on her a decade ago. Her body tensed at the memory.

She moved away from the workbenches and ambled toward the back of the laboratory. In the farthest corner, the almost-*Gene odor dropped off and she was about to turn around when she sniffed something curious. Actually, it wasn't the smell itself that was unusual—it was the same* almost-*Gene smell—so much as its place-ment. It was coming from the floor. She sniffed. No, it was coming from* under *the floor.*

She cocked her head, stared down.

A second later, she was ramming her arm through the floor-boards. Her fingers touched the metal top of a small trunk. She tore out a few more floorboards and lifted the trunk out.

She ripped open the lid. There were stacks of paper inside. An-cient papers, musty, yellowed, and frayed at the edges, they har-kened back to an era not decades but centuries ago.

It was not the content of these papers that immediately drew her attention—the ancient typeface was utterly indecipherable. In-stead, her eyes lit on the insignia of the crescent moon in the top corner of each sheet:

There were other papers, as well, modern and crisp with relative newness, covered in the almost-*Gene scent. She flipped through them, glancing at the handwritten notes. These were apparent tran-*

*scriptions of the ancient documents. She read hurriedly at first, think-
ing there would be little to hold her interest. But soon she was
taking in every sentence, swallowing every word. Blinking at the
truth they revealed. A half hour later, she had read enough. To understand. Everything.*

*She took out a sheet of paper, a crumpled letter, from her pocket.
She'd been carrying it for many nights since finding it in the
Pit, and she now placed it next to the handwritten notes. It was
the same handwriting.*

She felt nothing but a deep pity for Gene.

*She gazed through the opened doorway to the outside. The black
of night was shading gray now as it had done millions of times before. But it felt as if the world, the universe, had irretrievably changed.*

*Sunrise caught everyone by surprise. Dawn light radiated into
the streets, breaching the walls like a flood of acid. Many never woke
at all—their inebriated bodies melted without so much as a twitch
and their liquefied flesh dribbled between the stones of the fortress
wall and into the dewed grass of the meadows. Others awoke screaming and scrambled into nearby cottages, seeking a refuge that was to
be—like the remainder of their lives—short-lived. Within minutes,
the strengthening sunlight slipped into the interior of the cottages
through windows, smashed doors, breaks in the walls. It was a slow,
agonizing disintegration for those inside, and some soon preferred
the quicker death of full-on sunlight exposure. They ran outside into
the onslaught of sun rays, dashing along streets and racing down
meadows, as far and as fast as their disintegrating legs could take
them. Those who had not melted away by the time they reached the
ledge of the cliff threw themselves dramatically into the ravine and
were seen no more.*

*Only Ashley June, ensconced safely in the darkness of the labo-
ratory, survived. When dusk finally arrived, she opened the tightly
sealed laboratory door and walked out. She found the village
empty, its streets polka-dotted with yellow crusty stains, like vomit
baked into the ground. She did not stop to genuflect or to mourn,*

nor did she even step around the crusty puddles. She walked right through them, the soles of her feet stepping on the sticky, slightly crunchy texture of what was once teeth and eyes and skin and bones.

She was crossing the bridge when she stopped. The train tracks would indubitably be the straightest path to Gene's destination, but they were also the riskiest. The mountain foliage would initially offer her partial reprieve from the sun, but once the terrain leveled out and the tracks fell across the spare barren desert of the Vast she'd be fully, and fatally, exposed.

No, she would use a different route. For she'd already figured out the train's destination. It had to be the Ruler's Palace. Rumor had long circulated of a secret stash of hepers kept in underground pens, a rumor now corroborated by what she'd read in the laboratory. She would head to the Palace via a circuitous but safer route: return to the caves beneath the mountain, then backtrack along the Nede River the way she'd come. Several of the sun-proofed dome boats were docked at various points along the river with mechanical issues, and if she timed it right she could run at night and find shelter in these boats during the daytime. And in so doing, skipping like a rock across the surface of a river, she would make it back to the metropolis. And from there, to the Palace.

To Gene.

Wherever he was, she would journey there. No matter how far, how many miles and suns and days stood in her way, she would find him. And if she could not go to him, she would somehow lure him to her. For she had something to tell him: a truth that was both a curse and a miracle, the truth of the crimson moons.

Ten

F EAR SPILLS OUT of each enclave, collectively clotting the catacomb corridors. Matthew told us somebody is always taken after the sirens, and I can feel the hundreds of bodies on edge. A terrified pause, as if everyone is holding their breath in their hot and dark enclaves. How long before one of us is taken? Minutes? Hours?

Time passes unseen, unfelt, unknown. It feels like hours, but it might be mere minutes. It might be whole days.

A light suddenly shines. From across the corridor. It is bright, spilling into, then fracturing my blackened space.

It is coming from Sissy's enclave. From *only* her enclave.

Too bright. I see only a firestorm of brilliant white light, a dark shape swimming in it. Sissy, trapped within. She swings around, her arms cutting through the shafts of light.

Her enclave starts to vibrate ever so minutely. Now my eyes are adjusting to the brightness. Her limbs, pressed against the walls, are racked with fear and tension. Panic ripples across her face. On her back, she spins around, then pistons her legs out, pounding her feet against the glass, slamming it harder and harder. But she makes not a dent, not a crack, not even a sound.

She shouts, but her muffled voice is swallowed up by harsh,

metallic clanks. And then her enclave starts to shift and move. She slides over to the glass wall, her hands splayed against it, eyes swinging wildly, trying to see.

She's trying to locate me, needing to see me. Our eyes meet for just a second.

And then the wall behind her opens up, and her whole enclave starts to retract into the wall. Into the dark void behind.

I scream out her name. Throw myself against the glass. I won't let her go. I can't let her go. I'm done with desertion. I will never do to another what I did to Ashley June. As long as there is breath left in me, I will never abandon Sissy. Ever.

She starts hitting the glass over and over, but the impact is silent and useless. She is pulled farther into the darkness behind the wall, getting smaller and smaller, until she is recessed so far back, I can see tracks now exposed under her diminishing enclave. One last time our eyes meet, and I try to stare comfort into her eyes. And then the back wall slides down into place and she is gone as if swallowed whole. Only a gutted recess exists where her enclave had been only moments ago. The faint vibrations in the walls come to an end, the metal clanking ceases, and all I can hear is her name being shouted over and over, and only after a minute do I realize it is me who is shouting, the syllables of her name cutting and grating against my throat.

Eleven

Hours later, it's my turn. The enclave is suddenly seared with blinding white light. The metal-plated walls about me grow warm as the enclave starts to vibrate gently. As if coming to life. None of this comes as a surprise. I lie still, eyes closed and heart racing, not resisting or attempting to escape. Trying to stay calm.

In fact, this is what I want. What I have been hoping for since Sissy was taken away. I only wish it could have happened hours ago, that wherever they took Sissy I could have joined her sooner. Even if it is in the Palace kitchen.

Something latches into place under the enclave, and then the whole coffin-like structure starts to shake, rattling slightly as if on a conveyor belt. My breathing grows faster despite my resolve to stay calm. I flick my eyes open. I'm being pulled into the wall, am now past it, swallowed into a wide-open void of darkness. I draw a sharp breath as my stomach knots.

Fear, until now tamped down, starts to boil over. I lash against the sides of the enclave, but the walls remain sturdy as ever. The gap in the wall through which I've just been pulled narrows into a slit. It closes, sealing me in a completely different universe.

The enclave lurches over rises and dips, and for a few harrowing seconds I'm actually upside down. Then I'm tossed to the bottom of the enclave, spun dizzyingly around as the enclave careens through the darkness. And as I'm pummeled from side to side, disoriented in the darkness, I now know fully what I've been trying to deny. I'm no longer in control. I'm at their mercy. A scream rips out of my throat.

Twelve

THE ENCLAVE TRUNDLES to a stop. For several minutes, nothing happens. Then a crack forms in the darkness above, a razor-thin slice of gray light. Not bright, but my eyes—too long in the darkness—blink in surprise. Then I'm suddenly being lifted up toward the widening crack of light.

Silver light bathes me and I force my eyelids open despite the sharp jab of pain. Dark silhouettes of thin, long-limbed figures hover over me. Their ovoid heads almost touch as they peer down at me. They don't speak, only stare. I catch my own reflection in the pairs of shades they have donned on their faces. I look so small. So frightened. Their shadows glide over me like dark clouds erasing my reflected image.

A hiss. Then the glass wall begins to pull away. Fresh air pours into the enclave, and it is a sweet clarity that fills my lungs, clears my head. I shudder in the relief of it.

Whispery words, quiet and detached. Then they touch me. They push aside my arms, hands pressing against my chest, fingers poking between my ribs. Then they're hoisting me out of the enclave. Cool air splashes against my skin, chilling me. I try to stand, but my legs are jellified. I collapse to the metallic floor. Immediately I start crawling away from these men, my legs scrabbling over the slippery tiled floor.

They don't stop me, don't utter a word to me. They only pace beside me, their feet mincing along with unnerving calm beside my frantic, crawling body. I bump up against the wall, spin around. The men—three of them, reedy and swaying slightly as if blown by a breeze—surround me. Their pale skin glows with a sour-milk complexion.

White cubicle curtains hang from tracks on the ceiling, sectioning us off from whatever lies on the other side. I squirm up into a sitting position. In the far corner stands someone tall, broad shouldered, his face blurry.

"Do not be afraid," the man immediately in front of me says. Cold, detached, clinical.

"We mean you no harm."

"You're safe now," the third man says. His thin upper lip slips up his row of teeth, exposing a pair of sharp incisors.

Instantly I'm leaping to my feet, my fist connecting with his soft, effeminate cheek. The man collapses to the ground, offering as much resistance as a daffodil. But the other two are on me in an instant, their speed compensating for their lack of strength.

One of the men is holding a hypodermic needle.

I smack it away. It shatters, its contents—a dark-green fluid—splattering on the wall. I need to escape through the part in the curtains, but before I can get my legs in motion I feel a sharp prick on the side of my neck. I grab the nearest man by the scruff of his neck, push him against the wall. His shades smack into the wall, crack into two, and fall to the floor.

I feel something dangling from my neck. I reach for it, pull it out. Another hypodermic needle, the syringe fully depressed, a dark-green droplet hanging off the tip of the needle. The man squirms, trying to escape.

"Where's Sissy?" I shout, pressing him against the wall, keeping his fangs away from me. "The girl! What have you done with her?"

Face smushed against the wall, the man shakes his head vigorously from side to side, stammering.

"Take me to her!" I shout, my words slurred and thick.

The man begins to turn. He has found a surge of strength, his arms now able to break out of my hold. A wave of dizziness hits me. The man extricates himself from my grip, faces me. The room tilts, canting at a harsh angle. My legs wobble with sudden weakness. Leering, he shoves me, causing me to stumble and almost completely lose my balance. My vision swims. He hasn't gotten stronger; I've gotten weaker. Whatever he injected into me, it is working quickly and powerfully.

Then a set of hands clamps down on me from behind. "Do not resist." This voice is masculine, authoritative. His grip on my shoulders is strong and assured. I turn around, realize it is the man who just a moment ago was standing in the corner. My legs fail me, and I start falling. He catches me, lowers me to the ground. "We are not *them*. Do not resist. We are not them." He speaks these words softly now, with tenderness.

"Father?" I murmur.

But it is not. It is the burly man I'd seen in the catacombs an hour ago, the one who'd spoken to me in the restroom weeks ago. He looks exactly the same as he did back at the Heper Institute, even wearing the same prissy pair of glasses. Except now he's dressed not in a tight-fitting tuxedo but in the regal attire of the highly ranked.

"Do not be afraid," he says gently. "Nothing is as it seems."

And then I fade out.

Thirteen

G<small>ENE!</small>"

I fling my mind upward trying to break through a dome of sedated darkness. The room tilts and spins; it takes a second before everything stills.

I'm in the same sectioned-off cubicle as before. I recognize the same curtains, even see the faint splotch of green on the wall where the hypodermic needle had shattered earlier. I'm in a bed. My ankles and wrists cuffed to the metal bed rails flanking me. How much time has passed it's impossible to tell.

"Gene, wake up!" It's Sissy, right next to me.

The restraints prevent me from sitting up completely. But Sissy's cot is pushed up against mine, at an acute angle, the head corners touching. Her fingers reach out for mine through the bars of the railings. I maneuver my hand until my fingers are intertwined with hers.

That's when I notice. A thin plastic tube is inserted into the crooks of our arms. The tubes lead into transfusion bags hanging on each side of our beds. They're filled with blood. Our blood.

"How did you—"

"These cots have wheels on them. I was on the other side of that curtain in another area also sectioned off by curtains. It took me some time, but I was able to swing-push it over. Inch by inch." Sweat beads dot her wan face. She looks exhausted.

"They're draining you of your blood. We've got to get these tubes off."

She shakes her head. "I tried earlier. It sets off an alarm. They came storming in within minutes. Don't do it. Not yet. We need to talk."

"Are you okay?"

Her fingers clasp mine tighter. "I think so. Do you think David and Epap are okay?"

"They're fine," I say, even though I don't really know. I try to raise my head, but it feels bloated and heavy. "Who were those men?"

"They're human. That much is obvious. Else we'd be eaten by now." A bead of sweat glides down her face. She wants to wipe at it but can't; her cuffs clang loudly against the railing. "They know everything about us, Gene. They know we're the Origin. And they're going to keep drawing our blood for who knows how long."

"How many of them are there?"

"I think there's only four of them. They call themselves the Originators. They've been working undercover here for years. One of them, the leader, is pretty high ranking, I think."

"We need to reason with them, Sissy. If they're really one of us, we need to tell them we can escape from here. Us, the kids in the catacombs, and them, the Originators. We can take the train back to the Mission, then head east from there."

She shakes her head. "What do you think I've been trying to do for hours? But they wouldn't listen."

"Why not? Did you tell them—"

"I told them *everything*, Gene. Detail by detail. I left out nothing. I spoke of your father, his instructions, the hang gliders, the Nede River, everything. They just nodded and stared blankly at me. And continued to draw blood. When I raised my voice and got combative, they . . . shot me with another injection."

I pull on the restraints, but they feel, in my vanquished state, even sturdier than before.

"You need to know something, Gene." She turns to me. "When I was telling them everything about the past, the history of the duskers, there were a few things that didn't add up."

"Like what?"

Her jaw clenches in frustration. "I don't know. If I wasn't so exhausted and hungry all the time, if I wasn't thrown into weirder and weirder environments before I can gather myself, maybe I could put my finger on it. But my head's spinning, Gene. I can't collect my thoughts for even a minute."

Sissy's suspicion echoes my own. Even back on the train when we were fleeing the Mission, similar questions had troubled me. "What do you think is going on here?"

She pauses. "I don't know." Her eyes focus on mine. "But I'm not about to simply lie here while David and Epap are still in the catacombs." She curls to her side and with her teeth rips out the tube from one arm, then the other.

Two Originators charge in less than a minute later. They rush to Sissy's side without speaking, attempt to reattach the needles into her arms.

"Stop moving your arms," one says in a stern, clinical voice. They try to pin her arms down, but, even restrained, she's able to break out of the grip of their spindly arms.

The men stare blankly at her. One of them goes to a phone on the wall. "We need you," he says. Then he hangs up.

He rejoins the other. They stand solemnly at the feet of our beds, waiting in silence.

A minute later, we hear the door open, then locked. I instantly recognize the broad-shouldered man as he pushes through a part in the curtains. He does not look particularly upset or in a rush. More bemused, almost apologetic. He's since put on a velvet frock coat decorated with Palace regalia. Judging from the number of crests and badges, Sissy's right. He's highly ranked.

"What's the matter?" he begins to ask, then sees the ripped-out transfusion cords. "Oh. Oh, I see." He strokes his left eyebrow with his right thumb, once, twice.

"Obviously," he says, "by now you realize we're your friends. We're on the same side."

I tug at the restraints, making them clang nosily. "You have a pretty low bar for friendship."

The men scratch their wrists. "He has a sense of humor, this one," one of them says, monotone and deadpan.

"Where are David and Epap?" Sissy demands.

The highly ranked man ignores Sissy's question and places his hand on my shin. I try to pull away, but the restraints prevent movement. He strokes my leg, his palm sickly smooth and cold to the touch. Like chilled plastic. "Seventeen years you lived among them, yet how quickly you revert to heper ways. You've let your leg hair grow out. Stubs and prickles of hair everywhere," he whispers with naked disdain. "On your arms, in your armpits, even a stubble on your face."

The other men, fascinated and disgusted in equal parts, also touch my leg with their fingertips, probing, rubbing the short stubs of leg hair, trailing their fingers down my ankle.

"Stop touching me."

Their fingers pause. They look at their leader. He nods, and they remove their hands. He regards me for a long time.

"Do you remember the first time we spoke?" he says. "Back in the Heper Institute, in the restroom?" His hands move to the bag of blood on the side of my bed. He expertly seals the bag, careful not to spill a drop, and hands the bloated bag to one of the men. "It was the eve of the Heper Hunt. I was, if you recall, giving you invaluable advice. To let the Heper Hunt take its course, then use the FLUNS on the other hunters. But you were too smart for your own good, weren't you?" He titters. "That would have made things *so* much easier."

He moves over to Sissy's bed, checks her bag. "And yet, despite it all, here you are. Both of you. Both halves of the Origin, safely tucked away in the Palace. That's just one example of your father's genius. Even when things fall apart, it all somehow seems to work out in the end."

At the mention of my father, everything in the room seems to still. Everything except my heart, beating fasting now, harder.

"He was the mastermind behind it all, you know. Our leader." The man glances at me, scratches his wrist. "I can see by your obscenely readable face that you don't believe me. Well, doesn't surprise me. You thought your father only a janitor. But he was so much more. Obviously, he had to keep you in the dark out of concern for your safety."

I turn my eyes to the floor. I suspected, but never fully knew, the passions hidden in the maze of my father's heart. Not for the first time in the last few weeks, I wonder if I ever really knew him at all. "Tell me about him," I whisper. "Tell me everything you know."

The man studies me with unnerving concentration. He sees the urgency in my eyes, senses my need to know, and draws out the silence. Clearly, he is enjoying this. "There's a lot to know. And we have a lot of time. Later—"

"No," I say. "Now."

The man stares back, rakes deep scratches into his wrist. "Very well. To show that we truly are on the same side, that we are comrades in arms, I'll tell you what you want to know. In bite-size portions for now." He places his hand on the bed railing. "Your father and I grew up together. Up there in the mountains. The Mission was our home, the only home we'd ever known."

His eyes roam across my face. "You look so much like him when he was younger. Your studied gaze, your thoughtful eyes. But I doubt you're nearly as smart. The kid was a genius. While the rest of us were romping around the mountains, he preferred his textbooks. He was constantly studying into the wee hours of the night. By the time he was—why, probably your age—he'd come to believe that a cure for the duskers was possible."

"The Origin," I say.

He nods, examines his fingernails. "Fast-forward a couple of major setbacks and not a few frustrating years and your father was ready to lead a team into the metropolis. To collect samples of dusker fluid, gallons of it, and bring it back to the Mission. It was crucial for his research and experiments. But it was a dangerous operation. Didn't think he'd get even a single volunteer. As it turned out, he had to turn away dozens. He had that way with people."

I nod. So far everything is consistent with what Krugman had told us.

"How large was the team?" Sissy asks.

"About thirty of us. Made up of mostly young men hardy—or foolhardy—enough for the dangerous mission. Women wanted to go, of course, but it was too risky for most of them. The operation was supposed to take anywhere between a fortnight and a month, and menstrual bleeding was going to be an issue. Imagine having your period in the middle of the metropolis populated by millions of them."

"But my mother went," I say.

He nods. "Along with five other women. They were all in the early stages of pregnancy—two, maybe three months along. That was the one condition. You had to be pregnant, but not *too* pregnant, if you know what I mean."

"My mother," I whisper. "She was pregnant with me then."

For the first time his eyes soften. "She was. They'd recently married, your father and her, and he didn't want her to go. But she insisted and . . . well, she got her way."

"And my mother, too," Sissy says. "She was part of this group?"

He nods.

"What happened next?" Sissy asks.

"The operation was a total catastrophe. We were so naive and idealistic! We had no idea of the dangers. Everything fell apart, and quickly. Many of us perished that first awful night. Those who survived—we hunkered down, afraid to come out even in the daytime.

That first week, we were just trying to find a way to escape the metropolis and return to the Mission."

His voice quivers slightly, the first time his monotone voice has shown a hint of emotion. He grabs the railing tighter. When he speaks again, he's regained control.

"And perhaps we may have escaped. But it was your father who galvanized us. He warned us that fleeing back to the mountains would lead the duskers straight to the Mission. That history would judge us for such a cowardly and selfish act."

A heavy pause.

"And then he asked us to believe in him, in the cause. *Put your eyes on me,* he'd said. *Listen to me.* How his eyes had burned! How his words pierced into us. He told us there was no higher purpose than to heal the sick, to purify the impure. That there was no nobler calling than to save the duskers. And with the same kind of charisma and passion that convinced us to leave the Mission in the first place, he persuaded us to stay in the metropolis. And so we did. And so we did. We merged into dusker society and over the years became masters of blending in. And every day that passed, every month, every year, every decade, we got closer and closer to finding a cure."

"What about the women?" I ask, thinking of my mother. "You said they were pregnant when they left the Mission."

"They survived the first wave of attack. And the births were six, seven months away, distant enough to prepare in advance, to build a triage out in the desert. Afterward, the women nursed their babies for as many years as they could, as much to feed their babies as to ward off their own menstrual bleeding. And when their breasts ran dry, a year, two, even three years later, and bleeding again became a problem, they made sure to get pregnant again, and quickly. Later, we were able to develop a medical procedure—"

"That's why we had siblings," I say in horror. "That's why the women kept bringing babies into this fallen, forsaken place. It was only to protect themselves."

52

"It was to protect you!" he retorts. "Because if a mother had been discovered, it would have led quickly to not only her death, but her whole family's."

Another silence, weightier this time.

The man blinks rapidly, as surprised by his outburst as we are. He touches his throat with his fingertips.

"We were discussing your father," he finally says after a moment, his voice recaptured, keen to get back on topic. "As I was saying, he was our leader. Getting his position as janitor at the Domain Building was instrumental to the cause. It gave your father access to the labs, the computer mainframe, the highly classified files. Even placed him close to the top-secret fifty-ninth floor, although he was never able to break in. Later, he rigged the system and had some of us transferred here to the Palace. To have eyes on the Ruler, and, eventually, to have his ear." He puffs his chest out, the insignia on the breast of his frock coat jutting out. "That would be my role. Chief advisor, in case you were wondering."

He pauses expectantly, waiting for Sissy or me to say something. He clears his throat. "And then, of course, the miraculous day. Your father found some archaic data embedded in forgotten files in the computer mainframe. He wasn't sure what he was looking at, but from those cryptic equations he was able to patch together a formula. For the Origin. Eventually, he converted the Origin formula into an actual serum. The process wasn't perfect—it was extremely complicated, in fact. The Origin had to be separated into two halves, injected into two different carriers, and only after the gestation period—over a decade, mind you—was completed could they be later conjoined by mixing the blood of the two carriers."

"Sissy and me," I whisper. "We're the carriers."

He nods.

"But something happened," Sissy says, "before the gestation period was complete. What went wrong?"

He exhales silently through his nose, the waft of air grazing my face. "One of us got careless. Whole families were captured, imprisoned in the dome at the Heper Institute. Including you," he says to Sissy. "Right from our midst."

A flash of anger crosses his body, barely contained. "Together the two of you were a weapon. Apart, useless. You were a gun without a bullet; she was a bullet without a gun. And there was nothing we could do about it. We couldn't simply steal her away without her absence being noted. The dome was under video surveillance twenty-four/seven. If she vanished, they would simply play back the videotapes, and see everything! Questions would be asked, suspicions raised, investigations launched. And the trail would lead right to us, the Originators. And from there, the trail might have led them right to the Mission itself. No, stealing her away wouldn't have been worth the risk."

The room spins. It's all the blood being drained from me. It's making me light-headed, woozy. "You've taken too much blood from me."

But he only continues speaking, his words coming out faster, with less precision.

"So we did what we had to. Which was simply to keep you both alive until you were both past the gestation period. Your father protected you, Gene, trained you. Indoctrinated into you the need to stay in the metropolis, that escape into the Vast was never an option. And you, Sissy, were with other adults in the dome, so you were fine."

He rested his aqueous brown eyes on her. "But then, of course . . . the Heper Hunt ten years ago. It caught us by surprise. As you well know, all the adults in the dome were hunted down, killed. Leaving you alone in the dome. With a bunch of useless babies. You needed help. And that's why your father left you, Gene. He went to her, to the Heper Institute."

"Why him?" My voice, though fatigued, is tinged with anger. "Why didn't someone else go? Why not you?"

He scratches his wrist. "You think it's so easy, don't you? You think it's a little chess game and you can simply move pieces where you want, when you want. But it's not like that at all. Your father was the only one who had the knowledge to convincingly play the part of a scientist."

He stops, pauses, forces himself to breathe slower. "Besides, he knew he'd trained you well enough by that point. Even if you were still a little pipsqueak. But he was worried about Sis. Thought she mightn't have the necessary survivor skills. Turns out he was wrong, of course. She's every bit as tenacious as you, isn't she?"

"But why did he have to fake his death?" I ask. "Why not just tell me the reason he was leaving?" I ask.

"Because unless you believed him dead, you'd have gone after him." He turns his eyes to me and for the first time I detect a kindling of warmth. "Isn't that the truth, Gene?"

My eyes drop.

"It was a tortured decision, okay?" the chief advisor says. "Your father was against it initially. Does that make you feel better? Only when he realized there was no other choice did he go along. It was the only way his brainchild would work."

"What brainchild?"

"A plan to make the two of you disappear *without any suspicions raised*. That was key. And the Heper Hunt was the keyhole. Because out there in the Vast during the Hunt, hepers are devoured. Nobody is taking inventory or recording the kills. It's a bloodbath. If we were able to extricate Sissy during the Hunt, no one would give her disappearance a second thought. Nor would anyone question your disappearance, either, Gene. Everyone knows the Hunt is violent, with hunters turning on one another, hunters left to melt away in the sunlight. What happens out there stays out there, no questions asked. Ever. It was the perfect plan to extract you two without suspicion."

"Doesn't make sense," Sissy mumbles, deep in thought.

"What doesn't?" The chief advisor stares down his nose at her.

"If this was the Scientist's plan," Sissy asks, "his life's goal, why did he disappear from the Institute mere months before it was executed? Before the Heper Hunt was to take place?"

A flicker of uncertainty in the chief advisor's eyes.

"You don't know, do you?" she says.

His voice comes out strained. "I'll admit it. I don't. When he disappeared, we were flummoxed. Why he would suddenly leave at that point, so close to seeing his life's work come to fruition . . . I don't know." He falls into a sullen silence.

I frown. Sissy's right: my father's disappearance defies logic. And it makes his subsequent disappearance from the Mission—so shortly before we were supposed to arrive—all the more inexplicable. My eyes swim uncertainly around me, at my feet, my wrists, at the bags filling with my blood.

"But all that is academic now, isn't it?" the chief advisor says. "Why he disappeared doesn't matter. What does matter is the fact that his dream has been realized. Look around you. At the Origin weapons. At the Origin blood! At the Origin together and intact at last!" he says. "His dream come true!"

I stare at the curtains sectioning me off from the rest of the room, from the rest of the world. At the handcuffs chafing my wrists. At the bags, dark and full with my blood. This is the destination my father's grand plan brought me? This is why he raised me, why he protected me all those years? This is the life he envisioned for me? This is all I meant to him?

"There are children beneath us," Sissy whispers as if to herself, but her eyes are trained on the chief advisor. "Living in horrifying conditions, waiting for a gruesome and certain death. How can you call this a dream come true?"

The chief advisor stares at her without answering. He sniffs.

She turns to look at me, and her large eyes reflect shock and horror. Her face, wan and drained, frighteningly sapped of color. They've pumped too much blood from her.

"Sissy," I say quietly. "Are you okay?"

She shakes her head. Something is erupting in her eyes, and it takes a moment for me to realize it is fury.

"I wouldn't worry about her," the chief advisor says, noting my concern. "It might *feel* like we're draining life out of you both, but trust me, we aren't. And over time, we'll calibrate our transfusions more efficiently and maximally. Can't kill the hand that feeds—"

"We never agreed to this," Sissy whispers in a voice much softer than his, almost inaudible under his loud tone. But somehow that whisper cuts him off, silences him. She meets his cold stare, doesn't blink. "And we never will. Not while there are young boys and girls in the catacombs."

The chief advisor stares at her for a long time. Not quite with a glare, but with a clinical look bereft of any warmth.

What he does next takes Sissy and me by surprise. He removes a key from his pocket and unlocks our cuffs. Sissy and I sit up, rubbing our wrists and ankles, wary.

"This younger generation," he says, scratching his wrist, "unable to think of anyone but themselves." He walks to the curtain, pulls it wide-open. "Coming?" he asks.

Sissy and I stare at each other.

He and the other Originators walk away from our beds. They know we will follow.

And after a few seconds of indecision, we do.

Fourteen

O<small>N THE OTHER</small> side of the curtains we step into a pool of darkness, the size of which we're not fully aware of until—

"Lights coming on in three, two, one," the chief advisor says in a surprisingly tender voice.

White light washes over us.

We're in a large room with two distinct halves. On one side is what appears to be a laboratory. Test tubes, vials, burners, incubators, microscopes, blenders, dry block heaters, compressors, centrifuges are placed in orderly fashion atop workbenches and inside glass storage cabinets. On a shelf that runs the entire length of the wall test tubes filled with blood sit in racks. A soft hum emanates from several machines, gently shaking flasks half-filled with our blood.

On the other side of the room are shelves of artillery and weapons. There are rows of guns, all in varying shapes and sizes, pistols and revolvers, as well as double-barreled and long-cylindered weapons gleaming in the light. Boxes of cartridges and shells and bullets sit on the bottom shelf.

"As you might have guessed, this is a top-secret humans-only section of the Palace," the chief advisor says. "Humans-only, as in only humans know about it, only humans enter it. Specifically, only the four us," he says, indicating the other three Originators.

"Four?" Sissy says incredulously. "Any reason why you're not counting those in the catacombs? As in, the *hundreds* of other humans?"

The chief advisor. His face smooth and unreadable. He pulls on the cuff of his left sleeve, once, twice. "If not for the ones in the catacombs, there would be none of us up here. And if none of us are up here, there would be no hope for those in the catacombs. That is to say, they are necessary. For our existence as much as their own."

"Fancy talk," Sissy says. "A nice cover for your betrayal. Let's be honest. You're sacrificing them for your own protection. And as I said before, I won't have any part in it. You won't be getting another drop of blood from me until everyone down there is free."

The chief advisor walks over to a desk, picks up an electronic tablet. "We tried to be civil," he says to us. "We tried appealing to your better senses, being rational with you. We even tried the Father-angle, hoping you'd see how this was your father's lifelong dream and passion. Clearly nothing has worked." He taps on the tablet screen, punches a sequence of buttons.

"Listen to us," Sissy says, stepping toward him. His right eyebrow arches slightly higher, a minute but rare slip of emotion. "It doesn't have to be this way," Sissy continues. "I told you before! We get on the train, escape from here, all of us, including everyone in the catacombs. No more humans have to die. You have access to the Palace controls. You'll know how to open the right doors, how to get the train moving. From there—"

"Well, you're right about my access to the controls. This tablet really does control everything. The movement of the enclaves, the train." A muscle under his left eye twitches. "So, yes, let's. Let's all get on the train. Let's squeeze into the train cars, ride off into the mountains, and live happily ever after." He strokes his wrist. "What pretty dreams you have. Let me guess, do we head east on purple ponies under the wide arches of brilliant rainbows?"

"Why don't you—" Sissy begins to say.

His eyes settle on her before flicking to me. I know why Sissy has fallen silent. It's the look in his eyes: like dead fish floating on the surface, scales gleaming but lifeless inside.

He punches a few buttons on the tablet.

Nobody moves.

"Let me disabuse you of these fantastical notions. Take a look at the lab. It has been primed and ready for years now. *For what?* you might be asking if you weren't so besotted with your silly notions. Well, so glad you asked. All the equipment here is for one purpose: to produce Origin artillery. Your blood will be combined, then congealed into all manner of weapons: bullets for pistols and revolvers, dissolvable pills, shotgun shells. Once we have enough of your blood, of course."

He gazes fondly down at a line of darts on the table. He picks one up. Its translucent length is filled with a dark-red liquid. "For now, we're starting with darts and grenades. In fact, these darts have just been filled with a serum of your combined blood, plus some preservatives. They're good to go. And take a look at these two grenades here, fully loaded. Pull the pin and they'll explode shrapnel of jellied Origin blood. Just prototypes for now, but awesome stuff." His tongue darts out, moistens his lips. "One dart or piece of shrapnel pierces its skin and the dusker is re-turned to human within minutes. That's how potent your combined, concentrated blood is."

He picks up a dagger, slides the broad side of the blade against the back of his hand. "I am telling you this because visuals are worth a thousand words. So look at the technology here. Think of the decades of work they represent, the lives sacrificed, the carefully calibrated planning that made all this possible. All set in motion years ago by your father. Now think: are we really going to jettison decades of work and sacrifice to help a few miserable wretches make a doomed attempt to escape to the mountains?" He places the dagger on a counter next to him. Deliberately, slowly, conspicuously.

"This big plan," I say, "to re-turn everyone. It'll take an arsenal a hundred, a thousand times larger than what you have here."

"We know," the chief advisor whispers. "Believe you me, we know."

"That's going to take a lot of Origin blood."

"Indeed."

Silence.

"You speak," I say, "as if Sissy and I are going to be around for years. Well, I have news for you. The Ruler knows about the Origin. We read a letter from the Palace. They know all about us. And they know we're here—they saw us down in the catacombs. There's no way they'll let us live past a few more days."

"Oh, that letter," the chief advisor says. "From the Palace? Written to Krugman and the elders of the Mission?" The chief advisor scratches his wrist. "Did you like my penmanship?" His nose lifts high, chest balloons out. "I told you, I'm His Highness's advisor. As such, I have access to his Official Seal. And we're quite capable of slipping a letter aboard the train if and when we need to."

Absentmindedly, he gently touches the lapel of his frock coat. "The Palace staff doesn't know a thing about the Origin. And yes, they saw and recognized the two of you when they'd earlier toured the catacombs. Your appearance stirred quite a ruckus—the hunter boy, the dome girl, found! In fact, in a scant forty-eight hours, the Ruler has plans to devour you. Both of you. For his birthday."

He pauses, takes in the look on our faces. Something humors him; he takes a long, languorous scratch of his wrist. "But you needn't worry. Before that can happen, tomorrow, in fact, I plan on relaying to him the sad, unfortunate news of your premature deaths. That you got into a kerfuffle with some boys down in the catacombs. Over what I don't know—perhaps over Sissy, say. Things got out of hand, and you ended up drowning in the cesspool, then flushed through to the sewage incinerator. Both of you."

"The Ruler won't believe you," Sissy says.

"Of course he will. He will fly into an apoplectic rage, of course, will sprint down into the catacombs. And of course, he won't find you. Nor will he—or anyone—later smell you up on the Palace grounds. Not so long as you remain in this hermetically sealed secret room."

He dabs the corner of his mouth with his pinkie. "We have just a few kinks to work out before our story becomes airtight. So we'll need to send you both back to spend one more night in the catacombs— just in case the Ruler decides to spring a surprise visit tonight to gawk at his catch of the century. But come tomorrow, after we've crossed our *t*'s and dotted our *i*'s, we'll have you back in this room. And then we'll inform the Ruler of your untimely demise."

He studies us for a moment; something about our silence irritates him. He picks up the blade, looks at me. "I think it's best if you consider something."

"What?"

"You and this girl," he says. "You're the Origin."

"Understood, but—"

"You're no longer *Gene* and *Sis*. That's no longer your designation or your name or your identity. You're the Origin. You're the cure for the duskers. Best to now think of yourself that way." He lifts the blade to his nose, sniffs. "We can inject you with sedatives. Render you into comatose blood-producing vegetables. And there you will lie, asleep, for years, no, for decades. Your eyelids will never open again while you slowly turn into withered plants, hair white, nails long—"

"But you won't," I say. "Otherwise you'd have done it, already. You need our blood pure. Not polluted by whatever chemicals you'd have to inject into us." It's all conjecture, but I seem to have nailed it.

His lips twitch ever so slightly.

"You need us awake, healthy, and robust for years. Not chemically jacked vegetables lying on cots, bodies atrophying away. You need—"

"Shut up," he says quietly. "Just shut up."

The air in the room stills.

"We Originators haven't survived in their midst," he says softly, "without becoming ruthless. Business done with the minimum of fuss. Risks avoided, deadweight sacrificed. So remember this word: *ruthless*. If you resist, we shall be ruthless. Ruthless in exacting your full, if not glad, cooperation."

When Sissy speaks, her voice is as calm and unflinching as the chief advisor's. "And you'll never have our cooperation. Not while you continue to send countless human boys and girls to their deaths. You claim it's for the greater good, but whose greater good?" She shakes her head. "So go ahead, shoot us up, inject us. That's the only way you'll get our blood. Go ahead and taint your precious Origin blood."

The chief advisor regards her coolly through half-lidded eyes. He picks up the tablet, taps the screen.

The group of men shift as one, moving several meters from a rectangular outline grooved into the floor. Two of the men slip into the aisles, grab weapons. Tranquilizer dart guns.

The floor starts to hum.

"We've been waiting, have had oodles of time to think and plan for every possible contingency that might arise." His cadence is slow, it is deliberate, it is hypnotic, and it is menacing for all these reasons. "Your little shenanigans which you probably think are so intelligent and quick thinking—why, we anticipated them *years* ago. And we designed a menu of options to deal with every possible response: A, B, and C, as well as iterations A One, B One, and C One." His voice is thick with smugness. "Your response right now calls for plan B One." He presses a button.

At once, the rectangular outline in the floor slides away, exposing a hole. An enclave emerges through it. The glass is fogged with condensation and it's impossible to see who is inside. Then a hand inside the enclave wipes across the glass, revealing eyes, then a face. The face is frightened. The face is young. The face is David.

"We have our ways of securing cooperation," the chief advisor whispers.

Sissy immediately tenses. As she springs toward the enclave, two Originators step forward. I grab her arm, hold her back. The other Originator is aiming the tranquilizer dart gun at her.

"These darts are loaded with heavy sedatives," the chief advisor says. "Please don't make us use them on you."

Sissy tries to pull her arm from my grasp.

"Sissy," I hiss, "don't."

She shakes with fury but stands her ground, her eyes glowering at the men. One of the Originators walks over to a shelf and removes a shotgun. He returns, stands next to the other two men, his face bereft of emotion.

The chief advisor scratches his wrist, his eyes shining with approval. He reaches down to the enclave, presses a button on the side. The glass partition slides open.

David coughs at the sudden infusion of fresh air, dry, grating heaves. The chief advisor pulls him out, then unceremoniously drops him to the floor. And kicks him in the gut.

"Hey!" I shout.

David curls around, grabbing his knees. The chief advisor pulls out of his coat pocket a pair of latex gloves, then withdraws from another pocket a hypodermic needle. It's filled with a sudsy yellow fluid. He grabs David's hair, snaps his head back.

Sissy leaps forward. As do I. But the armed Originators move forward, shoving their shotgun and dart guns in our faces. We stop.

The chief advisor stabs the needle into David's neck, depresses the syringe fully. Within seconds, David's body goes limp, his head flopping to the ground.

"What did you inject him with?" Sissy yells.

"It's a concentrated compound," the chief advisor says, placing the hypodermic needle into a ziplock bag. He strips off his latex gloves, balls them into the bag before carefully sealing it. "Made up of saliva from five different duskers. Centrifuged together, the middle two—and most potent—layers of the mixed compound then removed, a few preservatives added, and voilà, the yellow liquid. Which is now flowing in David's bloodstream. Which is now seeping into every organ, every molecule, inside him."

Sissy and I together spring toward David, no longer caring about the men and their weapons. They apparently don't care, either; they lower their weapons. David has already begun shivering, his skin frigid to the touch, streaming with hot sweat. Then he starts convulsing, his arms flopping against the floor, the flesh of his sweaty skin smacking the smooth tiles.

"I'm sure Gene already knows this," the chief advisor says softly, his eyes riveted on David, "but let me spell it out for you just in case. Once infected, a human will turn into dusker in anywhere between two hours and two days. Saliva from several duskers will exponentially increase this rate of turning."

David suddenly arcs his back, his body taut as a pulled bow. His jaw gapes wide, then judders, teeth snapping. The man with the shotgun swings his weapon nervously at David.

"David, poor child, has been injected with the blood of *five* duskers. He will turn in less than forty seconds. Fifteen seconds have already passed."

In my arms, David is plummeting off a cliff. Sweat is pouring out of his pores, his temperature is dropping precipitously, and he's shaking so hard, his fevered face is a hazy, vibrating blur.

"Twenty seconds before he turns," the chief advisor intones, gazing at his watch.

Sissy screams, leaps to her feet. She pounces toward the chief advisor, but he doesn't move. Doesn't even flinch when she snatches the dagger from his hand.

She slices the palm of her hand true and deep. Blood floods into her cupped hand.

The chief advisor scratches his wrist.

And then she's kneeling beside David, tilting his head back, and pouring the blood into his parted mouth. She tosses the dagger at me, and I snatch it out of the air. In less than a second, I've sliced my own hand and I'm pushing Sissy's hand aside, letting David drink my blood. Over the next minute, we take turns hand-pouring blood into his mouth. David stops shaking, collapses into a rest. But his body yet rages hot, sweat drenching his shirt. It will be hours before he's completely healed.

The chief advisor, exuding silent elation, nods to one of the men. The man switches his dart gun for another—one of the Origin dart guns. He aims, pulls the trigger. The dart pierces into David's thigh.

"This will speed things up," the man says.

In seconds, David stills. His breathing slows, deepens. His skin already cooling.

"As you can see," the chief advisor whispers, "we can be . . . *ruthless*. We know about David. We know about Epap. We know—"

"Shut up," Sissy says. "Just shut up, already."

The chief advisor stops, stunned. Then, with a glimmer in his eyes, he curls the corners of his lips, widens his mouth, shows teeth. He's mimicking a smile. It's a grotesque contortion clearly meant to taunt Sissy.

She snaps her eyes away, burns holes into the floor with her gaze. She's saving her fight for another day.

The chief advisor's tablet starts to flash and beep. He flicks his eyes down, reads quickly. "Now, you'll have to excuse me." He sighs dramatically. "His Highness needs me. Some kind of emergency, apparently."

He walks toward the door, programming the tablet. "You'll both be returned to the catacombs now. But just for tonight, remember? We'll see you back here tomorrow." He pauses at the door, glancing at the room. He pastes another crude smile on his face, then gives off an eerie trill of fake laughter. "Welcome to your brand-new home."

Fifteen

A BURROWED DARKNESS, a heavy sleep. I break out of it slowly, merging from sleep sludge. I touch the sides of the enclave—they're damp with condensation. I'm still locked in. Hours ago, after the chief advisor transported me back to the catacombs, the glass wall had remained shut. Such was my blood-drawn fatigue that despite everything, I drifted into a deep slumber.

A grayness surrounds me now. I can just make out the rows of enclaves across the corridor, the frames of each unit glowing dimly. Everyone is still locked in. Quite a lot of time has passed; how much I'm not sure. But judging from my deep-seated grogginess, I'm guessing it's been at least three, four hours since Sissy and I were transported back here.

Sissy—where is she?

I look directly across to the enclave facing mine, but it is occupied by a boy. As is every other enclave I peer into. No sign of Epap, or David, either. The boys in their enclaves across from me stare at me with wariness. They're wondering if I'm the cause for the irregular alarm, curious as to why I'm being shuttled back and forth. Wondering why they're still locked in their enclave after so many hours have passed.

They're about to get even more curious.

Because my enclave starts to hum. Then vibrate. All their eyes snap to my enclave, some eyes widening in surprise, most eyes narrowing with suspicion.

I'm being taken back to the room with the Originators, I think. But a part of me knows that can't be right. The chief advisor had said I was supposed to stay in the catacombs for another day. And though I don't have an exact handle on how much time has passed, I do know that it hasn't been a day. Not even close.

I try to rise, but my body is too heavy. An electronic beep sounds from inside the enclave, followed by a hum. Then the enclave starts moving again.

I think to kick at the glass, to try to break through. But I know it's futile. Instead, I save my breath, conserve my energy for whatever's coming next. Blood rushes in my ears. Something like panic begins to rise in me, but I stem it. I breathe in, out, gathering myself.

The enclave suddenly drops into an almost free fall.

Sixteen

AGAIN, I'M TOSSED from side to side as the enclave careens around hidden loops. All I can do is brace for the next drop or turn. As with every trip thus far, the enclave stops for a brief spell in a centralized location where it is flooded with lights. Then it is once again racing along the rails.

A minute later, it slows to a crawl, starts ascending. For a long time.

A gap in the darkness above me opens up. The enclave trundles through it and into a darkened space of indeterminate dimension. I hear the gap narrow, then shut beneath me; the enclave comes to a rest, lying flat on this now-closed floor.

I don't move.

Everything is very still in this room.

And dark.

And very wrong.

A row of wall sconces on the adjacent wall begins to glow dimly. It's not the seven-meter-high stucco-decorated ceilings that gives the room away, or the thick, lustrous area carpet, or even the stately, regal aura of this cavernous room. But it's the large commissioned portrait painting hanging over me. Of the Ruler, his face inert and pale, his eyes cold and stern.

I'm in the Ruler's Suite.

The chief advisor had underestimated the Ruler's ability to restrain himself. The Ruler doesn't want to wait forty-eight hours. He wants me now.

The lid of the enclave starts to slide open.

This is when I die, I think, tensing my body.

"You may step out."

I startle at the voice. Because of its proximity, hidden in the nearby shadows. And because of its familiarity. It's a voice I've heard many times over the years, the silky cadence instantly recognizable. Over school PA systems. In my bedroom over radio airwaves.

"Please," the Ruler says, his voice slightly nasal, "step out. It's safe. You have nothing to fear."

I squint into the darkness, can only barely make out another shade of black.

"Please, step out. If we meant you harm, you'd be dead now."

I pull myself out tentatively, planting first my right foot, then my left. And stop. Now I'm standing on the lush royal rug, completely exposed. I've never felt more naked, more vulnerable, in my life.

And what I see next: A crowd of people, standing oddly in a line, facing me. Perhaps as many as a dozen hazy, indistinct silhouettes.

But they don't move. They are growing restless, I can see that, in their bunching shoulders and flicking heads. I can hear their excitement, too, in the cracking of bones, the *slish-slash* of saliva. But they haven't moved a step toward me.

Then one of them gives out a wail, shaking, losing control. He leaps toward me, his face distorted with desire.

My guts clench inside.

I hear the thud of a body hitting glass. The dusker has leaped right into a glass wall I'd failed to see earlier. He slides down the wall, his skin screeching, claws scratching against glass.

"As you can see, my staff are securely barricaded behind that glass partition." The Ruler's words slip out with what sounds like a lisp. "It was built decades ago when my aquarium tanks were constructed. To keep the staffers from, um, breaching them. So don't worry. My staffers are all safely behind that glass wall. You're in no danger. No danger at all."

His voice sounds too close, almost intimate. He can't be on the other side of the glass partition. He must be on my side. I squint in his direction, trying to see.

"You can't see me, I've just realized. Forgive me, I should have been more considerate. Turn on the aquarium lights," he orders.

Immediately five large floor-to-ceiling cylindrical aquariums, stout as columns, begin to glow. These aquariums, located on this side of the glass, encircle me. Dark, murky shapes float within them. But something steals my attention away from them.

The Ruler. Standing a mere five meters away.

He's strapped to a tall, X-shaped steel beam. His arms are lifted up and secured to the beam with metal bracelets around his wrists, elbows, and biceps. Almost in perfect symmetry, his legs are spread apart and similarly restrained by bracelets around his ankles, knees, and upper thighs. Thus constrained, the Ruler takes on the near-perfect formation of an X. He's even been secured around his chest by what looks like an expanded metal rib cage. A metal peg is pinched over the bridge of his nose.

"As you can see," he says nasally, "I've been securely fastened. You have nothing to fear." It's not a lisp affecting his speech but saliva accumulating in his mouth. And splattering out of his mouth like hot spit out of a boiling kettle.

"You'd think after a steady lifelong diet of hepers, my salivary glands wouldn't be quite so sensitive," he says, his voice unaccountably sweet and tender.

The five cylindrical aquariums continue to glow brighter. Now I'm seeing other things, inside them. Things that, as frightening as the sight of the Ruler is, are even more chilling.

"I've placed pinchers over my nose so as not be quite so . . . distracted." His eyes squint with pain as he speaks, a pair of crow's-feet fanning out from the corners. It's the light: though dim for me, it's too bright for him. And because he's tied up, he can't put on his shades.

The glow from the tanks has transformed the glass partition into a mirror that veils the many staffers standing behind it. The overall effect is to render this half of the Ruler's chamber into an intimate private setting. Just the two of us.

"Now that I've placated your fears," he says, "perhaps now would be an appropriate time to put to rest some, er-r, ideas that might be cropping up in your head." He breaks his gaze, shifting his eyes downward. I realize, with a shock, that the Ruler is, of all things, shy.

"I'm truly sorry for having to mention this, but my advisors were quite insistent. You might notice in my right hand a control. It's a simple control, one fat button, easy to depress with my thumb. One push and instantly the glass wall separating us from my staffers will lift. They will be on you in less than a second should I find myself . . . jeopardized." His nose crinkles in distaste. "Forgive me for bringing up such an awkward topic, but we really did have to get that unpleasantry out of the way."

"What do you want with me?" I say, taking in more of the chamber. No exit doors. No windows, either, at least not on this side of the glass partition. My eyes, like reluctant magnets, keep getting drawn to the tanks. To the dark shapes floating inside, in particular.

In the nearest tank, a gray blur gains size and definition as it drifts slowly toward me. And even as my mind is telling me to look away, I see. The dark mass sharpens into the shape of a body. The emergence of an ear, strands of hair, then the side of a face, pressing against the curved glass.

I flinch, almost cry out.

"The truth is," the Ruler says again with an apologetic tone, "my love for the taste of hepers is so insatiable that I have to keep a few accessible at all times. For a midday snack to munch on, when insomnia once again claims this overburdened and overtaxed ruler. The taste of heper on my tongue relaxes me. I don't need a full feasting, mind you, just something to tide me over to the next devouring."

The body inside the tank slowly rotates. Distorted by the curvature of the glass tank, its features stretch sideways, smeared into an oblong. It is a girl. Her eyes are half-lidded, vacant, lifeless, arms drifting by her sides like useless, sodden rolls of paper. Cords dangle down, connected to her elbows. A face mask of some kind is attached over her mouth and nose, covering almost her entire lower half of her face.

"The liquid in these tanks is a technological marvel," the Ruler intones with quiet awe. "It acts as a preservative—hepers remain edible for upward of three months. The liquid also functions, as you can see, as a source of light, illuminating this room evenly, and, in the right setting, quite seductively. And take a look at the base of the tanks. You might have already noticed the keg taps. I give myself a sip at least a few times during the daytime. I have to tell you, the natural secretions of the heper mixed with this liquid render an exquisite taste. Delectable, really."

The girl's eyes suddenly blink.

I cry out, an unintelligible gasp.

She blinks again, and consciousness and awareness seep into her. Her head drifts up; her fingers press white against the glass.

"What? . . . How?"

"Oh, I assumed . . ." He blinks in confusion. "They're *alive*, of course they're still alive; how else would they be able to produce the natural secretions I just mentioned? We pipeline oxygen to them. And transfuse liquefied foods. After they die—usually they stay alive a couple of weeks—we keep their bodies afloat in the liquid. During that time, their dead flesh ferments rather nicely. Preserved, pickled heper flesh—quite a delicacy, actually." His eyes light up with an idea. "Would you like a sip? Go ahead, just use the keg taps. I'd serve you myself if I weren't so . . . tied up." His fingers scratch air, unable to reach his wrists. "Or how about a little bite? I could instruct you on how to use the pincers. The tanks are really tricked up. Really, try some; go ahead. It's wonderfully soggy, simply melts on your tongue—" His mouth drops open, then closes. Opens again, flabbergasted. He's trying to find the next words. "Oh dear. I'm sorry. I'm so, so sorry. I just didn't; I mean I kind of forgot that you're . . ." he says with genuine self-reproach.

The girl in the tank rotates slowly around, floats thankfully out of focus.

"Tell me why I'm here," I spit out. "I know you didn't bring me here just to gloat about these tanks."

"Why, yes, of course," he says, relieved to move past the awkward moment. "Why you're here." He starts to speak, pauses, trying to find the right words. "Well, you see . . . it's just that . . . Well, there's no other way to put it." And still he pauses.

"What?"

"We need your help," he says. His fingers scratch empty air again, trembling slightly with nervousness.

Seventeen

You need *MY* help?" I say, certain I must have misheard.

His fingers continue to scratch air, only faster now. "Do you mind," he asks, "if I have the lights dimmed down? It's rather painful. . . . Why, yes, thank you. Lights down, please." Within seconds the tank lights dim. The glass partition loses its mirror quality, and the group of staffers emerges from behind the glass. Only now, the group has doubled in number. And standing in front, with a look of mild panic that is evident even with shades covering half his face, is the chief advisor.

"I like you," the Ruler says with gentleness. "Can I just say that first off, before we get down to business? And if I ever do eat you one day, know it's nothing personal, because I really do like you. You've got ingenuity and pluck, loads of it. Would we all shared your qualities." Shadows pool into his eye sockets, hiding his deep-set eyes.

"What do you want with me?"

"What I *want* with you and what I *need* from you are, unfortunately, two very different things. What I *want* is your flesh, to devour it. What I *need* from you, however, is quite entirely different."

I nervously glance at the crowd of staffers, at the tanks that are now thankfully too dim to reveal their interior. "Go ahead."

He pauses. It is a pause tinged with embarrassment. "Quite simply," the Ruler says, "we have a situation."

"What kind of situation?"

His face remains bland, but his chest expands, pressing against the metal constraint. "First some background. During the Heper Hunt, we know you got away by boat. We know you were followed down the Nede River by the HiSS organization. You are familiar with the HiSS organization, yes?"

I nod. HiSS stands for the *Heper Search Society,* an underground grassroots organization that seeks to root out hepers rumored to have infiltrated society. Despite the Ruler's best efforts to snuff out this group (its very existence was an affront to the Palace's position that hepers were extinct), it had in recent years not only survived but also thrived. I remember Ashley June telling me she had joined the HiSS in order to both escape suspicion and keep tabs on suspected heper activity.

Seeing me nod, the Ruler continues. "Now, judging from the fact that you were forced to beat a quick escape by train, we can safely assume that the HiSSers hunted you down in the mountains, yes?"

The girl's body inside the tank rotates slowly toward me again. Her face, her eyes, turning round as if to look at me. I turn my gaze from her.

"Those damn HiSSers," the Ruler says, his lips curling. "Took us by surprise. The depth of their organization, their membership numbers, their ability to secretly build a fleet of sun-proofed boats. Must have decimated the heper farm." His voice is bland, but the words come out as if marinated in acid.

"But having our farm raided is the least of our problems," he continues. "It's the train tracks that concern us the most. Any nincompoop would realize they lead to the Palace, and that the Ruler must have been hiding a secret stash of hepers for generations. News like that gets back to the metropolis and . . . it'd be all over for the Palace. And for me."

The Ruler banks his eyeballs to his right, stares at the crowd assembled behind the glass. He's staring in particular at the chief advisor. "But, as my chief advisor has informed me, there's reason to be optimistic. A sufficient number of sunny days have passed since that raid to lead us to believe that all HiSSers have perished in the sunlit mountains. And with all the HiSSers dead, the gentle citizens of the metropolis shall never learn of the heper farm or the train track or the catacombs filled with hepers below."

"I'm happy for you," I say, not bothering to hide my sarcasm. "Congratulations. But you still haven't told me why I'm here."

He's quiet for a moment.

"Turns out," he says, "our optimism may have been a little premature." His eyes swivel left and look to the far wall. "Would you do me a favor? Would you turn on that TV monitor over there? Hanging on that wall?"

Everyone stares—I feel their wet eyeballs on me—as I walk in front of the glass wall to the TV monitor. I push a button on the side of the screen. Immediately it blinks on.

"This is a recording of a live television report," the Ruler says. "Breaking news that came through the airwaves only a few hours ago."

I hear sounds before the images blur in. Of mass pandemonium, people shouting. With breathless excitement. Then images sharpen into focus onscreen. I see people rushing along one of the main avenues in the metropolis. Streets overrun with mobs, horses and carriages forced to come to a standstill, passengers leaping out of them. More images from different locations, likely from security cams, nonsensical and fragmented, as if the broadcasting producers were having a hard time piecing it all together. For no more than a couple of seconds I see a shot of the Domain Building where my father used to work. A shot of the Metropolis Hospital. A shot of the Convention Center, capturing the water show from the large fountain out front.

I don't know what's happening, but goose bumps nevertheless break out all over my skin. Voices whisper in my head, excited, frantic, overlapping one another, growing louder until I realize they're not in my head but coming from the TV monitor.

". . . incredible news that has shocked the citizenry of the metropolis . . ."

". . . nobody believed anyone could survive so long out in the Vast . . ."

"—a face familiar to all as one of the selected hunters—"

And then the TV image suddenly shifts and we're inside a studio; no, the décor is too bland, too clinical. It's the inside of the Metropolis Hospital. Uniformed nurses and doctors line up against the walls. The curved, fish-eye quality of the footage tells me the shot is likely from a convex hallway security camera. A medical team is hurrying down the hallway. A trio of doctors in the lead, their arms swinging wildly, frantically waving aside reporters. They're pulling a wheeled hospital stretcher. As the stretcher—a horizontal beam supported by two vertical poles on wheels—passes the camera, at first I can't see the person hanging upside down on it. There're too many reporters blocking the view, too many nurses and doctors surrounding the patient. I see only the patient's feet secured in the footholds of the stretcher.

And then there's a clearing, a millisecond of a second when a crack in the wall of bodies allows me to catch the briefest glimpse. But it's all I need. I know who it is. The stretcher is pulled away, down the hall.

I close my eyes in disbelief. I still see her hair secured into a bun, a few loose, dangling strands dragging along the tiled floor. A fervent ripe redness glosses them, like arteries filled with blood. I see the high bridge of her nose, the soft protrusions of cheekbones, the stark line of jawbone pale against the dark tiles of the hospital floor.

Ashley June.

Eighteen

S<small>HE IS THE</small> problem," the Ruler says, an acerbic tone replacing his softness. "Your fellow classmate at school. Your compatriot on the Heper Hunt. Your date at the Gala. And, as we're finding out now, an important member of the HiSS organization."

The screen fades to black.

"She is a huge, gigantic problem." He enunciates the words slowly, distastefully, with deliberation. "The writing was on the wall back at the Heper Institute. During the training period. Of her rebellious streak, her wily nature."

"What are you talking about?"

The Ruler snorts, a quick blow out of his nostrils. "She pulled off an infantile stunt right before the start of the Heper Hunt. Displayed an enormous lapse of judgment, decided she wanted to be the center of attention. Must have sprayed herself with some fake heper odor, and got the Institute staff all riled up chasing after her. Locked herself inside the Pit in the Introduction. After she sobered up, after all the faux-heper spray had dissipated, she emerged out of the Pit. She would have gotten a beat down from the administration if it hadn't been so distracted by the Heper Hunt. As a result, they failed to discipline her."

The Ruler's eyes stare directly at me. "And that was a mistake. Because she slipped away, back to the metropolis, notified the HiSS leaders. Told them everything she knew, which, according to our informants, had something to do with a getaway boat on the Nede River. It would transport the hepers to some far-off paradise made out of honey and milk shake. This information didn't come as a complete surprise to the HiSS leaders—in fact, they'd gotten a whiff of such rumors a decade ago and had been steadily amassing their own fleet of boats. But the girl gave them all the motivation they needed. They quickly set sail down the Nede River. In their pretty little boats." He inhales. "But for all that, that isn't the reason why she's such a problem."

His fingers twitch with agitation. Even his thumb, held above the button, spasms slightly. "She's done the unthinkable: she survived the journey back," he whispers. "That's why she's a problem. She was there. At the Mission. She must have seen the train tracks."

"How do you know this?" I ask. "Maybe she didn't even make it to the eastern mountains." I know this isn't true. I saw her with my own eyes at the Mission—where I was clawed and almost turned by her—but I'm curious to know how the Ruler got his information.

"Your friend," he says, calmly, slowly.

"Who?"

"Your friend. He told me."

"Who are you talking about?"

"The one you designate 'Epap.'"

"When—"

"A few hours ago. After news first broke out. We got concerned. Perhaps she saw the Mission; perhaps she didn't. Then we realized— *I* realized—we had new arrivals from the Mission who might know for certain. So we had Epap brought up."

"Where is he now?"

"He told us he saw her at the Mission," the Ruler says, ignoring my question. "And so now we know. That she knows. About the Mission. About the train tracks." He snaps his wrist, cracking a bone.

"Already, she's called for a big event. At the Convention Center, tomorrow. One hour after the crack of dusk, she'll disclose something 'mind-blowing' and 'earth-shattering.' Twenty thousand online tickets for the event were sold out in fifteen seconds."

"Where is Epap?"

The Ruler doesn't reply immediately. Fatigue circles his eyes. "There's no way we can allow the girl to speak. She blabs about the Mission and the train tracks and everyone will connect the dots. Within minutes, five million citizens will be gunning for the Palace. They'll shred this place to pieces looking for hepers."

"Where's Epap?"

But still the Ruler barely seems to notice me. His next words are spoken in a whisper, not with the kind of hushed tone gossipers employ but with the disquiet of disgust. "Let her knowledge die unspoken," he whispers hoarsely. "Let her be silenced forever." He looks at me. "We need to kill her."

His eyes slide across my face. "You are stunned into silence, I see. But I think you're already one minute along in this conversation. I think you realize why, at last, you've been brought to my chambers." He studies me. "See how your eyes search the walls for a clock, or even an unshuttered window to peer through. See how keenly you seek the time. Because you want to know if it's daytime or nighttime. Allow me to confirm what you already suspect. It's three hours past dawn."

"And it's sunny today, isn't it, not a cloud in the sky," I say in a barely audible voice.

"The most toxic blue sky imaginable."

I don't move. The bodies in the tanks drift and float. Their hair swirling, their limbs moving in slow motion.

"You do know, don't know?" the Ruler says. His voice has regained its timidity, and he asks with genuine shyness. "You know what I'm asking of you."

Two rows back, the chief advisor stands amidst the staffers, his face cast in shadows. But his shoulders are tense with barely contained panic. He stares at me, at his precious, suddenly precarious Origin.

"An impassable barrier of sunlight, miles long, stands between us and the metropolis," the Ruler says. "It is an impenetrable wall between us and the girl. Desperate as we might be, try as we may, there is simply no way we can reach her. Not before she appears at the Convention Hall shortly after dusk. Not before she spills to the whole world the fatal secret." He cracks his neck. "But we are not without our options."

"I won't go. Don't even think about it."

He gazes at me with apology. "I know how you feel. I know." His thumb caresses the button. "I'm really sorry how quickly this is coming at you. In an ideal world, it would be dusk and we'd be able to send out our own team of assassins. But we're not in the ideal world, are we? We're forced to be practical, pragmatic. The way I see it, the only person who stands a chance of successfully assassinating the girl has two qualities: first, he must be able to withstand the sun, and second, he must know how to disappear in a crowd, even despite his newfound fame. And that," he says, looking with admiration at me, "is you."

"I won't do it. I'm not at your beck and call. Let them come and—"

"I'm *really* sorry to have to say this, but I can easily depress this button here. If you don't comply, I mean."

"Go ahead."

"Hm-m." He considers. "I'll bring up one heper after another to be sacrificed until you accede to my request."

"Go ahead."

He pauses. "Okay. I'll bring up just one. The girl. The pretty dome girl. The one you designate 'Sissy.' Once she's arrived, I'll push this button. The staffers will have at her."

"Go ahead." But my reply comes a fraction of a second too late, the slightest pitch too high. They know. On the other side of the glass, they scratch their wrists.

"Yes, I can bring her up right now. Will take no more than two minutes. Then the feeding will begin. Nom. Nom nom nom." A chorus of wails sounds from the other side. The Ruler is tantalizing them, egging them on.

"Go ahead," I say. "We're all dead anyway."

"Really? What if I told you that was not the case? What if I make a promise to you?" He gazes at me with an innocence that defies cynicism. "What if I vow that if you successfully assassinate the girl before she reveals the truth I'll grant you freedom? To both you and 'Sissy.' And just to show you I mean well, I'll throw in the young dome boy as well, if you want. The one who you designate 'David.' We'll release all three of you."

"Epap as well."

The Ruler pauses. "Ah, yes. Epap." He purses his lips. "There might be a slight problem with that."

"What do you mean?"

"He . . . well, listen, I'm truly sorry. I am. Please accept my apology."

Alarm ticks in my throat. "What did you do to him?"

The Ruler pauses. "Well . . . it's just that I . . . This is really hard. . . ."

With a sudden, horrific realization, I turn my gaze to the tanks around us. Darkened bodies float, some facing me, others away. But none have Epap's physique. Which leaves one other possibility.

"Did you eat him?" I say.

The Ruler licks his lower lip. "I did not." He doesn't say anything more.

"Did somebody else?"

"No. Well, I don't think so. I don't know."

Saliva drools out of the corner of his mouth, sliding down to the tip of his chin. The droplet hangs there, growing pregnant, but does not drop.

"I'll be honest with you," he says. "I'd slotted Epap for that tank over there. The tank's been empty for a week now, been begging to be occupied. Epap would've been perfect. We usually don't get boys that old and tall; he would have been a nice addition to my collection. So different from the usual little runts."

"Just tell me where he is," I demand.

The Ruler withers under my berating tone. "We s-s-ent him out," he stammers. "We thought him a solid choice. Older, more mature, like I'd just mentioned, smarter than all the little boys here. He seemed capable, of course, like he could handle the assignment—"

"You sent him out? You sent *him* to assassinate the girl?"

The Ruler's silence is answer enough.

"How could you send *him*? He doesn't know the first thing about the metropolis. He doesn't know how to meld into the scenery, how to remain inconspicuous in a crowd. He'll be devoured within seconds of stepping into the metropolis, if not before."

The Ruler flinches at my outburst. "I'm sorry. I am. You were our obvious first choice, but my chief advisor was dead set against it. Said that you, being so muscular and cut, would possess a taste second to none. And that I shouldn't deny what would be the most exquisite of heper meals for my birthday tomorrow. My chief advisor strongly urged me to send in Epap instead. The boy seemed capable, no?"

The chief advisor. Trying to protect me, his precious Origin, and so he sent out Epap instead. I stare into the crowd trying to locate him, but he's merged into the dark mass of bodies.

"It looks like he's no longer viable, so we're left with no choice but to send you," the Ruler says. "A more logical choice, really, given your experience living there. You know the metropolis; you've acquired all the necessary skills. My chief advisor, bless his heart, is still against it. Can you believe he even volunteered himself to go? He said he would don all the SunCloaks necessary to traverse the sunscorched land. I scoffed at that idea. It would be *suicide* to venture out there. He wouldn't last ten minutes, even with the SunCloaks."

"When did you send out Epap?"

"It must have been about three hours ago. We gave him a bag of weapons—really cool stuff, daggers, snipers, a Moonlight Visor to hide his face, shotguns, stuff the denizens know nothing about—along with a map of the metropolis, the location of the hospital and Convention Center circled. Then we put him on a horse. And away he went."

"But you think him dead already?"

His eyes slid off me uneasily.

"We do. I'm sorry."

"How do you know this."

"We gave him one other thing. A TextTrans. It's cutting-edge stuff, really. With it, he was to type messages to us—which we received instantly—and we, him. We were checking in on him every hour or so, and everything was fine. For the first two hours, anyway." He pauses. "But about an hour ago, we lost all communication with him. The last TT message indicated that he'd just entered the metropolis limits. Then nothing."

"I'll go," I say.

"You will?"

"Contingent on your meeting my demand."

"Go on."

"I don't go in alone. If you want this done right, if you want the girl assassinated, I'll need help. I need two others to come with me."

"Two others? Who?"

"Sissy and David."

He pauses. "No."

"Then forget it."

"Understand my reasoning. You'll all three be spotted in the metropolis almost immediately. Your pictures are everywhere. It's bad enough sending you in alone, but at least I know you have the skills to go unnoticed. But the three of you together will simply be a screaming signboard."

"We'll wear MoonLight Visors. They'll sufficiently cover our faces."

He pauses. "We've packed only two Visors. So you're short. In any case, nobody wears those Visors indoors. What happens when you need to go inside a building?"

"Leave that problem to us. But it's *us*—all three of us—or none at all. The girl, with her combat skills, gives us a lot more kill options. And she won't do it unless the boy goes."

"Like I said, no."

"Then we can just wait for the millions to storm these walls. In about ten, twelve hours, right?"

The Ruler's hand on the control tenses. "I'm trying to be accommodating," he says after a while, "but I'm not a fool. If I let you three go, you'll simply take off and flee. I'd have lost the only leverage that ensures your commitment and cooperation. Because I know what they mean to you. My chief advisor does his homework, see."

"You already know it was a mistake to send in one alone," I say, trying to sound convincing. "Don't make the same mistake twice. Because you and I know both know: this is your last shot. You don't get a third chance at this."

He stares at me with dispassionate, unreadable eyes. He puckers his lips. "Very well," he says after almost a minute. "We'll compromise, meet you halfway. We'll give you one. The other we will keep as insurance."

"As a hostage, you mean."

"Let's call it *incentive*—for you to return, that is—and leave it at that. We'll let you have the boy."

"No," I say. "The girl comes. That's non-negotiable."

"I said we'll give you the boy—"

"No deal, then."

He glares at me, his eyes smoldering in their sockets. "Very well," he says, his voice tinged with resentment. "You can have the girl. But we'll keep the boy here."

In my peripheral vision, someone moves behind the glass. A tall, broad-shouldered silhouette—the chief advisor—is rushing to the side, where he picks up a boxy contraption that's attached by a curly cord to a wall panel.

"Your Rulership?" His voice booms into the room through a PA system.

"Turn down the volume before you blast out my eardrums!" the Ruler yells.

"Sorry, Your Rulership." When the chief advisor next speaks, his voice is softer yet clipped and anxious. "We ought not send out the girl, Your Rulership. For that matter, let me once again reiterate my advice against sending out either of them."

"We've already discussed this, and the matter is closed. The boy is is staying. The girl is going. Now, don't try to dissuade me. Simply make all the necessary preparations."

The chief advisor's silhouette stands very, very still. "May I suggest an action that will further incentivize them to return?"

The Ruler, his patience running out, says quickly, "What, what is it?"

"Transport the young boy into Your Rulership's chamber. Keep him in that empty tank until they return. Only then do we release him."

"No way—" I say.

"An excellent idea," says the Ruler. "Make it happen."

"This may have been presumptuous, Your Rulership, but I've already remotely programmed him to come. He's on his way." The chief advisor's head bends down to look at the tablet. "In fact, he's due to arrive here in four, three, two, and one."

And like clockwork, something starts to happen inside the empty tank. Air starts bubbling out of the submerged face mask. Then the floor disappears and a body is torpedoed into the tank from below. The tank is momentarily filled with a surge of bubbles; only after the floor is resealed does the liquid inside calm.

David is scrambling within, his head snapping from side to side, his arms swinging, legs kicking in panic. I rush over, start slapping the outside glass. "David! The mask, put the mask over your mouth!"

His eyes meet mine, and I see the panic and raw fear swimming in them.

"The mask, David!"

He finally understands. He grabs it, pulls the strap over his head. He sucks in huge, desperate gulps, his pale, thin chest ballooning with need and relief.

The chief advisor's words, though whispered, blare through the room's speakers. "The boy will remain in the tank until you return. After you *both* return."

"After you've successfully killed the hunter girl, of course," the Ruler adds.

David's breathing steadies. But not his composure. His eyes are agog with fear. I imagine what it must be like for him: suddenly floating in a glowing liquid, confined inside a tank, a mob of duskers gawking at him nearby, the Ruler bizarrely tied up mere meters from him. No wonder his arms begin to lash about, his legs kicking the curved glass wall around him.

"David!" I shout, not sure if he can even hear me through the glass. When he looks at me, eyes wrecked with despair, a resolve fills me like molten gold. "I'll come back for you, David. I won't desert you. I. Will. Come. Back. For. You."

Bubbles push out of his face mask as he starts hyperventilating. There's nothing more I can do but press my hands against the tank. He places his own hands on the glass opposite mine.

The Ruler speaks from behind me. "We're running out of time. You must depart immediately, I'm afraid. Wish we had more time to chat."

I turn around, face him. Anger brews deep in me.

"We've already made the arrangements," he continues. "You'll be transported to the outside via your enclave. There'll be a horse waiting for you there. It's been prepped for the two-hour gallop to the metropolis, and loaded with all the supplies and weaponry you could possibly need. A few bottles of water, too, because we know your needs. Oh, one more thing. In a small pouch tied to the saddle, you'll find a TextTrans. It's linked up with Epap's. Just in case."

"And what about the girl?"

"I'll see to it that she's transported outside immediately. There won't be time to prep another horse for her. The two of you will have to ride double."

A pounding on the glass behind me. David is kicking at it, trying to get my attention. Then his eyes lock on mine with understanding. But instead of panic, a strange clarity fills them.

"Let me tell you what will happen in the event you fail your mission, or fail to return here," the Ruler continues. "I will prolong the boy's existence in the tank as long as possible."

David reaches up and pulls the face mask off. I shake my head at him, but suicide by drowning is not what he has in mind. He pushes against the glass with both arms, works his body downward until our faces are level.

"I will take my daily sips, of course," the Ruler says, his voice dreamy, unaware that I'm no longer paying attention. "But I will also take my daily bites, too. Using pincers, I'll pull off bite-size nibbles of his flesh. I've found that after a few days, the flesh gets very soft, simply pries off with only the gentlest of teasing."

David's eyes lock on to mine. They once looked at me with sweet innocence under bright blue skies, and I had seen the man this sensitive, tender boy would grow up to be. A man who would learn to laugh with sadness, and cry with joy.

"I will initially partake of the ancillary flesh, of course, avoid the vital areas . . ." The Ruler's voice drones on.

David's lips open and move, with emphasis. He's mouthing words to me.

Run. Run.

I shake my head at him.

". . . especially the earlobes, so filled with succulent fat . . ."

It's okay.

I choke back tears as I turn away.

". . . if you can avoid the tangy areas of the arms or the gamy texture of the biceps, I have found that . . ."

"Enough," I say, my voice hard and gritty. "Enough."

The Ruler's mouth freezes mid-speech.

I walk over to the enclave, step inside.

"Transport me, already," I say through clenched teeth.

Nineteen

THE ENCLAVE IS transported directly to the Palace wall. A narrow slit widens and that's all I see before I'm scorched with piercing sunlight. I throw an arm over my eyes. There's an electronic beep, and I hear the glass lid of the enclave sliding open. Blinded by light, but afraid the lid might close on me, I step out.

My feet meet nothing but air and I fall a short distance, a meter or so, to the hard, baked desert ground. The fresh sting of sunlight on my skin, after so long underground, feels like life itself.

Gradually, my eyes get used to the brightness. I see skies saturated with the purest blue, the endless stretch of the desert plains. A breeze blows past me, refreshing despite the grains of sand picked up and thrown into my sweaty face. I've changed; now I crave all those things I once avoided: sunlight on my skin, open space, warm winds blowing through my hair, the feel of sweat pouring down my back. They make me feel alive.

A horse nickers. Right up against the Palace rampart, tethered to a hitching post. I walk over, clouds of sand kicking up at my feet. The horse perks up at my approach, nervous, and I slow my pace and move directly into its line of vision. I stroke the side of its neck, clucking softly. Next to its front hoofs are two upturned bowls of food and water. Some of the water has spilled on a backpack.

The backpack is filled with weapons. Lots of weapons. Four handguns, a couple of daggers, Moonlight Visors, a handful of pre-loaded magazines. Several boxes of ammunition. And a small metallic briefcase that I don't open. Not yet. Now it suddenly feels real. These are weapons of death, of Ashley June's death. These are the triggers I must pull; these are the cold bullets that must pummel through her body.

I think about the deal struck with the Ruler. How forcefully I'd insisted that Sissy come with me. Of course, it had to be Sissy. I wanted to be with her. But it never occurred to me—until now—that my choice might have been more calculated than emotional. That there might have been an ulterior motive. My lungs go cold.

The sound of screeching metal disrupts my thoughts. Next to my enclave still jutting out of the rampart, another enclave suddenly protrudes out of an opening. It's Sissy, arms spread against the glass walls of her enclave, trying to stabilize herself. A hiss, then the side facing the outside slides open. Her arms are thrown in front of her eyes.

"Who's there?" she demands, her voice filled with both fear and warning. Trying to see, but blinded by the light.

"Sissy."

Her head snaps toward me. "Gene?" She steps out of the enclave and, like me, mishandles the short drop. She falls awkwardly, sprawling on the ground.

I go to her, and the heat of her skin singes me with guilt.

She tries to open her eyes but can't. "Where are we? What's going on?"

"We're outside. It's okay."

"What? Why did they let us go? One moment I'm in the catacombs locked in the enclave, the next moment I'm transported outside." She slants her head to the side. "David? Epap? Are you guys here?"

"No, Sissy, it's just you and me."

She grips my forearm harder. "What's wrong, Gene?"

I shake my head.

"Tell me what's happening! None of this makes any sense!"

I tell her. I don't hold back—you don't hold back from Sissy, she'll insist everything out of you anyway—so I tell her everything, everything, the Ruler's Suite, the aquarium tanks, the hours passed since Epap last sent a TT message. You give her everything and more, hoping the flood of information, the deluge of words, will conceal the secret agenda. You stand with the sun on your back and the light piercing into her eyes, hoping your face is obscured by shadow. And when she hugs you back, tightly and fiercely, and speaks words of corded steel that the two of you together will find Epap, together kill Ashley Junc, and together return to save David, you return her embrace with your own, only tighter, harder, to mask the self-hatred and self-loathing inside.

And minutes later, galloping away, you are only too glad she is sitting behind you and unable to see your face. And though her arms clasp around your waist and her inner thighs press against the outside of your legs—their intimacy a torture—you are at least relieved she does not see your face, that you do not have to look her in the eye. Because then she might see right through you, and realize why she is with you at all. Then she might discover your hidden motive.

That you are going not to kill Ashley June.

But to save her. To re-turn her back to human.

And in order to do that, you cannot do it alone, for you are insufficient. By half.

You need someone else. You need Sis.

Twenty

WE RIDE HARD across the desert land that is blazing copper and blasted with heat. I push the horse at full gallop for the first thirty minutes, relishing the hard, jaunty bounce, the impossibility of coherent thought in my rattling skull. I try to ignore the feel of Sissy's arms and legs around me, the soft press of her on my back whenever we take a hard bounce. The wind in my ears, the harsh glare of sunlight in my eyes, it is all a welcome distraction.

When the Palace has shrunk to a distant dot behind us, we stop by a pile of large boulders. We disembark, lead the hard-breathing horse to the shade by the boulders. Its eyes are wild with exhaustion, it muscles bunched with fatigue.

"You're pushing the horse too hard," Sissy says, concern on her face. "It'll keel over and die before we reach the metropolis. Go slower, Gene."

I don't reply. She's right, but I'm not in the mood to admit it.

She stares hard at me. "Something's different about you. What's going on?"

I ignore her, and busy myself tending to the horse. She sighs with frustration, then scrambles up one boulder, then another.

The horse side-gazes me with large, accusatory eyes as if it knows my true motives. It snorts, spraying me. I return a hard stare, then climb up the boulders to join Sissy. The granite is blistering to the touch, almost singeing my hands. Sissy is staring into the horizon, through wavy bands of heat undulating off the boulders.

"You don't have to worry about the Originators chasing us down," I tell her. "The chief advisor can't leave the Ruler's side. Not at a time like this. And the other Originators won't leave without him."

But she's not looking in that direction. Instead, she's staring toward the metropolis, her hands placed over her eyes like an awning.

"I can see buildings. The metropolis isn't too far," she says. "Maybe an hour away."

"An hour and a half," I say. "I'll slow down. You're right."

She doesn't reply, but her expression softens a touch. "What's that sparkle over there?" she asks. "That glimmer in the distance."

I follow the trajectory of her pointing arm. There. "That's the Domain Building. The tallest skyscraper in the metropolis."

"Where your father worked."

I nod.

Sissy whistles. "Look at all those skyscrapers. The metropolis is so much bigger than I imagined, Gene." She looks at me with awe. And deep pity. "How did you ever survive? Living right in the midst of them? For all these years?"

"You just learn. Adapt. Survive."

"It's so massive," Sissy says in a quieter, subdued voice. "How are we ever going to find Ashley June in there? It'll be like searching for a needle in a haystack."

"We don't have to search. We have a time and place certain where she'll be. The Convention Center. At dusk. We go there and let her come to us. Then we take her down."

She doesn't say anything, but I can see the idea taking hold. "And how do we find Epap?"

I reach into my pocket, take out the TextTrans. "We keep trying to reach out to him," I say. I quickly explain how the TextTrans functions as I type out a brief message.

→ It's Gene and Sissy. Where are you?

"Let him know we're heading for the metropolis," Sissy says. "Tell him we'll be there in about an hour and a half."

I pause. "I don't know. Maybe we should leave out the details. Just in case his TextTrans has fallen into the wrong hands. It'd be better not to give away too much."

She looks away. She knows what I'm insinuating about Epap, that he might not be alive. She gives a quick, almost imperceptible nod.

I hit SEND. "We do this every few hours," I say. "Maybe we'll get a reply."

Her jawline juts out. "He's probably dead, isn't he?"

I don't say anything.

"He is, isn't he?"

"I won't lie to you, Sissy." My voice is softer now. "He probably is. But we can't let that get to us. We need to think of David, okay? Even if we can't find Epap, we still have David to rescue. Which means we still need to get to Ashley June. For David's sake."

Sissy stares hard at me. A wind gusts then, blowing the hot air rising off the boulders through our hair.

"I keep thinking of David," she says. A vertical line creases down the middle of her forehead. "That right now while we're free under blue skies, the sun on our faces, able to talk, able to breathe fresh air, he's confined in a tank. He's submerged in liquid, alone, in almost pitch-darkness." She clamps her jaw, her teeth grinding. "It's more than I can bear."

Sissy gazes back at the Palace. Muscle juts out of her arms, tinseled with sweat. "I feel like I'm deserting him. I'd do just about anything to take his place; I'd be willing to die a thousand deaths. I should go back for him."

"You can't," I say, almost too quickly.

She pulls her hair behind her ear. "You go to the metropolis, get Epap. I return to the Palace, get David."

"No, Sissy," I say urgently. "We stay together." I can't let us separate; I need her; I need her blood. How I get it—how I'll explain why to her—that I haven't figured out yet. But I can't rush things, not without a proper container to store her blood, not with so many hours for her blood to spoil in the heat. Not while she still has a chance to walk away.

She squares her body with mine, and her look is surprisingly tender. Sweat droplets bead her forehead, dot her upper lip. She sees the desperation in my face, and something in her relents. She presses her forehead against my collarbone. I wrap my arms around her damp back.

"We stay together, okay, Sissy?"

She nods against my chest.

I close my eyes, swallow hard. Hoping she'll forgive me when this is all over.

We test out the weapons. Better to practice firing the weapons here at the boulders than in the metropolis where the loud bangs would attract attention.

Sissy is a quick study when it comes to the handgun. She figures out how to load it and, after only a few minutes, is able to do so with eyes closed, her fingers snapping in cartridge after cartridge, all in under five seconds. She picks out a rock as a target, and after only a few practice rounds she's nailing the target each time.

My weapon of choice is the sniper rifle, which I find only after opening the silver briefcase. Also embedded in the case are two tube-like cylinders.

"Silencers," Sissy says with awe, taking one. "I read about them in the dome." She stares down at the handgun. "I think this silencer is compatible with both the sniper rifle and this handgun!" she exclaims, screwing it in. "I always wanted to try one of these." When she shoots, instead of an explosive report a whistled *zip* is all that sounds. She nods approvingly.

"You keep that one," I tell her.

Turns out, I'm a crackerjack at the sniper. From the moment I place my eye on the eyepiece and stare down the scope, the stock pressed snugly into my shoulder, it feels right. I'm overeager at first, too hungry to feel the sniper's power, and end up pulling the trigger too hastily. But after the first few shots, I steady my breathing, slow my finger on the trigger. My shots are still a bit off, a touch to my left each time. I make some minor tweaks on the scope, and from that point on I bull's-eye every one of my shots.

"Hotshot, you are," Sissy says, smiling. Her face turns serious. "This is good. In terms of strategy. When we take out Ashley June, we'll position ourselves both close and far from her. You get the first shot, from afar. I'll be up close with a short-range weapon, in case you miss. Two chances at the same target."

I nod in fake agreement, glancing up at the sun. "Let's get going," I say. I break down the sniper and pack the parts back into the case.

"Check the TextTrans," she says.

But there's nothing.

Silently we slide down the boulder, untether the horse. But despite Epap's TT silence, I can tell that Sissy's mood has lifted. Her skin glows; her body seems more vibrant. The weapons, the shooting, the sense of working toward a goal—these have all buoyed her spirits.

I secure the backpack to the saddle and am about to mount the horse when she puts her hand on my shoulder. "This time," she says with a grin, "I'll ride in front. It's your turn to sit behind and be the useless seat belt wrapped all around me."

Twenty-one

ITIS ALREADY late afternoon when we trot into the business sector of the metropolis. Heat lies oppressive in the empty asphalt streets. Skyscrapers tower over us, and their slanted shadows cut diagonally across the street, offering us spurts of reprieve from the scorching sun that has unremittingly pounded us the whole journey here. These buildings, looming tombstones of sun-blasted concrete and shuttered metal grates, are silent spectators to our slow, cautious progress.

The horse's clip-clops echo back at us, an eerie sound. And though I used to walk these same empty daytime streets many times when I was younger, they spook me in a way they never used to. More than once, I glance back, half-expecting to see a figure silently chasing us down, bounding on all fours.

"Turn left at the next intersection," I tell Sissy, and she guides the horse with a gentle pull on the reins. We pull up in front of a large circular building. A wide driveway loops up an elevated bank to the entrance. In front of the building is a deep, wide body of water larger than the municipal pool. Not that anyone would ever swim here, not with the water at a depth of almost six meters. A dangerous depth—duskers easily drown in much shallower water— but necessary for the majestic water shows at night. I'd seen a few shows before, on school field trips and on television. An awesome spectacle of high arching coordinated jets of water, colored lighting, sprays and splashes everywhere.

We dismount, lead the horse to the water. It sticks in its snout, drinks in messy gulps.

"Is this the hospital?"

"No. The Convention Center."

"A little early, don't you think?"

"The horse needs to drink. As do we." I cup water into my hands, take in large swallows. It's warm and metallic tasting but a salve to my thirst. I douse my head underwater, then flick my head back up, letting the water stream down my neck and under my shirt.

Sissy's done the same, and water drips off the tips of her bangs, dampening her shirt. She squints at the Convention Center. "Look there. At the roof. It's shining like glass."

I nod. "People rave about that glass roof. On rainy nights, it sets the perfect ambience. The raindrops hitting the roof, just the right amount of filtered light. If there's a full moon, they'll darken the tint of the glass. Push of the button." I douse more water over my head.

Sissy cups another handful of water, combs her bangs to the side. "It's hours before dawn. Find a place to hide out here?"

"We can't stay here."

"Then should we head to the hospital? Find Ashley June's room, take her out there?"

I shake my head. "The hospital's likely to be packed. With journalists. Doctors, nurses. We won't get far before being recognized."

"We can put on the Visors. They'll shield our faces."

I take another gulp of water. "Won't work. People don't wear them indoors. And besides, look at us. We stick out in other ways. Our hair's disheveled, we're caked in sand and dirt, we've got streaks of dried sweat along our faces and necks. I'm badly in need of a shave—not just the facial hair, but I've got hair on my arms and legs, too. And then there's our odor. When's the last time we bathed?

Trust me, they'll smell us a block or two away. A Visor isn't going to conceal our smell."

Sissy's eyes scan over my face, my body, as if for the first time noticing the dirt and hair. "We could use a wash, I suppose. But honestly, I don't smell any odor."

"We've gotten used to each other's smell. We reek."

"So we wash ourselves with this water?"

I shake my head. "It's not enough. Our odor is too deeply recessed into our pores. We need soap, scruffy pads, detergent. Paling cream for our sun-darkened skin. Whitening agents for our teeth. And I need razors."

"And something tells me we're not going to be able to walk into a neighborhood store and find these things. Where do we go?"

I rub the horse's neck. "We go back home. My home."

Twenty-two

I T'S STRANGE TO be walking in my neighborhood again. We'd tethered the horse to a road sign as we entered the suburban district, worried that its loud clip-clops might wake the light sleepers in curbside homes. We're glad to be walking, anyway, the first time in days it feels like we can stretch our legs, get the muscles working again.

We walk in silence. This is all new to Sissy, and the scale of civilization has both spooked and awed her. She's never seen streets aligned in perfect grids, flanked by houses that are perfect copies of one another. Never walked out so fully exposed, without protective glass encasing her, with so many hundreds of duskers in the immediate vicinity, so many millions more in every direction around her. She stares at the shuttered windows and doors, looks anxiously at the sun that will soon begin to set.

"Not much farther," I whisper.

We turn the last bend, and now we're on my street. Nothing has changed since the last time I was here only two, three weeks ago. But I have. The person who once walked in my skin and on these streets no longer exists. Everything is familiar, everything is alien, all at the same time.

Until we get to my house. Then nothing is familiar; everything is a devastating new. Because my house is barely there. The windows have been shattered, the front door smashed off its hinges. Even the walls have been pummeled, whole chunks of cement blocks pushed out and ground to dust. The house has been ransacked. Virtually everything has been stolen, to be later sold on the black market. What remains is only fragments, shards of glass scattered on the floor, splintered wood from the table and chairs strewn everywhere. The sofa has been gutted, and only the twisted metal skeleton frame remains. The walls, the floors, the corners where dust once gathered— all of it has been licked clean five times over by people trying to find a molecule of heper: my dead skin, my hair follicles, my fingernails, my droplets of mucus from a wayward sneeze, anything. The walls are covered with hundreds of swirls of dried dusker saliva, gleaming like prickly coats of dried varnish.

The bathroom, where I'd hoped to find the cleaning agents and shavers, is in even worse shape. Mirrors cracked, floor tiles ripped out, the secret tank of water cracked like broken pottery. The cabinet of cleansing supplies gone. Every tile, crack, line of grout, licked by hungry tongues hoping for a strand of heper DNA.

"Gene. We should go." Sissy's hand on my shoulder, gentle, offering solace. "There's nothing here for us."

I wipe at my cheeks, nod.

Before we walk out, I take one final look at the husked carcass of my home. The last few years here, all alone, were not happy years. They were not. After my father was gone—after he faked his turning and misled me into thinking he perished by sunlight—I had missed him terribly. With a physical aching. The daytimes were the worst, all alone in the house. Its empty spaces were painful reminders of my father's absence.

In those days, to dull the ache, I had imagined him still alive. It was the only way my seven-year-old mind and heart could cope. I imagined he had somehow, miraculously, escaped to some place far away. Perhaps he had fled east, all the way across the Vast, to where the eastern mountains rose on the distant horizon. He had once flown a remote-controlled plane toward those mountains and had told me to remember that. Wasn't it possible, my seven-year-old mind reasoned, that he had escaped there? I held on to this lie because it was a footbridge—rickety and frail though it was—across the chasm of my loneliness.

On days when the pain could not be managed (and there were many), I left the house and walked the streets. Walking for hours at a time, I would remember the way my father would walk next to me, how he would warn me to stay out of the sunlight or to hug close to the buildings. That is what I remembered most: his voice, his words. And what I had wanted was quite simple: I wanted to hear from him. I would not be demanding nor even require an explanation—a simple message would suffice, sent to me all the way from the eastern mountains on one of those remote-controlled planes. *I'm alive. I'm okay.* A sentence or two. That's all.

And so, as I walked the streets, I would—despite knowing better—occasionally gaze upward. I wanted to see a tiny dot growing bigger and bigger as it sailed over the Vast, hear the small whirring buzz of its motor, see it fly between the maze of skyscrapers. Watch its descent toward me, its landing on the street as it taxied slowly toward me, to finally bump softly against my feet.

But I never saw a plane. No matter how many times I set out, how many miles I walked, how many shoes I wore out, how many times I looked up, I never saw a thing. And so I changed my expectations; I did not need a message. I would accept the mere sight of a plane; it did not even need to land. If it merely sailed in the skies above, never descending, and passed over my head, that would be consolation enough.

But I never saw a thing. I never knew what it felt like to fall under the cool, comforting shadow of a passing plane.

Twenty-three

Sᴉꜱꜱʏ ᴀɴxɪᴏᴜꜱʟʏ ɢᴀᴢᴇꜱ at the sky. A pale outline of a full moon is already etched into the blue but darkening canvas. "I'd say we have a couple of hours before sundown. And we still stink." She glances at the neighborhood houses, her brow furrowing. She's imagining the doors and shutters opening at dusk, the houses' occupants—toddlers, teenagers, parents, the elderly—racing out onto the street, hunting us down.

"Follow me," I say. "I know where to go."

We walk with quick, nervous strides. The houses around us are casting longer shadows now, and the sky's saturated blue is now brushed with a hint of crimson.

"Check the TextTrans," Sissy says.

Nothing. I type out another quick message:

→   Epap, you there?

After I hit SEND, we wait for a minute, staring at the blank screen, hoping for the best. I put it back into my pocket. "C'mon, let's go."

A short while later, we arrive. The house is at the corner of the street, exactly as I remember it.

"What is this place?" Sissy asks.

"Ashley June's home."

"Oh." Sissy tucks her hair behind her ear. "What are we doing here?"

"Ashley June didn't survive all these years without her own supply of cleansing agents. We can use hers."

She stares at the house, intact and shuttered, the walls unmarked. Ashley June was never suspected of being a heper, especially after she emerged from the Introduction turned into a dusker. There's been no looting or vandalism here. "How do we get in?" Sissy asks. "All entryways are shuttered."

"It's not what it looks like." Bending down, I grab the bottom of the door shutter and hoist up. It grates up along the rails. "These shutters are meant to keep sunshine out, not people. You don't need to lock them in the daytime."

Sissy nods, understanding. She reaches for the doorknob, turns it. The door swings opens. She pauses.

"It's fine," I say. "Ashley June lived alone and she's at the hospital now. Nobody's home."

The gauzy slab of late-afternoon sunlight filters into the interior, festooning it with strips of red and orange haze. I walk in, Sissy right behind me. Inside, I find something unexpected.

Ashley June did not live scared. That much is evident. In the safety of her home, she did not live as if she had anything to hide. Hung and taped on every wall, from ceiling to floor, are colorful paintings and pictures. Of imaginary places described by her parents, probably: Green hills dotted with colorful flowers where blue streams rush into mythic seas. Places where the sun always splashed down in torrents of yolky yellow. Where it was always day, never night.

And photos. Of her mother, her brother. These surprise me the most. My father had burned all our family photos and drawings, but Ashley June did not seem afflicted with the same level of cautiousness. She was brazen in her own home.

"Look," Sissy says from across the room. "There's a photo of you."

She's pointing at a class photograph. From years ago, when I was only nine. I remember that night clearly. The night of the lightning storm. It had caught the whole school by surprise. We had assembled on the school steps outside when the skies suddenly coagulated with dense clouds. The lightning, forking across the skies, flashed hard and fierce. It sent everyone into a frenzy, eyes clenched shut against the pain searing through their eyeballs. Pandemonium broke out. Children cried out in terror. Teachers screamed. The photographer's camera was knocked over, and the impact on the ground somehow triggered the continuous auto-shoot mode.

Those shots, uploaded online later that day, revealed something stunning. A small girl, standing in the middle of the storm, her face seemingly unaffected by the bright light while every other face around her was twisted in pain. But she was staring right at the lightning with uplifted face, smiling at the falling raindrops. A few hours later, she was eaten. At the crack of dusk, hordes of neighbors who'd viewed the photos online during the day hours stormed her home. Too late (it is always too late, it is never in time) I found out there lived another just like me.

"Is that really you?" Sissy says, smiling, oblivious to my ashen face. "You were a cute little runt, weren't you? You had cheeks like Ben!" Her eyes water with laughter. She rests her hand on my shoulder.

This whole wall is covered with school photographs. Some of the students I recognize, some I don't, some group shots, others capturing only a single person. There's no rhyme or reason to this random assortment of photos. Perhaps they were students Ashley June once suspected were human. Perhaps she got lonely at night, and wanted to see the company of faces on this wall, no matter their lack of expression or warmth. No matter their inherent difference from her.

"Oh, look, there's you again," Sissy says. Then her voice trails away. "Oh . . . weird." It's another class portrait, one I instantly recognize. It was taken last year. I see the faces of my classmates, our bodies standing formal and erect, arms stiff by our sides. There I am, standing in the second row, eyes plain as cardboard. All our eyes depthless, emotionless. But none of this is what grabs my attention.

It's what Ashley June's done to the photograph. Marked it up. Not only in one place, but on every face. A chill slides down my back.

Over every mouth in the photograph, she's glued on a small cutout of another mouth—a smiling mouth, lips drawn back, exposing fangless rows of pearly white teeth. Instead of a class of duskers, we've been transformed into a group of smiling humans. She placed the identical smiling mouth over the teacher's mouth, over my mouth, over every mouth but one—her own. Over her face, she's instead glued on a different shot of her, and in this one she is radiant. I have never seen her look this way—a wide incandescent smile, the sunlight glinting in her auburn hair, her eyes moist with happiness, her whole face cracking free with abandon. I lean closer and stare at her smiling mouth. It's the same smiling mouth that she photocopied and glued over everyone else's mouth.

Exuberant, smiling mouths set under dead eyes. Grotesquely, eerily at odds with one another. But perhaps in the semi-dark and from the other side of the room, you could convince yourself otherwise.

"She was so lonely, wasn't she?" Sissy whispers.

I stare at Ashley June's image. "All of us were."

Twenty-four

ASHLEY JUNE

When ashley june *was almost eight years old, her mother began looking at her in a funny way. At dusk, as her mother scrubbed her down and checked her body for any visible scratches before sending her off to school, she would pause in a way she never had before. As Ashley June dressed, her mother's eyes would examine her naked chest with a seriousness that made her feel self-conscious.*

"Hold on," her mother said one such evening. It was getting late. Fifteen minutes had passed since the shutters had automatically opened. Stars glimmered outside. The moon was brightening.

"Mama?"

"Just turn sideways." Her mother's eyes flicked back and forth. Ashley June wanted her mother to meet her eyes, but she didn't. Her mother's eyes scanned her chest, as if reading tiny letters on her bare skin, and never once rose to meet Ashley June's gaze.

It wasn't until her mother's forehead suddenly creased that Ashley June began to genuinely worry. Her mother never frowned—it was a forbidden expression. Those lines looked so foreign on her mother's forehead, they looked as if tiny sewing strings were pressed into her skin.

"What is it, Mama?"

She shook her head and didn't say anything. She helped Ashley June pull down her shirt and put on her shoes. When Ashley June walked out the door, her mother didn't even warn her to be careful as she always did. Her lips were pressed into a tight line, her eyes a thousand miles away.

It weighed on Ashley June's mind the whole night at school. When she returned home, the first thing she wanted to do—even before taking off her shades—was give her mother a hug.

Except she was nowhere to be found.

"Mama?"

Ashley June stood very, very still in the foyer. Her mother was always home when she returned. She'd greet Ashley June in the foyer, help her out of her shoes, and when the door clicked shut run her hand over her cheek. "Don't grow up," she'd often say, squeezing Ashley June's chubbiness a little.

But today, her mother wasn't in the foyer. Confused, Ashley June took off her shades. And that is when she heard the voices, hushed and urgent, coming from her parents' bedroom. She walked over. From behind the closed door, she heard her mother's raised voice—high-pitched and panicky, a tone she'd never heard her speak in before. Then came another voice, and this caught Ashley June by complete surprise. It was her father's voice.

He was never home so early.

She knocked on the door, but they must not have heard, because they began to speak again, over each other.

She turned the knob and pushed the door open.

Her mother was standing with her arms folded across her chest, her head bent. Her eyes were puffy and rimmed red, and her hair— usually pulled in a tight ponytail—was disheveled. Ashley June's father was standing in front of her, listening, an arm outstretched, holding her shoulder. Despite the volume of their voices, his touch on her was tender and comforting. And it was this last fact that transformed Ashley June's curiosity into something that bordered on fear.

"Mama?"

Her parents startled at the sound of her voice. They turned slowly until they stood side by side, their arms hanging awkwardly at their sides.

The front door opened. Her older brother was back early from school. The clump of shoes kicked off, the click of the front door closing and locking.

"I'm home!" he declared in his jovial voice. "Practice was canceled!" After a whole night of keeping his voice even-keeled and monotone at school, it was freedom to be back home. All the pent-up emotions finally released. Their parents allowed a short burst of emotion when they came home, as long as the door was locked and the shutters were down and they weren't too loud. And after dinner— for ten minutes and only if they'd completed all their homework— they let Ashley June and her brother play. It was a wonderful time when they could smile and sing and frown and burp and fart. When they could let it all out.

Her father would not look at her. Then her mother began to do something she had expressly forbidden Ashley June to ever do. She started to cry. Tears rushed to her eyes, lined down her face.

And before too long, Ashley June was crying, too, for although she did not know why, she somehow knew enough.

A few days later, a man—whom Ashley June had never set eyes on before—arrived sometime between dawn and noon. She spent as much energy staring and trying to figure out the reason for his visit as she would later—for the rest of her life, in fact—spend trying to erase him from her memory. Through the opened front door, she saw the hot sun still rising in the hazy, stone-gray skies. The man— who carried his broad shoulders and muscled body with surprising grace—carried a large steel briefcase, which he set down carefully on the dining table.

He was accompanied by a woman with a little girl—his wife

and daughter, Ashley June surmised. She stared at them. Ashley June's family never received visitors. But she noted the beads of sweat glistening on their heads, the sweat stains banding around their armpits, and so she knew they were like her.

She walked over to the little girl. She was carrying an empty tote bag in her tiny hand as if on her way to pick fruit. Shyly, Ashley June reached out slowly and touched the younger girl's hair. The girl flinched, gripped tighter her mother's hand. The girl's mother squeezed back to let her know it was okay. The girl's eyes were big and innocent.

Ashley June let a small smile form on her lips. The tiniest expression.

The girl's eyes widened with surprise. Then she began to smile in return, tentatively, the corners of her lips curling upward like the margins of burning paper.

"Stop it," the man barked. He was stricter than Ashley June's parents. Instantly the young girl's mouth straightened into a tense line. The man didn't say anything more. He went to the table, opened the briefcase.

And that is when Ashley June's mother quickly took the young girl and her mother into the bedroom. The bedroom Ashley June shared with her brother, where he'd been the whole morning. This was odd, Ashley June realized. Why hadn't her brother come out?

But not as odd as what happened next. It was only her father and the other man in the dining room now.

They laid out strange objects on the table, carefully, as if setting the table for a meal. But these weren't forks and knives and spoons. These were scalpels and needles and other things she didn't recognize. They were small things with sharp edges. They frightened her.

Ashley June moved to the corner of the room and stood there.

The men murmured to each other in low voices. Ashley June strained to hear and she caught the sounds of foreign, odd words like anesthesia *and* bilateral *and* ovaries. *The strange man picked up a glass cylinder with a long needle and dipped it into a clear* liquid. He pulled back a syringe, drawing liquid into the needle. He nodded at her father.

And her father turned to her.

"Come here, honey," he said to her.

She took a step forward, stopped.

"I need to tell you something. Come here." He sat down on the sofa, patted the empty spot next to him.

She thought about sitting in his lap. Sometimes, when he was in a good enough mood and had drunk too much, he let her sit in his lap. He'd bounce her up and down, letting her giggle and laugh for three seconds. For Ashley June in those moments, his lap became the funnest and safest place to be in the whole world. But she did not sit there that day. She sat next to him. And for weeks afterward she wondered if things may have turned out differently if only she'd sat in his lap instead.

"Honey, there's something we have to do," he said. His hand on her shoulder, usually warm and comforting, was clammy and shaky.

"What, Daddy?"

"You'll hardly feel a thing," he said.

"What, Daddy?"

He was quiet and turned his head to the side. Away from her, as if he didn't want her to see his face.

"You're getting older," he said, still looking away.

Ashley June didn't say anything.

"And when you get older, your body . . . changes. Things start happening beyond your control."

Ashley June felt her cheeks turn hot. "I get boobs," she said timidly, quickly, hoping for this moment to disappear. "Mama already told me. She said it won't happen for a few more years. And not to worry when it does. It's natural."

The strange man tapped on the dining table. It was to get her father's attention. The man's broad shoulders hummed with impatience. He flicked his chin at the clock on the wall.

"There's something Mama never told you, though," Ashley June's father said. *"She never told you about another change that's going to come upon your body. Soon. Maybe. We don't know when exactly, it might not happen for another two, three, five years. But because your diet is almost all meat, it might happen soon. A month, a week. Tomorrow."* There was a hardness in his voice and a foreign quality to his taut body that made him seem like a different person. *"And we can't chance being caught off guard, having this . . . change suddenly arrive at school, in the classroom, on the bus, on the streets. In the midst of a crowd, in the middle of the night."*

"What kind of change?"

"Better to do it now rather than later, it'd have to be done anyway. Might as well be now before the change comes." He was rambling. As if trying to convince himself.

"What kind of change, Daddy?"

He jolted as if surprised by her presence next to him. "You'll start to bleed."

She didn't say anything for a while. "I'm always careful. Just like you and Mama always tell me, Be careful not to get any scratches, any cuts, I—"

"You can't stop this one. It's not from a cut."

"A nosebleed? I know what to do if—"

"No."

"I don't get it."

"You don't have to. Not after . . . we do this."

"Now, Tobias," the strange man said from the dining room. He had moved all the utensils to the side and placed a large plastic sheet over the table.

"Who is that man, Daddy?" Ashley June asked. It was odd to hear the man address her father by his designation.

Her father paused. *"He's one of us, dear. He works at the Domain Building and he's very, very smart. He knows a lot about the body and today he's going to be your doctor, okay? He's going to help you be safe. He's brought his wife. She'll help him later, if necessary."*

Ashley June stood up. "What's happening?" She glanced at the closed bedroom door. "Mama? Mama!" she cried out, fear suddenly surging in her. "I'm scared!" But the door did not open. Her brother, her mother, the little girl, none of them came out. It was silent behind those doors.

The doctor stepped toward Ashley June and her father. The needle in the doctor's large hand looked ridiculously small and thin, and he carried it with great care.

"You won't feel a thing, honey," her father said as if that were the only thing that mattered. His eyes were glistening, but there was nothing beautiful about the tears she saw welling up. He stood up, and a line of tears coursed down his cheeks.

The two men stood before her.

Ashley June started to shake.

The doctor took a step toward her. Something snapped inside her, and she spun around to sprint away. But his hand grabbed her arm.

She resisted; she did. With flailing arms and kicking legs and biting teeth. They restrained her anyway, her arms and legs pressed firmly down on the floor like a pinned, encased butterfly. She felt the prick of the needle somewhere below her waist, and then the world went murky and her body went soft and lax.

"You won't feel a thing, you won't feel a thing, you won't feel a thing," her father kept saying a million miles away.

He was wrong.

She came to. She was lying on the living room sofa. The pain was a smoldering fire within her, affecting even her vision: a film of purple, like a bruise, covered over everything she viewed. She felt weak. Drained. The air was thick with the smells of ammonia and cleaning agents.

"Mama?" she whispered weakly, each syllable a burden to utter. Tried to speak louder, but her voice was even frailer than before.

She heard the men speaking. Her father. And the doctor. She glanced over the back of the sofa, saw them by the bookshelf. They were speaking in hushed tones, their bodies hunched.

"Are you serious?" her father asked the doctor.

"Somebody has to go. Those kids can't survive all by themselves in the dome."

"Joseph, I don't know."

For a long moment, the two men stared at each other, neither folding.

The doctor's hands clenched and unclenched. Flecks of dried blood dotted his hand. Her blood. "It's either you or me, Tobias," he said. "We both know that. We're the only two left who can pull off being a scientist at the Heper Institute. And I'm not about to give up my position at the Domain. It's strategically too vital. Besides, I've almost compromised the security safeguards to the fifty-ninth floor."

"You can always go back," her father said. "Even if you did move out to the Institute, you can always go back to the Domain in the daytime."

"You know what, you're an idiot," the doctor lashed back. "There's no way I'm leaving my family to fend for themselves."

Her father's upper lip snarled upward. "Oh, so you're just going to let the girl fend for herself in the dome? Do I need to remind you that she's one half of the Origin? And that she's only seven, that all the dome adults are dead now, that she's got no one else around but a bunch of babies? That it's another ten years before she's past the gestation period?"

Indecision flickered across the doctor's cheekbone. "And do I have to remind you that the other half of the Origin is my son? Who is young, who is prone to making mistakes, who we keep at home as much as possible, like today. I'm not about to up and leave him for weeks, months at a time!"

"He'll still have his mother—"

"No!"

"Then we go in and grab the girl now. You leave us no choice. We take her back to the Mission with Gene!"

"No!" the doctor yelled, so loudly her father flinched. "We swore never to do that. If we simply pluck her out, they'll know, they'll come after us, all the way to the mountains—"

"Then go to the dome!" her father said. He stepped forward until his nose was almost touching the doctor's face. "No one but you can pull it off. Only you can handle being in their midst, rubbing shoulders with them at the Institute. You've proven as much at the Domain. Because you have ice water running through your veins. No one else holds up under those conditions. Certainly not me. Only you. And deep down, you know that."

The doctor did not blink, did not soften his expression. He only uttered, "I have my family to consider."

Her father snorted. "Whatever happened to the Origin first? That nothing else—not even family—can get in the way? Whatever happened to your priorities?"

"You go to hell." The doctor pulled his broad shoulders back. "Never question my commitment," he whispered in a steely voice. "Nobody is more devoted to this cause. You know I place it above all else."

They spoke more, and Ashley June tried to listen. But strength leaked out of her, and she could no longer hold up her body. She sank back down into the sofa and drifted into an unconsciousness that felt like death.

When she awoke again, the house was filled with the harsh glow of daylight. This was unusual. In the daytime, their house was always shuttered to keep out the dangerous sunlight that could tan or even burn their skin. But now the door was wide-open, and from where she lay she could see the dusk sun, hanging low and bloated over the line of rooftops across the street.

The doctor's family was leaving. Even though they were on the street outside, she could hear the fear in their frantic whispers. Something was wrong with the horse. Perhaps it was all the blood, her blood—now all safely burned and bleached away—that had unsettled it.

"Maybe you should just stay," her father said. "You're cutting it too close."

The doctor glanced at the sun, assessing. "No, we can make it back. Better that we not deviate from routine."

They set off, all three of them, the report of the horse's clip-clops growing dimmer and fading, even as it quickened in pace and rhythm.

Ashley June thought she'd never see that family again. But she was wrong. She saw them only twenty minutes later. She was awakened by an incessant knocking on her door. It was muted, deliberately, meant only for her family to hear and not the neighbors, but she heard the urgency behind it.

She sat up. The pain between her legs made her vision swim. The shadow of her father flew past her to the door. He'd been getting ready for the day, washing up and shaving. A set of fake fangs was gripped in his hand.

"Stop making such a racket!" her father said, his mouth cupped against the door.

"Let us in!" A muffled cry came from outside. It was the doctor's voice. But it was hoarse now, bereft of composure and dispassion.

Her father was about to unlock the door when he paused. A grayness settled into him like a layer of sediment. He moved to the shutters next to the door and pressed a button to open them.

Ashley June could now see the doctor on the doorstep. Farther down the street a block away was his wife. She was carrying the young girl in her arms. The girl did not seem to be awake. Her head was slung backward, her hair dragging on the ground. Except Ashley June did not remember the girl having long hair. She peered more closely.

It was not hair.

It was blood.

Long strings of blood streaming from an open wound on the girl's head. Trailing to the ground.

It was dusk. It was past dusk.

The girl's legs dangled out of her mother's cradled arms. Something was wrong with one of her legs. It was misshapen and bent at an acute angle.

The man pounded the door on the other side. "Hurry up! It's almost night!"

"Why did you come back?!" Ashley June's father responded angrily.

"The horse bucked. Something spooked it, threw us off before running away. A hoof caught my girl, broke her leg. We were too far from our home—we'd never have made it. Returning here was our only option."

"You should never have—"

And then he froze. As did her father. At a single sound.

Howling. From somewhere across the street. Joined, a second later, by another howl.

The neighborhood was waking up. To the smell of heper blood.

Her neighbors were probably still dangling in their sleepholds, their half-asleep minds unable to comprehend or believe what they were smelling. But very soon, they would rush out of their homes in their pajamas and into the darkening dusk light.

Ashley June, her body still wracked with pain, sat up.

"For heaven's sake, open the door!" the doctor shouted.

Her father: "No."

A pause. Then the sound of pounding ensued, only louder, more urgent, even angry. "Open up! They're coming!"

"No."

"You can't do this. You leave us out here, we're all dead. You hear me? All of us."

Her father did not say anything. He only pressed his hands against the door, his head hung low like a man pushing uphill against a *heavy boulder. Ashley June glanced at her brother's room. The door was still closed, her brother and mother staying behind it, willfully blind.*

"You let us die out here and you lose me! You lose everything we've worked so hard for."

Her father did not reply.

"Think of the Origin! He's only seven! How long do you think he'll last alone? Now let us in!" The rest of what he said was drowned out by the sound of pounding. It was her father pounding the door now, not the doctor, three, four times, tortured with indecision.

More howls broke out.

"I can't let you in!" her father said. "She'll leave a blood trail right into the house."

"It's nothing! Just a scratch. We can stem it. It—"

"No! She's left a trail. There has to be an explanation for the trail." And the next words from Ashley June's father came out lower, the quiet of guilt. "I'll let you in. But not the girl. Do you understand? Not the girl."

There was a long silence on the other side of the door.

More howls screeched into the dusking sky.

Ashley June moved to the other side of the sofa. Her legs dragged along, paralyzed like lifeless sacks. From there, she was able to glimpse out the unshuttered window, see more of the street. She observed the doctor hurrying back to his wife and daughter. He pulled his daughter out of his wife's arms, let the young body fall misshapen onto the ground. The leg, bent at a hideous angle, lay on the ground like a broken twig. The mother screamed, her high-pitched screech joining with the wails of the neighborhood.

The man grabbed his wife from behind, pinned her arms down, and began dragging her down the street toward the home. The little girl was left lying in the street and her mother screamed and shouted, and tried to extricate herself from her husband's grip. But he was too strong. Already, the distant sound of doors and shutters automatically opening hummed in the air.

Ashley June's father opened the front door for them. Quickly, just enough for them to slip inside. The doctor entered first. But as he twisted his body to slide in, his grip on his wife loosened. She torqued her body and fled from his grasping hands.

"No!" the doctor shouted, spinning around to go after her.

But the door slammed shut in his face. Ashley June's father pushed his body against the door, faced the doctor. "No! It's too late!" her father said, spit sputtering out of his mouth. "For heaven's sake, you open the door, we're all dead! All of us!"

The doctor pushed back, shoving Ashley June's father against the door.

A scream from outside. The woman's scream.

The doctor, hand frozen on the doorknob, stood rigid. Whatever he was feeling, anger, fear, panic, it was expressed only through the bunched muscles of his back and bulging veins along his neck. He did not move.

Outside, the woman ran to her collapsed daughter. Neighborhood shutters were fully opened now, revealing thumbprints of pale faces peering out windows. Within seconds, front doors were slammed open, windows smashed right through by people leaping out. Their flannel pajamas fluttered like ripples across a windblown puddle as they raced down the street. Faster and faster toward the mind-blowing discovery of two live hepers lying right there in the middle of their street.

The mother had draped her body like a blanket over her daughter. Ashley June would forever remember how the woman gazed at her child as if there were nothing else in the universe. The woman's expression was not of panic nor of despair. Rather, a maternal stillness—as if she were singing a soothing lullaby over her sleeping baby—glowed from her face. Then, a second later, the mother herself was blanketed, but this by the arrival of a dozen people, with *violence, with obscene force. They flung themselves at her. And a split second later more arrived, pummeling her with the force of a hailstorm that separated her from her daughter, separated the mother from even herself in a thousand bloody pieces.*

Inside the house, no one spoke, no one moved. But everyone found a wall—or a door, or the floor—against which to press their faces and shield their eyes and cover their ears from the loud mauling of flesh and spillage of blood.

And all Ashley June could think about was the doctor's poor son at home, how he was oblivious to what was happening, how he did not know his mother and sister were being ripped apart, how he did not know that his life had just irretrievably changed. And a sadness clamped around her heart, for she felt for him, and for just a moment she wished she could absorb some of the pain and loneliness that would shortly and surely visit him like the cold, stark arrival of night.

Twenty-five

ASHLEY JUNE'S BATHROOM is as I'd hoped it would be. Intact, filled with cleaning agents. Her homemade concoctions are similar and in many ways superior to mine. Everything is placed in orderly compartments, on shelves, racks, in cabinets and hampers. Skin powder, odor neutralizers, bars of soap, nail clippers. Next to the mirror on a glass shelf are bottles of a translucent liquid I realize is hair soap—in liquefied form. Ingenious. In the top drawer of a small sundry tower are her fake fangs. Over a dozen of them, varying in size, all the fangs she's worn since she was a toddler. She'd kept them, for whatever reason. I rub my thumb over the blunt tip of one of the smaller fangs. So tiny. She was maybe only five when she last wore them. The sight of these fangs, the span of years they represent, make my throat go suddenly thick.

"We should start," I say, my voice low. "Sundown is less than an hour away." I check the water level for the shower. Good. The two overhead containers are filled to the brim with rainwater. They haven't been used in weeks. *Since the night of the Lottery,* I think to myself. That was the last time Ashley June was here, in the predusk hours before the Lottery.

"I'll go first," Sissy says.

I nod, walk out.

A minute later, I hear the sound of water splashing. Sissy will need a change of clothes—what she's been wearing is grungy and stinks. Shouldn't be a problem finding clothes. She and Ashley June are close enough in size. I browse through a chest of drawers, grabbing a pair of roll-up capri pants, a casual denim shirt. And underwear, quickly chosen, which I fling between the shirt and pants, sandwiching it.

I knock gently on the bathroom door. "Hey. I picked out some clothes for you." She doesn't answer. Concerned, I push the door open and step in.

She's fine. There's no shower curtain and I see everything. Her soaked hair, dark as a horse's mane, pressed halfway down her back. Water streams down, pooling briefly in the small of her back, then over her pale-white buttocks. Glides down over the curvature of her calf muscles. Her face is upturned inches from the showerhead, her mouth gaped wide, drinking in some of the water as it splashes noisily over her. That's why she didn't hear me knock.

I quickly drop my gaze. I place the clothes on top of the hamper, turn to leave. But not before I notice she's holding the bar of soap in her right hand, is softly grazing it across her left arm. Too delicate, too soft. She's not cleaning herself.

I begin to step out. I'll speak louder from the other side of the closed door, tell her that she has to scrub harder.

"What is it?" she asks, jolting me. "What's wrong?"

I'm sorry is on my lips, one foot already stepping out. When I stop.

She's turned sideways to me. There's no shame, no embarrassment, no shielding. Just her eyes, honest and open. Her arms by her sides, the water splashing on her shoulder, creating a mist of tiny water droplets.

I shift my eyes away. Cold tiles, metal frames, gray containers. Swing my eyes back to hers and the warmth in them is like a flame suffusing me.

"You have to really scrub hard," I say.

"I am."

"You're not."

She holds my eyes. "Show me," she says softly.

I walk over, take the bar of soap from her hand. I remove the coarse rag from a hook on the wall, soak it in the water.

"Turn around," I tell her. My voice sounds hollow in the confined space, the words muted by the splish-splash of water.

She does. Water flows in waves down her back, coursing down the vertical dip of her spine.

"Don't think of it as washing," I say. "Think of it as erasing."

I lather her back with the soap, moving in small circles. Trying not to let my fingers touch the skin of her back. "Erasing everything that makes you different. Erasing everything that is human."

With my other hand, I press the towel against her skin. I rub down, gently at first; then I scrub harder and harder until her skin is chafed red, until it must feel like I am scraping her raw. She does not complain. She does not move.

"We have to erase everything. The smells. The oily secretions. The dead skin cells. And later, we need to cut our fingernails and toenails, pluck our eyebrows, shave the hair from our legs, arms, armpits. We erase all signs."

"You did this every day?"

"Every night."

She stares ahead at the tiled wall in front of her, not speaking. The water comes down, washing away the lather, curtaining over her skin. "I can't imagine doing all this every single night. I don't think I can do it even now."

A fine spray of water, soft as mist, drifts onto my face. "I'll show you how," I whisper. "I'll help."

She turns her head to look at me and her eyes are dove soft.

I take her arm and slide the soap down its length. She shivers at the touch, goose bumps protruding out. I press the bar of soap harder into the soft give of her flesh. She keeps her gaze on me, and a film of something translucent layers over her eyes. A flash of doubt, suspicion even. But just as quickly as it appears, it vanishes.

"Okay?"

She nods. I rub the bar of soap over the ridge of her forearm. Then to the soft underside. She flinches.

"I'm sorry. I forgot about that." I turn her arm over. The X branding has scabbed over into what will become a thick scar. Softly, I guide her arm under the showerhead, letting the water sweep down her arm, over and over, as if the water will wash away, will smooth, will erase away all the unwanted marks and protrusions.

And she turns fully around, cups my face with her hands. Her eyes pierce deep into mine. Dark circles rim her eyes, slanted black half-moons, and the sight of them stirs a protective instinct in me. Her eyes never waver from mine, not so much for even a blink. They hold mine, damp yet strong, like a long embrace in the rain.

This is what draws me most to Sissy. Not so much her beauty or inner strength. Nor even her loyalty to those she loves. It's her utter lack of guile. This openness—it is something I'd over the years tamped down and shunned. For the sake of survival, I have instead worn a mask, thick and impenetrable as a calloused scar. And, denied exposure to the elements, I've shriveled beneath it.

Sissy stands naked and open before me. She strokes the side of my face, over and over, as if trying to peel something away. I feel the outer layer slipping off, and the sensation is akin to how I felt when I leaped off the mountain on the hang glider. Frightening and exhilarating.

Her fingers stroking my face. My hand trying to wash away her scar.

And in that moment, something breaks in me. I brush her upper lip with my thumb, follow the gentle curve of her cheek.

And that's when I realize. My plan to use her for her blood, to put her at risk in order to save Ashley June—that is a plan I could never follow through on. I won't do that to Sissy.

Not even for Ashley June.

We will go ahead with our plan. In a few short hours, I will put a bullet through Ashley June's skull.

"Gene," Sissy whispers. As if she has finally found what she has long been searching for.

And I lean my head forward into the jet of water. So that when I close my eyes the salt of my tears will be washed away and the evidence of my guilt will have been forever removed.

Twenty-six

AFTERWARD, CLEANED AND shaved and clipped, we sit in the living room on the threadbare carpet. The last rays of sunset slip through the opened door. We sit facing each other, so close that our legs cross over one another. Sissy runs her fingers through her damp hair.

"We can't go to the Convention Center by horse," I say. "People—duskers—don't normally ride double on them. We'll take the bus, instead." Seeing the confusion on her face, I add, "It's like a long carriage pulled by at least a pair of horses. Fits over a dozen passengers."

Her frown lines deepen. "I'm not crazy about getting into an enclosed space with them."

"If we walk, we'll build up a sweat. And a stink." I place my hand on her kneecap. "The bus will be okay. I used to take it all the time. Don't get freaked out if the horses turn to sniff you. Just remember—get a window seat and open the window wide. That should help dissipate any smell. And sit in the last row so nobody will catch any odors downwind. I'll sit close but not next to you. Better if we're not seen side by side, it might trigger recognition."

"How long is the ride?"

"Only about fifteen minutes. But it'll seem like an eternity, especially if it's crowded."

She squirms, clearly unhappy.

"Remember. Watch your lips—don't let them be expressive. Don't pull the corners down. And whatever you do, never smile or grin."

"I don't think I'll be finding much reason to do either."

"And don't speak if you can help it."

"Okay, got it. Just be a statue."

"That's the right idea. Except be a low-key, invisible statue. Don't do *anything* that will attract attention. Keep this Moonlight Visor on at all times," I say, taking two pairs out of the backpack and giving her one. "Even inside the Convention Center where it'll be dark and you'll be tempted to take it off. Without these Visors, we run the high risk of being recognized, Sissy. Never take it off."

"Won't we stand out if we're the only ones wearing them indoors?"

"We don't really have a choice."

She nods thoughtfully, her lips lining with determination.

"Your lips—"

She shakes her head, annoyed at herself. "Got it."

"You can't be so careless."

"I know, I know. But anyway, won't the Visor shield my face?"

"It only blurs. It doesn't completely block your face. And besides, it only covers from your nose up. Your mouth is fully exposed. You need to remember that."

She sighs loudly, but before I can reprimand her she says, "What about walking form? Anything special?"

"Walk with a glide, slow arm movements," I instruct her. "Go with the flow, not too fast, not too slow. Slink into the background. Don't speed up or slow down too quickly. Their eyes snap to irregular, inconsistent speeds."

"Got it."

"Don't walk too close to anyone—"

"Gene! I got it!"

"No, you don't, Sissy. This is going to be a huge challenge for you. We're going to be surrounded by thousands of people on the street, tens of thousands once we're inside the Convention Center. And you don't realize how much you stick out. Your demeanor, even when you're merely standing, screams *different*. I'm trying to help here."

She exhales with annoyance, stands up, flustered, taking deep breaths.

I rise with her. "See this reaction you're having? Standing up in a huff, sighing audibly? Out there, you're dead now."

"Just stop it, already."

"I'm trying to—"

"Hey, I'm not the only one who's going to find things difficult."

"Sissy, not to boast or anything, but I'm good at fading into a crowd. I've been doing this my whole life."

"I'm not talking about blending in. I know you'll be fine with that."

"Then what are you talking about?"

She pauses, her face filled with regret over bringing up the topic. But when she looks at me her eyes are unwavering. "Are you sure you're going to be able to take the shot?"

She keeps her eyes centered on mine, daring me to look away.

"You know what I mean. You get the first shot at Ashley June with the sniper. Long-range, hidden in the rafters. When you've got her in your crosshairs, are you going to be able to pull the trigger?"

I push out the next few words, quickly, letting them tumble out of my mouth. "Of course. Not a problem. I just put her in the hairlines, and squeeze the trigger. Done."

Sissy shakes her head, but with sympathy, not acrimony. "Really, Gene? Because I'm not so sure. I know what she means to you. I know the special place she has in your heart. Just being here in her home, I see the effect it's had on you."

"What she *meant* to me." I tug on the bill of my cap. And I return Sissy's gaze with a conviction I know is genuine, glad that I had made the decision back in the shower. "Because that person I'm going to shoot in a couple of hours? That person may look like her, sound like her, but it's not her. Ashley June is no longer. Ashley June is gone. I'm shooting a dusker, that's all. It'll be a mercy killing."

The setting sun dips below the line of roofs across the street. The room plunges into a dark gray. Night is almost upon us.

"Back at the Mission," Sissy says, her voice lowering, "when she attacked us. She paused, Gene. She *paused*. She was leaping up to attack you, but then she changed course and attacked me instead." For a second, Sissy's fingers instinctively move up to her neck, touching the tiny scabs where Ashley June had fanged her. "I don't know if she's changed completely the way you say she has. She may have retained a few things, Gene. Like her feelings for you."

The house darkens even more. The sun a fading memory now.

Feelings of defensiveness rise up in me. "I will take the shot, Sissy."

"Really?" She touches my hand, gently. "Because you're also weighed down with a lot of guilt. You still feel responsible, justly or not, for what she's become." Sissy's eyes penetrate the thickening darkness, piercing into me. She's searching, probing. "Are you certain you'll take the shot? Because if you're not, we can change positions. Let me take the sniper."

"No. I can do it—"

She puts her hand on my forearm. A soft grip, but tight nonetheless. "Understand why I'm saying this, Gene. If you can't pull the trigger, I'll be forced to take the shot. From close range. You know what that means, right? I shoot near the stage, and the crowd around me turns to me. Within seconds. I won't be able to make a getaway in that crowd. They'll jump me before I can even drop the gun."

I look at the paintings, the photographs, all their lines and bright colors, disappearing into the deepening darkness. I meet Sissy's gaze, straight on. "I can do it. Like I said, it'll be a mercy killing. I'll be putting her out of her misery."

The house darkens. And then, like a mournful elegy, the neighborhood dusk siren sounds. Within a minute, shutters are raised, windows and doors opened. The metropolis is arising, and the thin, frail barriers separating us from them removed. Nothing stands between their millions of fangs and our skin.

I pick up the backpack filled with weapons, put on the Visor. "Time to do this, Sissy. Time to go."

Twenty-seven

PEOPLE RUSH OUT of their homes within a minute of the dusk siren. Everyone is already dressed and eager as they head out, all in the same direction. Toward the Convention Center.

"Wait for more traffic," I whisper to Sissy. "We'll stick out less."

Horses trundle by, all single ridden, as more pedestrians hit the sidewalk. Within minutes, it seems like the whole neighborhood has hit the pavement. A few of the wealthier families rattle past in their carriages.

"Okay," I say in a low voice. "Now."

We walk down the path, turn left at the sidewalk. I stay ahead of Sissy about ten paces as per our plan. We need to stay apart to lessen the chances of being jointly recognized, and she doesn't know the way. But now I wish we'd reversed our positions—I want to keep an eye on her, monitor how she's doing.

I move off to the side, bend down, and pretend to do my laces. She passes me a few seconds later. I stand up, and slowly—slowly— catch up with her. Nobody speaks, nobody makes small talk, nobody offers a greeting. Nothing is wrong: This is just the way they are. Bland, sullen faces, everyone donning shades or Visors at this early hour of the evening.

I can tell the silence of the crowd is unnerving Sissy. Her gait is too stiff, tight, not enough to attract attention, not yet, anyway. I walk to catch up with her. She senses me beside her, doesn't turn her head in acknowledgment (good), but she's breathing too fast (bad). It's the proximity of fangs and claws, the potential for brutality to erupt in a split second, that's unsettled her.

When we find ourselves in a slight clearing, I whisper to her, "You take the lead. The bus stop is two blocks down. Look for the yellow sign."

She doesn't reply, but she starts walking too quickly, her arms swinging too high.

"Slow down. Arms," is all I'm able to murmur before the crowd fills in around us. But she gets it. She slows her pace, stabilizes the swing of her arms. I slowly drop back.

There's already a line at the bus stop, about seven people. Standing perfectly still, their pale faces turned sideways in our direction. I'm paranoid, on edge, and for a moment I think they're staring at us. But they're only staring down the road, past us, looking for the long carriage of the bus.

Sissy gets in line, and I stand behind her. Perhaps it's my imagination, but the people queuing up seem to stiffen slightly. In front of us, horses and carriages roll by, the clip-clop and occasional squeaky wheel breaking the monotone thumping of boots on concrete.

The bus arrives, an extra-long carriage used on special days when ridership is high. The six horses are already chuffing with exertion, their combined heat radiating out. We board. And as we do, the nearest horse suddenly swings its head toward me, nostrils flaring wide and wet. It smells us. Hepers.

Discreetly, I nudge Sissy from behind. A *hurry up, get on already* prod. She ascends the two steps, glides down the aisle slowly but deftly, avoiding body contact. No easy feat considering how crowded it is. She finds a seat in the second-to-last row. Opens the window quickly. Good. Wind gusts in. A few passengers, annoyed, turn to look at her. Sissy only stares out the window. Even after they look away, she keeps her head perfectly still, face turned looking outside. Perfect. She's doing great.

I find an empty seat across the aisle from her. Place the backpack down on the aisle seat, carefully. I open the window wide, feel the glorious rush of air. So far, so good. Everything according to plan, not a hitch yet.

Behind my Visor, I glance sideways at Sissy. She's rock still, holding strong. Her breathing controlled, her shoulders not too tense. Only her hands give away the stress she feels—her fingers are fidgeting in her lap. But nobody's sitting next to her; nobody can see her hands.

The bus moves along, the sound of the horses' hoofs on concrete synchronized almost perfectly with one another. The wood-shelled carriage creaks as we move forward.

Several stops along the way. More people pile in. Somebody approaches. Points to my backpack on the seat next to me. I ignore him, stare out the window. He doesn't say anything, only stands in the aisle. He reaches up and grabs a strap dangling from above. Bodies fill the aisle now. Somebody sits next to Sissy. Then a wall of bodies in the aisle blocks my view of her.

People staring at me, annoyed at this young punk who's too self-absorbed and selfish to move his bag so others can sit down. I keep my head facing outward, even as my eyes scan from side to side behind the Visor.

A sudden turn at an intersection. The bodies tilt and sway slightly and I catch a brief glimpse of Sissy. Her shoulders bunched and taut, her neck unnaturally canted. She's tense. But she's still got her wits about her. She's facing outward, pushing her breath through the open window. Capable, this girl. Something like pride swells in me.

Minutes pass. More bodies pile in. Then we've made our last residential stop, and the bus-carriage is flying along the street. The road is filled with other horses and carriages, the sidewalks bursting with the pace of thousands walking to the Convention Center.

No one speaking, everything quiet except for the sound of hoofs and the pounding of thousands of boots on concrete. The buildings grow taller, no longer the low domiciles of the residential zones. We've entered the business sector.

And minutes later, we arrive at the Convention Center. A water show is on full display in the large fountain out front. High arching, spiraling streams of water jet out of the pool, twenty, thirty meters into the air before splashing into the rippling, frothing surface. Music is piped in through outdoor speakers, synchronized with the water show. Sissy gets off the bus before me, walks with the flow of pedestrian traffic. Everyone's pace faster now, the start of the event drawing closer, the excitement level building. She walks slowly, knowing it'll be easy to get separated in such a crowd.

She stops in front of the fountain. I sidle up next to her. Our eyes stayed fixed on the water shooting up in wide symmetrical arcs above us. Phosphorescent liquids have been added to the water, and the soaring twirls of water glow lightly in the dark.

"Okay?" I whisper.

"Okay."

"No. Really. Are you okay?"

She doesn't respond immediately. "There's so many of them. Too many." Her voice catches, hitching. "How are we ever going to pull this off? What were we thinking?"

"Sh-h-h. Don't stand so close to the fountain. They're afraid of it—the water, the depth, the lights."

"Why do they have it then?"

"The danger's a huge part of the thrill for them."

She takes a step backward. "I don't think we can do this. There're too many of them. They're everywhere."

"No, we're doing fine. Just remember the game plan. Focus on that. And on nothing else, not the people around you. Okay?"

After a moment, she whispers, "Okay."

"Stay close," I say, and we rejoin the crowd streaming into the Convention Center.

Twenty-eight

To enter the main arena of the Convention Center, the crowd must first filter through a large tunnel that breaks into smaller and smaller tributaries leading to higher levels and sections. Here in the main tunnel, every sound is amplified and echoed and the thunder of footsteps makes it seem like there are many more than the thousands heading into the auditorium.

Despite our best-laid plan to remain apart, Sissy and I walk side by side. It's simply too dark and too crowded to risk losing each other. We even take off our Visors, a dicey move but given the near-pitch-black environs, a necessary one. I comfort myself in the knowledge that this throng of thousands is facing the same direction, with no one glancing backward or sideways at us.

Sissy starts trembling next to me. It's barely discernible, invisible to most. But I see the way her fingers are quaking. She's trying to tamp down her fears and give off a calm demeanor, but she's overcompensated. Her lips are torqued into an odd curve, and her arms swing with disjointed jerks. We can't go on like this. Sooner or later, somebody's going to notice.

On our right is a small food court, mostly empty. It's surrounded by concession stalls selling light fare, slims of synthetic meat and artificially flavored sludge. I nudge Sissy toward a table in the far corner where we can keep our faces from view. There are a few other couples at other tables, conversing and sipping their drinks. That's good. We fit in.

"I'm sorry," she says as we sit down. "It just got to me. Too many of them, penning us in. The air went thin, I felt suffocated."

"It's okay. Let's take a minute to regroup."

She takes slow, deep breaths. Shakes her head in frustration, catches herself. "Thought I was stronger than this," she says, a hoarse whisper issuing from her throat. "What's wrong with me?"

"You're not used to it. Listen, we can stay together. Maybe it was a foolish idea to separate."

But she's already shaking her head. "No. We stick to the original plan."

"Sissy—"

She touches my hand. Withdraws it quickly, remembering. "No, Gene. We decided it was best. You in the upper levels. Me down on the floor. You take her out with the sniper, make a quick getaway. If you miss, or your sniper jams, or . . ."—she bites her lip for just a second—"I'll take her out."

"That's not going to happen, Sissy."

"We just have to—"

"I won't let it happen. I won't miss. I'm not going to make you take the shot on the floor because we know what that means. Down there, you have no escape."

"I know. But we should plan for every exigency." She brushed her hair to the side. "Regardless of how it goes down, we try to meet out front by the fountain. And worse comes to worst, we'll meet back at the boulders in the desert."

I want desperately to run my hand under her jawline where the hardness of bone and softness of flesh meet. But all I can do is stare at my stationary hands.

"We should check the TT," she says after a while.

I take out the TextTrans. Nothing. I type out a quick message.

→ Epap, we're at the CC. Where are you?

It's risky to give away our position like this, and my finger hovers over the SEND button, hesitating.

But Sissy urges me to send it. "It's the right move," she says. "Maybe his TT's broken, can receive but not send messages. If that's the case, we need to let him know we're here. Give him at least a chance of connecting with us."

"You really think he might be here?"

She nods. "If he wasn't able to kill her last night—and judging from the fact that the event is still on, he didn't—he'd want to come here. For the very reason we're here: she's here." Sissy nods. "Let's send it. Play big, win big." She taps on SEND.

Or lose big, I think, but don't verbalize.

Behind us, the crowds grow larger by the minute. Their footsteps are thunderclaps bouncing off the walls and ceiling.

Sissy half-turns to look at them. Under the table, she clenches my hand tighter.

"This is not something we didn't anticipate," I say.

"I know. But this is so much worse than I thought it'd be."

I lean closer to her. "We can still leave. Just forget about—"

"No. Let's do this."

"Sure?"

She nods, tensely.

Someone sits at the table next to us. The food court is getting crowded, filling with people who walked here on empty stomachs. "We should move on," I say reluctantly. "Before we attract any attention."

Her hand squeezes mine one more time before letting go. "But this is where we part ways, Gene."

"Don't put it like that."

A flicker of a smile. "I'll see you later then, okay?" she says.

"Okay."

But neither of us moves. We don't want to separate.

Using her body as cover, she takes out her handgun and pockets away a silencer. "We stick to the plan, Gene. Don't deviate, okay?" She slides the gun into her the waist of her pants, pulls her shirt over the bulge. "See you in a bit."

I nod, not trusting my voice.

One last look at me, and then she parts. I want to grab her hand, stop her from leaving. But I stay rock still, arms lashed to my sides, one of the hardest things I've ever done. She walks along the edge of the crowd—to her, it must feel like touching the sharp edge of a razor—then disappears into it like a raindrop into a river. She is there, and then she is gone.

A minute later, I join the masses. My feet fall in step with theirs. I want to catch a glimpse of Sissy ahead, but it is all darkness. I walk on, backpack slung over one shoulder, unable to shake the thought that, in letting Sissy go, I've made a fatal mistake.

Twenty-nine

Coming out of the tunnel, the throng of thousands moves efficiently and quietly along slate-gray walkways. At every level, thousands leave the ramp to find their sections on that floor. By the time I'm on the fifth and top level, the crowd has noticeably thinned.

I clutch the strap of the backpack. A different sort of crowd up here, better dressed, with more airs about them. The men in ritzy suits with wide velvet lapels, the women garbed in the luxuriant colors and swanky dresses of the affluent. The cream of society rising to the top where it's all about private luxury suites.

And not a Visor in sight. Other than mine, of course.

The layout of the arena is a mystery to me, and I'm unsure which doors lead where. When an announcement comes over the PA system that the event will start in five minutes, I start to panic a little. I don't know how to get to the rafters. I quickly decide to go to plan B: find an empty suite. Private and isolated, the suites are actually the perfect places to set up for the kill. I can still sight the target from a high vantage point. Then pull the trigger, drop the target, and escape quickly by merging with the panicking crowds.

The only problem is finding an empty suite. This is a packed event, and every suite I walk past is either fully occupied or fast getting there. I quicken my pace. A little too quickly. From the corners of my eyes, I observe two staffers conversing, their heads swiveling around to study me. They see a person walking too fast, whose attire and demeanor don't fit in with the upper-crust denizens of the Luxury Level. Who's wearing a Visor. Indoors.

I slow my pace, walk around the natural bend of that level. Once out of their view, I move faster, legs scissoring past each other with contained panic. My eyes again cut into every suite I pass, wishing for a miracle I know will not come. There's little hope of finding an empty suite.

An announcement is suddenly made over the speakers. "One more minute. Take your seats."

The small clusters of people milling about disappear into their suites. Leaving me virtually all alone and completely exposed.

There's one suite coming up. Unlike the others, the door is closed. As I draw nearer, the words *The Palace* embroidered in gold letters come into view. *It's empty,* I think to myself. *It's got to be empty*. The Ruler, his staffers, they're all stuck in the Vast, unable to journey on such short notice. I turn the knob. And like a gift, the door opens.

I glide in, shut the door quickly. Take off the Visor. The suite is empty, the air undisturbed. I press my ear against the door. Footsteps outside, too hurried to be anyone's but the security staff following me. The footsteps march quickly past the door, fade away. It'll be minutes before they circle back, if ever.

I take in the suite. It's larger than expected, perhaps the size of two typical suites, with a bar in the rear, velvet sleepholds on the ceiling, a sliding glass door that opens to two rows of cushioned exterior seats that peer into the arena. The dim lights go dark, enshrouding me in black. The show is beginning.

I slip through the door to the exterior rows of seats. Glance over the edge into the arena.

Only the stage is lit, dimly, an orb of faint gray gleaming off the bare floor. The arched glass roof of the arena, usually smoothly concaved like a dome, appears oddly granular and bumpy. It takes a minute to realize why: there are hundreds, thousands, of balloons bunched up there. I know what they have planned. At the climax of the evening's event, they'll drop all the balloons. It'll be quite the spectacle: thousands of colorful orbs descending to the floor while tinted moonlight beams down through the domed glass.

From the suites to my left and right, soft sounds. Clinking of wineglasses, restrained whispers of conversation. I edge back from the edge, not wanting to be seen, and slink into the second row. A good place to set up for the kill undetected.

The master of ceremonies takes the stage. He's yammering on, but I'm not paying attention. I need to focus on the task at hand. I take out the sniper rifle. Screw on the hollow, cylindrical silencer. Load and chamber two rounds. There won't be time to clear the shell casing, then load and chamber a third one. Pandemonium will ensue quickly, and I'll have to drop everything and book out of here in two seconds flat.

It hits me then, that this cool, clean weapon in my hands is the very instrument that will bring death to Ashley June. That the bullet will smash through her head, whipping past the fall of her auburn hair. I remember all those years in high school when I'd sat behind her in the classroom, how I'd longed to reach out and touch her hair. I think back to not long ago, back at the Heper Institute, the night of the Gala when we'd lain next to each other and I stroked her hair. I remember how those silky strands felt like a miracle, the warmth of her hand in mine, the lilt of her voice in my ears.

Applause breaks out from the crowd of thousands, deafening and raucous. They're alive, not just images on a screen. They're alive, they're here, everywhere around me, and the thought, cold and wet, prickles my skin. I stare down into the stage floor, a pit of blackness. Somewhere in that mass of thousands stands Sissy. How many times has she been inadvertently bumped, touched, had skin grazed across hers? How many times has she stifled a flinch, scream, jolt?

The master of ceremonies' voice is rising, building into an excited crescendo. I hear his words in the back of my mind, distant, as if miles away. He's talking about the Heper Hunt; he's talking about the hunters; he's talking about Ashley June. The winning hunter, that's what they're calling her now, the Valiant Victoress. The audience is impatient, starts clapping in rhythm, faster, louder, feet stomping the floor on every level.

Somewhere down there, Sissy is mimicking everyone around her. Trying to stay apace with the claps and foot stomps. One mistimed clap, one stomp too late, and eyes will turn, heads will pivot. Noses will twitch.

I should never have let her go alone.

I shake my head. Can't let these thoughts distract me. Let my mind slip one millimeter and that misaligned trajectory will send my shot a meter off-target. Need to blank my mind, sharpen my focus. Because if I miss, Sissy dies.

The arena lights dim further. Only one spotlight blazes through the darkness, a hazy beam that hits the side of the stage.

A figure steps into that light. A pearly white luminescence, and a cascade of red lava flowing from the top. That is all I see at first: red and white, brilliant, stark, vibrant.

It is Ashley June. In a crisp white frock, a pair of satin white pumps. And her hair, more voluminous and longer than I remember, a deep pulsating redness emanating from it. She walks to the center of the stage with confidence, her strides sure-footed and brisk. No shades. But something off about her eyes. She's holding something in her hand, small enough to almost fit into her palm. She stares up at the audience, drinks in the sight of tens of thousands of her new, adoring fans. She's a natural at this celebrity thing.

I kneel into position, place the barrel of the sniper rifle on the top of the seat in front, stare down the scope. Thumb the focus wheel slowly. Trying to locate Ashley June, finding her, the blurred, bloated outline of her body crystallizing into sharp clarity.

She is so close, she is only an arm's length away. Her skin is an iridescent white, her hair the color of a rose in bloom. She is glowing. Her beauty has ripened. She seems more real, more alive, than in all the years I've known her.

My hands tremble. I lose her in the sight.

She starts speaking in that inimitable voice that is both sweet and seductive. Except her voice is huskier now, more textured than before.

I close my eyes, inhale. Find her in the scope again, center her within the crosshairs. My index finger drifts along the trigger, curling around the metallic curve. I begin to pull.

Ashley June speaks, her head moving left to right and back left, along every level of the arena. Establishing eye contact with thousands, making every person feel personally touched. Even as I feel her eyes reach the Luxury Level, even as they careen toward my suite, I can't move. I'm frozen. My finger, pressed white against the trigger, comes to a stop.

She is not Ashley June. She has only the outward form, but Ashley June is no more. This is a mercy killing. *Take her out now. Take it out. Put it out of its misery*. Before its eyes swing around, center on me, before it puts me in its crosshairs. Because although everything is dark as night to me, it is clear as day for her.

Pull the trigger. Pull the trigger, already.

I can't. My finger's locked into place. Or maybe it is the trigger, maybe it's stuck. I pull harder, feel the trigger shift minutely. Any moment now, any split moment, and the sniper will recoil in my hands.

Its eyes swing across my suite. Then stop. For a split second, I think it sees me, its eyes meeting mine through the scope. Black beads for eyes staring at me. It is wearing black contact lenses to protect against the dim spotlights. The hair on my neck rises. A connection, thick as corded rope, forms between us. I feel it as palpably as the cold metal in my hands. Ashley June on the other side, tugging. Then her eyes shoot past me, past my suite, to the one next to mine.

Take her out. Take it out. Plug it.

But my finger can't seem to move.

Then a realization. Thumps me in the back of my head.

Sissy is still down there. My heart hammering again, a sick realization sinking in. Sissy is going to think I missed, she's going to start pulling out her gun. And if Sissy shoots, Sissy dies. There's no way she's escaping from the crowd on the floor.

I pull harder on the trigger. A millimeter. And another. One more, surely, and the bullet will be sent flying. It's centered in the crosshairs. Now. Now.

Then it's gone. Just like that. One second in my crosshairs; the next, vanished. I search the side of the stage. There: just behind the curtain, it is surrounded by uniformed officers who are pulling it away deeper backstage.

Fire off a shot, damn it. Just fire off a shot—maybe it'll hit her.

Another thought blazes into my mind.

Where's Sissy? Why didn't she take a shot?

Maybe Ashley June got off the stage too quickly for Sissy to react, to pull out the gun. Or maybe something's happened to Sissy. Something terrible.

Something vibrates against my thigh.

It's the TextTrans. A message has come in.

Ignore it, I tell myself. *Take the shot.* Before Ashley June completely disappears. I bend my head down, try to find her through the scope again.

The TextTrans vibrates with insistence, growing warm.

Exhaling with frustration, I release the trigger, fish out the TextTrans.

A message. From Epap.

→   It's a trap. Run.

Thirty

I CAN'T MOVE. Even as I feel valuable seconds tick by, all I can do is stare at the TT screen, try to thaw the layer of frost that's paralyzed my thoughts, my body. The audience suddenly starts stomping, snapping me out of my stupor. I type out a quick message.

→   Epap, where are you?

No reply. Inwardly cursing at myself for wasting time, I start to stand when the TextTrans suddenly vibrates again. Seemingly more frantic than before, it almost tumbles out of my hand.

→   Drop everything. Run.

→   Epap?

→   Run. Leave CC now. Get outside.

→   Where are you?

→   They're coming. They know where you are.

Something snaps in me, a panic, an urgency. Fury and adrenaline in chaotic tandem. *Finish the job, finish the kill. The* mercy *kill.* But when I bend to the scope again, I can't find her. She's gone. There's no sign of Ashley June.

The TextTrans buzzes in my hand.

→ They're coming. Run.

Need to move. I drop the sniper. For a moment, I consider taking the backpack with me, but decide its weight will encumber my getaway. Stealth and quickness are going to get me out of here, not a blaze of gunfire. Still, I grab one handgun, and affix the silencer from the sniper to it. Kick the backpack under the sofa, tuck the handgun down my waist. I'm rushing out the door when the TextTrans vibrates in my hand.

→ Turn right when you exit suite.

I shut the door behind me. Glance left: the curved corridor outside is empty, only one worker behind the concession gift stand selling T-shirts and magnets and posters and other Heper Hunt–related paraphernalia. Glance right: on the far curved wall, three shadows on the wall are speeding around the bend. *I have to turn right,* I think to myself. *Epap's telling me to go right.* The shadowy figures distort and loom larger as they race along the wall's curvature.

I head left, quickly, staying close to the wall.

I'm not going to make it. They'll come around the bend, see me walking briskly and suspiciously away. I sidestep in front of the concession stand, pretend to be examining the wares on display. My back to them, dillydallying as if I have all the time in the world.

Behind me, three security officers come around the bend, their boots clacking on the hard concrete, walking at a brisk pace. But they're *walking,* which means they don't believe they're on the lookout for hepers, for Sissy and me. If they did, they'd be sprinting, bounding, foaming, and hissing.

They open the door to the Palace suite, walk in.

Now.

I spin around, stride quickly. Only as I approach the open suite door do I slow down. I walk past slowly as if strolling, glance sideways. The three security officers are standing with bent arms at their waists, looking casually around.

I start running. With as silent strides as possible. Need to create distance, get around the bend before they exit the suite and see me.

Only then do I realize I left my Visor in the suite.

The TextTrans starts humming again.

The walkway is empty, the curving ramp bereft of people. I fish out the TextTrans, reading as I run.

→   Head down ramp to Level 2. Walk to Section 33, exit there.

Quiet. Everyone is still in the arena. I run down to Level 4. Level 3. The sound of my footsteps echoing around the walls of the curved ramp.

Then the sounds of other boots hitting concrete echo from above, throwing disorder and chaos into the rhythmic pounding of my own running.

Level 2, now. My legs are wobbly, kneecaps about to pop like a cork out of a wine bottle. This is the level where I should get off, find the exit by Section 33. I pause. A sign above indicates that Sections 40 to 32 are to my right.

Footsteps, louder now, slaps of soles hitting cement.

The TextTrans starts vibrating against my thigh.

Sissy. All alone on the arena floor. Surrounded by thousands. Right now, she must be sensing something is wrong. I see her in my mind's eye. Worry creasing her forehead. Her rib cage expanding, shrinking, expanding, shrinking, the air slack and insubstantial. Panic setting in. Stress odors chuting out of her pores. The crowd around her growing restless, beginning to press in. They will think it's because of this Heper Hunt–related event that they are involuntarily salivating, that their necks are beginning to crack, their lips wobbling wetly. But soon they will realize their heads are snapping toward a locus, toward one person in particular whose head does not snap, whose lips are dry, whose mouth is not salivating.

I bolt. Not to Section 33. But down the ramp to Level 1, down its dark throat, the thin floor lights running along the edges of the ramp like trails of glistening saliva. The TextTrans hums insistently again. But still no time to take it out.

Footsteps pound louder from behind as I get off at Level 1. I force myself to walk slower, fighting the urge to glance back every step of the way. A man, attention fixed on the program sheet in his hand, bumps into me. He regards me coolly, his nose twitching. Head cocks to the side at a slight angle. Shakes his head, is about to start walking when he gives me a long hard stare. But by then, I'm walking through the entranceway to the arena floor. I'm in. I'm safe. In here, there are thousands of bodies with which to merge and disappear.

And then it hits me with fresh horror. I'm *in*. In the midst of them. In full view, without a Visor, without shades. Rubbing shoulders with the thousands on the floor, with a fresh layer of perspiration slicking my back. With dozens close enough to touch me. Claw me, gut me, fang me.

I stare ahead. Somewhere in this swamp of darkness is Sissy. I push deeper into the crowd. They tide against me, washing over me. I'm in.

Thirty-one

EVERYONE IS PACKED in. Personal space is usually sacrosanct and transgressed only with consent during romantic interludes and social dancing. But tonight everyone in the arena has adjusted their personal preferences. Especially those crammed together on the floor, their shoulders occasionally touching, backs grazing against chests.

I push through the crowd, murmuring my *pardon*s and *excuse me*s. There's no room to slide between people. My secretions graze onto their skin, my odor wisps into their nostrils.

No sign of Sissy. She'd planned on positioning herself close to the stage, but with this crowd I'm wondering how far she was able to advance. Perhaps that's why she never took the shot. She wasn't able to get close enough.

A ripple of discontent is spreading through the crowd. Ticket holders were promised more than an appearance by the Valiant Victoress, resplendent as she is. They were told she'd give an earth-shattering disclosure. And so far, there's been none.

But something else is percolating among the crowd, something deeper than mere discontent. In the subterranean recesses of the crowd's subconscious, neural networks are detecting an odor. A heper odor. It is a mere ripple for now, but that ripple is ripening by the second into something like excitement, something like hunger, something like lust.

The master of ceremonies enters the stage, walks to the podium. There will be a slight delay, he says. The Valiant Victoress will return with more breathtaking stories after a costume change. In about fifteen minutes. The crowd grumbles.

I move faster now, grace jettisoned for speed (*slow down, take a breath, station yourself*). All my years of training going up in a flame of panic. I move quickly to my left to avoid a large man and bump carelessly into a woman. On high heels, she tumbles. The crowd about me shifts as they bend to help her up.

"Sorry," I whisper, giving her a quick sideways glance.

"You smell it, too?" a man next to me asks.

"What?"

He snaps his neck as if to shake himself awake. A dangle of drool ropes across the side of his face, over his ear. He looks very, very confused. Bothered. Excited.

I hold my breath, wait a second, then start to move forward, away from him, head down.

"Watch where you're going," says somebody next to me. His elbow jabs me in the rib cage. I move past, but his elbow, like a hook, holds me in place.

I turn. The man's eyes bore into mine. He is giving me an odd look, a glint of confusion that is being overtaken by recognition. But that's not what really scares me. It's what I see behind him. Dark shadows moving toward me, ruptured here and there by slivers of saliva, rapid head flicks, shimmering eyes.

The master of ceremonies now speaks with a distracted edginess. Saliva sloshes in his mouth, and his words slip out wetly. Spittle dots his lips and chin. He smells heper.

Everyone smells heper.

So much heper.

And like dark, wet clay hardening, the mass of bodies begins to encrust around me into a hard, impenetrable shell. And somewhere in the darkness is Sissy. She's losing it. I can sense it. *I* can almost smell her fear, growing, erupting, gaining on her.

I snap into action, shoving myself forward, out of this encircling, condensing mass of bodies. There. Ahead, about fifteen meters away, I see another such circle, a pool of blackness that more bodies are moving toward. Another center of gravity drawing people inward, pulled subconsciously by heper smells.

That's where Sissy must be.

I glide forward, pushing past—

I see her.

She is standing dead center in the midst of them. She is the only one who is perfectly still, her body rigid, her dry lips stretched taut below the Visor. I see her flinch—barely perceptibly—as someone hisses right over her shoulder. Pale faces swing in her direction, crescent moons turning horrifically full. She's trying to mimic them, but she's got everything all wrong. Her gait, the angles of her limbs against her body, tension and stiffness in all the wrong places. The nuances of her body language are completely off.

The master of ceremonies stops speaking mid-sentence. With the abruptness of a person who's given up any pretense of normalcy.

I push through until I'm next to Sissy. She turns, and her body literally sags with intense relief. Our hands discreetly touch under their line of vision, and I squeeze her hand for just a second, to reassure her. Her skin cold and clammy. Then I let go, and when her fingers try to find mine again I reluctantly push her hand away. She starts to shake with relief. No, not relief. Fear. *Fight or flight, fight or flight* written all over her. She's too wound up.

Someone hisses right over my shoulder, a blubbering snort, uncomfortably close. A line of sweat slicks down my back like a finger tracing my spine. I flick my head to the side, hiss, and spit. I'm trying to show Sissy how to release the tension, through movements that won't draw attention.

But she either won't or can't catch on. Her body is stock-still, her exposed lips an awful confluence of dread and horror. If one person sees her mouth, it'll be over before she can exhale her next breath.

Tse-tse-tse-tse! the person next to me clucks, a staccato sound that shatters through his slippery teeth. "I smell more than one!" he yells.

And at that, something unbuckles in the group. Whatever restraint has been holding it back completely disintegrates. The crowd closes the gaps, cements the cracks with the black tar of its bodies.

Sissy's hand drifts down to her waist. Where her handgun is tucked under her shirt. *Now or never,* her move tells me.

She's right. It's now or never. Wait another five seconds and we'll be found out. Dead in seven seconds. It's now.

But something halts me. I close my eyes, searching for the answer. It's somewhere in the dark of my mind, some—

It's already too late. That's what I realize. They're too many bodies clumped around us. There's no way the two of us—even armed—can blaze our way out of here. Even if every fired bullet inflicted a fatal wound, we'd be able to plug a dozen of them at most. Leaving thousands on the floor still alive, and tens of thousands more in the arena.

If we want to live, this plan can't be *now*. It has to be *never*.

There has to be another plan.

I swing my gaze to the stage. Nothing there to help us. Left and right, nothing. Look up. Only the flotilla of balloons assembled above us. Nothing. There's nothing.

A wail breaks out from balconies on the higher levels. Our odor rising, spreading. Heinous screams of hunger fling out. From the luxury suites. From the upper crust of society. They're not used to being deprived of choice action, and they want in. I see dark shapes, men in suits, women in upscale dresses, scaling down the walls like ribbons of saliva drooling from the luxury suites.

Sissy turns to me. Her hand is pulling up her shirt, revealing a glint of metal from the handgun. She's pulling off the Visor now for better vision, her bangs arching over her forehead like a pulled bow.

She's ready. To go down fighting, to cut holes into as many as she can on her way down.

The TextTrans buzzes manically in my pocket. So hot, it's burning a hole into my thigh.

Sissy starts pulling out the gun.

It comes to me, right then. The plan. An imperfect, deeply flawed plan. But the only one we have.

Sissy is cocking the handgun. And I'm reaching out, snatching it away. Her eyes widen with surprise as I aim it toward the roof.

And fire off six quick rounds.

Thirty-two

THE FLASHES OF light—six in quick succession—sear through even my shut eyelids. White splats of blinding brightness. Again. And again. With each flash, the gun recoils in my hand, the violent jolt felt all along my upright arm and shoulder. By the sixth shot, the handle of the gun is hot enough to brand my palm.

Fully discharged, I fling the gun away. It sails over the crowd; they lie collapsed like windswept grass completely flattened. Screams and cries of pain. Their corneas are burning.

Sissy grabs my arm. "Now," she says. "While they're all down."

But she's wrong. Only the people closest to us are incapacitated. The majority of the people, especially those on the outer rim who were shielded from the bright flashes, are already pressing forward. Toward us.

Instead of taking off, I grab her, pull her to the ground. "Not yet!"

"What? We've got—"

"Wait for it, wait for it!"

"Gene! For what?"

Then I hear it. The most glorious crack of glass, the sound of a thousand ice cubes thrown into boiling water.

"Duck!" I shout, and pull her into a crouch. Shards of glass rain down. As do massive plates of glass, slicing down and penetrating bodies like an axe head into wood.

Don't get cut, I think. One tiny slice and blood will pour out. It'll send this arena into a suicidal rampage.

Thousands of balloons drift down. Red, white, yellow, and green orbs floating down in slow motion. Thousands of discrete moving parts. The kind of cover we need.

Sissy starts to move.

I grab her arm. "A few more seconds, let the balloons reach us."

"*They* will reach us before the balloons," she spits out, pointing at the dark tide of people. "Damn it, Gene!"

"Wait for it. . . ."

The thousands of balloons flow down, spread along the arena floor. And then. An unexpected gift. Moonlight, no longer impeded by the thousands of balloons, or, more important, the tinted glass, cascades into the arena, flooding the floor with light.

The effect is immediate. Every eye in the arena shuts, every arm is flung across every face, every mouth cries out in pain. The sudden flush of moonlight is more startling than dangerous. But it's bought us cover, distraction, and maybe fifteen, twenty seconds.

We move.

Not back the way we came. The entranceways are too clogged with people rushing in from other levels. But forward, toward the stage, Sissy in the lead. Balloons still falling, bouncing every which way. We shove people aside. Our odor, our sweat, our fear, our desperation, wiped full bore on them. But we're past caring. A few swing back, arms slashing through the air, hoping to catch us with one swipe. But still blinded by the bright glare of moonlight, their aim is off.

Sissy slaps her palms on the stage, swings her legs sideways, up and over, clearing it easily. I'm right behind her, hoisting myself up. I glance back. What I see from this higher vantage point turns my insides cold. The whole floor is churning with the turbulence of thousands of shifting bodies, balloons bobbing in their midst. Pale moonlight layered on everything, casting everything in a sickly glow. And thousands of people streaming toward us like a turbulent river.

We stay low on the stage, and duck under the heavy train of the velvet curtains. The heavy, suffocating weight of the compressed folds pushes down on us as we crawl, disoriented, in the murky black.

And then we're through, on the other side of the curtains, backstage. It's empty, everyone having rushed out onto the stage moments before the moonlight poured down. Sissy is up and out first, turns to help me to my feet. No longer needing to pretend to be a dusker and allowed to be herself, she's in her element.

"Quick," she whispers. Already the stage is beginning to shift and move. The masses. They're climbing onto it. The curtain begins to stretch and pull from the other side.

"Where to?" I ask.

She looks left and right, her eyes burning with panic. She doesn't know. We have to move, to create distance. No, we need more than distance. We need bottlenecks and barriers. We need doors that open pull-ways, that lead to narrow corridors. We need a bottlenecking network of capillaries and valves of more doors and intersecting corridors and stairwells. A dozen duskers chasing us down would be logjammed by these doors and intersecting corridors; a horde of thousands would become clumped into impassable clots. "This way," I say, leading us through the nearest door.

Sissy gets it, immediately. Every doorway we run through, she's slamming the door shut behind us, locking it. The walls tremble as we run. Despite our best efforts, they're still coming at us. Right on our heels come the sounds of doors smashed in, wails and howls. The clatter of claws.

We stop. Chests heaving, legs burning. Sweat pouring down our faces. We stink. We absolutely reek.

"We're too easy to find," I say between pants.

Sissy sucks in air. "C'mon, we got to go faster."

I feel suddenly tired. It's not just a physical exhaustion from all the running, but something deeper, something wedged between the chambers of my heart. "Or not."

She looks at me. "What?"

"Maybe it's over, Sissy. Maybe it's finally over. We can't keep playing this cat-and-mouse game. They'll catch up with us. Within a minute at most. It's inevitable."

She shakes her head adamantly. "No, Gene. We keep running. We find a way out to the streets, we find a horse."

"A horse, even at full gallop, will be too slow. You know that."

Her face hardens with anger. "Okay, so what's your plan?"

"Maybe we just give up. Stop the running—"

She reaches forward. I think she's going to do something tender, like brush my bangs to the side, or caress my cheek, or touch my arm. Instead, her hand smacks me on the side of the face.

"What the—"

"Save the *feel sorry for me while I gallantly commit suicide* speech for someone else." She thumps me in the chest with her fists. "Stop thinking about only yourself! Think about Epap! Think about David!" Her eyes blaze hot. "Think about *me*!"

"Sissy—"

"We fight, Gene! We fight to the end. We *never* give in. Not while there are others depending on us. Not while there's still a chance."

"There is no chance! Okay? Even if we escape out to the streets, what then? Where do we go—"

"We'll figure it out! We'll improvise. We think quick on our feet, you and me together. That's what we've always done, Gene. We go down fighting!" And now she grabs my arm, but there's no tenderness in her grip. There's only resiliency and determination.

"Okay," I say to her. *Let's get out to the street,* I'm about to say, but she's already turned and is sprinting down the corridor.

It's easier than we think to find an exit. At the end of the next corridor, we come across an exit sign. From that point on, it's cake. We follow the arrows from one exit sign to the next until we're jetting down a stairwell, then out a side exit that spills us onto the street.

It's quiet, almost peaceful out here beneath the full moon. Everyone's inside for the big show. The only sound is the faint music piped through the fountain speakers for the ongoing water show.

I think the unexpected tranquility catches Sissy by surprise as well. She stops, stares up at the sky, breathing hard. But only for a moment.

"No clouds," she says. "Good. The moonlight glare will be tough on their eyes." She starts running toward a row of horses parked street side. "C'mon, Gene!"

There's got to be another way. This escape-on-horseback plan is fatally flawed. Anyone can see that. We reek. Our odor will leave a trail for them to easily follow. It'll be over before we cover fifteen blocks.

Another way, another way, there's got to be another way.

"Gene!" Sissy shouts, untethering two horses.

I glance across the street. Looming skyscrapers. Death traps, offering no escape at all. Useless as tombstones.

"Gene!"

But there *is* a way out. I can feel it in my bones. But I just can't *see* it. Not yet. I need time.

"Get on, Gene!" She's already sitting in the saddle of her horse, has trotted over another horse for me. "Gene!"

"Wait, give me time—"

"No! Gene, we have to—"

"Damn it!" I yell, and jump onto the horse. We start galloping down the street, the concrete beneath us turning into a blur. Past the corner, past the front of the Convention Center, past the water show.

"Which way, Gene?" Sissy shouts next to me.

And finally I see.

"Stop, Sissy!" I shout, pulling on the reins. "Do you trust me?" I say as she brings her horse around. I dismount the horse.

"What are you doing?"

"If you trust me, get off your horse."

"Is this your idea of committing suicide ag—"

"This is my idea of surviving. It's our only chance of seeing the sun rise tomorrow."

"What are you—"

"There's no time, just follow my lead." And I rub my sweaty face, arms, against the horse, spit gobs of saliva onto it.

"What are you doing?"

"Just do what I do, Sissy!" I shout as I slap the haunches of the horse, sending it galloping away—leaving a trail of my odor. They'll chase after it. So long as they don't actually smell my real trail.

Sissy jumps off her horse and does the same. Sweat, spit, rubbed on. She smacks the horse on the rump. It, too, gallops away, down a different street. Even better.

I start running. My direction takes Sissy by surprise because I'm not heading away from the Convention Center. But right back at it. As I sprint, I break out the handgun, remove the silencer. I let the handgun drop, clatter behind on the pavement.

"Your silencer, Sissy! Do you still have it?" She blinks, then pulls the silencer from her pocket, confusion and uncertainty written all over her face.

We reach the water fountain. But instead of running around it, I vault over the concrete edge and into the water. The water level reaches up to my shoulders. I spin around. Sissy is staring at me with incredulous eyes, then down at the silencer. Her mouth drops.

"It's the only way, Sissy. The only way we hide our scent. They won't think to look in here. The water splashing, the sprays, the ripples, the reflected moonlight, they'll conceal us. As long as we stay submerged underwater."

And again, she stares down at the silencer. The hollow, cylindrical silencer. About the length of a straw. "Until sunrise?"

I nod. Fine droplets of water mist down on us, soaking us.

"They'll look here."

"I don't think so. This is how this plays out. They'll chase after the horses, and it'll be sheer pandemonium. Storefronts smashed in, dozens of injured. The horses will get ripped apart, their parts splattered across five city blocks. Afterward, nobody's going to know what really went down. Hundreds are going to claim afterward to have devoured the two hepers. Or at least tasted a snippet of us. A nose, an ear. After that, everyone's going to simply assume we're dead. Nobody will think to look in here."

"I don't know."

Sounds break out of the Convention Center. A rumbling, the smashing of glass, screams.

"No other choice now, Sissy. Here they come."

She clenches her jaw, leaps over the edge and into the water. She glides right up next to me, takes my hand. Together we wade to the center of the fountain pool. We're in the very heart of the network of water propulsion snouts, rows of them lined in front of and behind us, encircling us like digits of a clock. Water plummets onto us like hard rain. Through the curtain of falling water, I see the crowd bursting out of the Convention Center, smashing through the glass lobby.

Sissy and I look at each other one last time. Her clothes soaked, sticking to her skin in random folds, her plastered hair framing her face. Fear in her eyes. But she blinks and there is in its stead a determination. I open my mouth, helplessly. I suddenly have so much I need to tell her. So much to confess, to apologize for. But it is all falling apart too fast. There is no time left to say anything.

I do the only thing I have time for, the only thing that matters. I kiss her.

Her eyes widen. Then they close halfway as she kisses back, her lips velvet and sweet and tender.

Then we separate. We take one last gulp of air under the open, naked sky. Together, we duck underwater.

Thirty-three

THE WORLD UNDERWATER is hell. Jets of water—arching high into the sky before crashing down—shatter through the swirling ceiling above us, churning bubbles. A low murmur rumbles through the fountain pool.

It is too dark to see Sissy clearly. She is only a murky form next to me. We half-kneel on the floor, clinging to several propulsion snouts, watchful that the tops of our heads don't break the surface. One end of the hollow cylindrical silencer placed in our mouths, the other end poking just out of the water. This is how we breathe. This is how we will survive. For the next eight hours. The length of time is unbearable; how we will endure, unimaginable.

Thousands pour out of the Convention Center and stampede down the streets. I feel their energy rumble through the water and quake the very foundation of the fountain pool. Their wails and screams and cries funnel into a collective deep moan that reverberates through the dark water. Several duskers are jostled into the water at the pool's edge. I see them flail with lashing arms; then, as the water level passes their jawlines, their joints lock, their bodies suddenly go inert, and they sink to the bottom. A minute later, they float slowly to the surface, quite drowned. The ripples of water push the floating corpses away from us and keep them thankfully pressed against the rim of the fountain pool.

The rumbling gradually fades. The stampede has moved on, away from the Convention Center, chasing after the horses whose eyes are rolled back, ears tucked flat, froth sputtering out of their mouths.

Over the next hour, Sissy and I adapt. We hook our feet into curled piping and float parallel to the splattered ceiling. This position's easier on our bodies, takes the pressure off our necks. And with other floating, dead bodies in the fountain—albeit around the rim—we don't really stick out, if we're even noticed at all in the glare and splash. We link our bodies by hooking our arms together.

Hours later, the crowds return. When I take a peek, slowly bringing my eyes just over the surface where the splashes are deepest, I see thousands milling about the open area of the Convention Center. The excitement of the evening's event palpable, prickling the air. The media out in full force interviewing people, photographers everywhere snapping pictures.

I sink back underwater. We'll take it one breath at a time, one second at a time. Try not to think about the cold sinking into our bones, or the stretch of hours ahead of us, the eternity it will be. Our arms hook tighter, her left leg snaking around mine. I close my eyes. The feel of her enfeebled, floating body next to me, her limp hand in mine, is like a silent lash of accusation.

If only I had taken the shot, I think. *If only . . .*

Then she wouldn't be trapped in this watery hell. If only I'd put a bullet into Ashley June's skull as I had vowed. Now, life and heat are draining out of Sissy, now her grip slackens by the hour.

I stare at the watery ceiling above me. I try to imagine the world past the swirl of froth where the moon and stars float free in the airy skies.

Thirty-four

DAYBREAK CREEPS FORWARD with ago-
nizing slowness. The waterspouts finally turn off. The swirling,
frothy surface quickly gives way to a windowed stillness. We do not
worry about being seen. The floating corpses now drift across the
fountain pool and offer us cover under a blanket of death. We watch
the sky yield from tar black to light gray.

When the dawn siren sounds, it is to us the ringing bells of
heaven.

Not a minute too soon. Especially for Sissy. Her skin has gone
pale and marble cold. For hours now, she's been trembling almost
incessantly. I've wrapped my body around hers as best I could, but
my own body is numb with cold. It's been ice on ice.

But we force ourselves to stay submerged for a few ticks yet. We
haven't suffered in this watery purgatory for hours only to throw it
all away by surfacing a few minutes too soon. Finally, finally, when
streaks of dawn rays shoot across the skies and cause the floating
bodies to smoke, Sissy and I finally bring our heads, shoulders,
chests above water.

Our bodies weigh a ton. The force of gravity seems to have grown
tenfold. Sissy leans into me, collapsing.

"Sissy?"

She doesn't respond. Her body sags and I pick her up. I carry her to the edge of the pool, pushing aside floating corpses. Wisps of smoke twirl up from these drowned bodies, and the sour-rotten stench of their sun decomposition fills my nostrils. I lay Sissy down on the concrete edge, brush her wet hair from her face.

"Sissy?"

She mumbles incoherently. Her chest arches up and she heaves, face turned to the side. White bile vomits out, turning yellow, then back to white. Eight hours underwater, she's been holding it inside all that time.

"Oh, Sissy," I whisper, stroking her face.

She murmurs, mumbles.

I look about. The glass entrance of the Convention Center is busted wide-open, shards of glass spit out in front. Metal frames and columns inside the lobby twisted out of shape, everything jutting outward as if by an explosion from within the lobby. The streets are a complete mess. Jackets, broken shades, hats, shoes scattered in every direction. Evidence everywhere of the wreckage left in the wake of the rampage.

Hazy beams of light slant between skyscrapers, spilling across the empty streets. The only movements are those of unclaimed horses, trotting aimlessly about. Theirs the only sound that punctures the dawn's quiet. A pair of horses, still harnessed to a carriage, waiting dutifully at the corner.

Sissy is not doing well. Even after I move her into the sunshine, her skin only grows colder, her body stiffer. I gather clothing strewn on the streets, sweatshirts and pants. Peeling off her sopping clothes, I flinch when I touch her back. Her skin cold and turgid. I hurry to dress her, my own hands trembling with cold. Her eyelids struggle to open, fluttering.

"Gene," she murmurs.

"It's okay," I say. "We survived. We did it. Gonna take care of you now, okay, Sissy?"

"Epap. Find Epap." And then her eyelids stop fluttering. She fades into merciful sleep.

I reach into my pocket, take out the TextTrans. Moisture has seeped into it, garbling the screen. I press a few buttons. Nothing. It's wrecked. *Let it dry,* I think to myself. I place it next to Sissy in the sun. It may yet be operable once dried.

As with Sissy. Give her sunshine, give her warmth, give her time, and her cold bones may yet arise. Most of all, give her food, nourishment.

"I'll be right back, Sissy," I say even though she's out. Putting a jacket under her head as a pillow, I steal back into the Convention Center. I'm cautious at first, worried about people who might be sheltering inside from daylight. But rays of sun, pouring through the smashed opening of the glass roof, are streaming through every floor. No one's going to be sheltering in here.

But there's no food here, either, not anymore. All the concession stands and food stalls are little more than mangled frames of metal. Food, whatever is left of it, is smeared onto the floor and walls, the raw meat already giving off the stench of spoilage. At every level, it's the same devastation. And everywhere I go, on every floor, I call out for Epap.

Only silence returns my cries.

Up in the luxury suites, I stare down into the arena, beams of sunlight falling on the twisted seat backs and ripped flooring. Nothing moves. I briefly stop by the Palace suite and retrieve my backpack. I didn't think it'd still be there, but it's right where I left it under the sofa. The handguns clink together when I sling the backpack over my shoulder.

I head back outside. The sun is higher and stronger now, stippling the surface of the water. Sissy is still lying where I left her. I feel a pang of guilt for leaving her but I know I'm only doing what's necessary. We need food. I'm about to rush headlong into another building when I stop. I realize something unsettling. Unlike the

Convention Center with sunlight pouring inside, these buildings are dark within, possible sanctuaries for the many thousands who, roaming the streets all night, were likely caught by surprise by the dawn siren.

And not just the buildings on this street. But, with so many thousands roaming the streets last night, probably every building in the business district is a black cave of stranded sleepers. I place my hand on the glass of the revolving door in front of me, hesitating. I push forward. The revolving door scoops me up, revolves me inside.

I never leave the inside of the revolving door. As it opens up into the dark lobby, I hear the sleep sounds of many hundreds, their raspy, grating *scrit-scrits*, their gnashing teeth. I make out the faint cluster of bodies dangling upside down from the lobby ceiling, a colony of stalactites. I stay between glass walls of the revolving door until I am outside again, backing away.

The buildings around us. They are not sanctuaries of food and recovery. They are fangs and claws jutting up into the sky.

Sissy is murmuring. I pick her up and hold her close, hoping to warm her. I pocket the TextTrans. We can't stay here. This place offers us nothing. No food, water that is quickly spoiling with the rot of melted flesh and only temporal safety until nightfall. And there's no sign of Epap. We need to leave. Sissy will hate me when she comes to, will accuse me of abandoning Epap. But I have little choice.

As I'm carrying her to the carriage with the two harnessed horses, it dawns on me. I know where to go. A place not so far away where there is safety and sunshine and, most important, nourishment. I lay her upon the plush velvet seating inside the carriage and tuck her snugly beneath a soft carriage blanket. Then I'm checking the harnesses, securing the horse collars and traces before grabbing the reins. One more wishful look into the lobby for Epap, then I snap the reins. The horses, perhaps glad for direction and order after the night's pandemonium, canter, then gallop, obediently away.

Thirty-five

A LITTLE LESS than an hour later, the metropolis far behind us, I sight the patch of soft green fuzz dotted with bright colorful spots. The fruit orchard. Bursting with an abundance of fruit, more than I can ever remember. I snap the reins, urging more speed into the horses.

I pull the carriage right up to the nearest tree, stumble off the seat. The horses, needing no prodding, are already grabbing for low-hanging fruit, their lips puckered and grasping. I join them, my hands desperate and clumsy. I ram the fruit whole into my mouth, skin and all.

A spell of dizziness hits me. It's the whiplash between the extremities of frigid water and now desert sun. I lie down, chewing and swallowing. The juice flows down my parched throat, silk on sandpaper, slaking my thirst. After even a few sips of the juice, I begin to feel revived. I chew more, working my jaws, reducing the fruit into a pulp.

I rise on shaky legs, pluck some fruit for Sissy. When I open the carriage door, I find her still tucked firmly beneath the carriage blanket. I place my hand over her forehead, the third time I've checked on her this trip. Her skin still cold. I squeeze the fruit, letting the juice drip between her parted lips.

Her mouth half-fills with juice before she reflexively swallows. She sputters, twisting to her side, the juice spraying onto the seat upholstery and down her shirt. She gasps, heaving in air, then shudders into a collapse. But her tongue licks her lips, tasting the juice.

I squeeze more juice, and this time she takes it in with eager swallows. After a few minutes, her pallor improves, her breathing steadies. I press my forehead against hers—no fever, no sign of turning. What she is suffering from is utter fatigue, a lack of nourishment, and perhaps hypothermia. All the classic symptoms of turning are thankfully absent.

I carry her out of the carriage, lay her on a plush carpet of grass the sun has warmed. For the next half hour, I work hard, collecting fruit, squeezing them, nourishing both of us as best I can. I'm squeezing the fourth batch of fruit when my head becomes heavy and my eyes fight to stay open. *How long has it been since I slept?* I am wondering, and then I am laying my head down on the grass, the softest pillow, and letting the sun soak into me, the warmest, coziest blanket.

I wake to the sensation of sweet juice in my mouth. Swallow. It's wonderful.

"Gene, are you okay?"

It's Sissy. She's kneeling over me, her eyes clear and alert.

"I am," I say, sitting up. The sun is higher in the sky now. Many hours have passed. "How about you?"

She nods. "Okay."

We gaze at each other. It feels like ages since we looked—*really* looked—at each other. We've been side by side all night, holding hands in the murky black water. But not directly, in full bright color. The feeling is mutual; both our eyes fill with tears of relief. We hug tightly.

"Epap," she asks, her mouth next to my ear. Except she says it not as a question. There is resignation, there is acceptance, in her voice.

I shake my head. "I looked. But I didn't see him. I'm sorry, Sissy."

She stands up on wobbly legs, stares at the distant skyscrapers of the metropolis. "Does it feel like he's gone? To you, Gene, does it feel like he's dead?"

I stand up, put my hand on her shoulder. "To the very end, he helped us." She turns her head to me, surprised. "He tried to warn us. Through the TextTrans. He told us it was a trap, that we should get away."

"He was there?"

"He must have been. He knew the layout of the Convention Center, seemed to know where I was."

She gasps softly. "We left him behind. All by himself."

"There was little we could do. We had no choice. We barely survived ourselves."

"Maybe he—"

"I don't think so, Sissy. I searched the Convention Center this morning. There was no sign of him."

"The TextTrans," Sissy says after a long, silent minute. "Let me see."

I take it out of my pocket. "Water got in, ruined it. Look, everything on the screen is garbled."

She takes it, presses a few buttons randomly. Her shoulders slump.

"Leave it out in the sun," I say softly, taking it from her. "Maybe it'll dry out, start working again."

She shrugs her shoulders disconsolately. Her strength suddenly vanishes; she half-collapses to the ground. She starts to laugh, and it is full of sorrow and torment. "Look at me," she says. "I'm pathetic. I've never felt so weak in my life."

I sit beside her and we lean against each other. The horses, still harnessed to the carriage, stand withdrawn under the shade of the tree. The sky is a pure cerulean blue, not a hint of a cloud across its wide, invisible dome.

"What now?" I say gently.

She leans her head against my shoulder. "Let's just sit here. For five minutes. Let's pretend everything is okay and we're just resting from a nice, leisurely hike."

"I think we can do that."

"Five minutes. We can talk about what to do next after that."

I inhale the air saturated with the fragrance of ripeness, of grass and fruit and leaves. Feel the soothing warmth of the sun, her body pressed up against my side, how she so perfectly and softly fits into the nook of my body. "Let's make it ten minutes."

She nods against my shoulder.

Ten minutes turns to one hour. One hour becomes two, then three. We nap, three, four times, sleep lulling us throughout the afternoon. We eat between naps, feel energy return. And now, in the late afternoon, we're at last restored. We chew the slices of orange slowly, savoring the taste. There's more than enough other fruit dangling from the trees, but neither of us wants to get up.

Sissy looks much better, her complexion returned to normal. Alertness again shines in her eyes. "This is where you got your fruit? Your whole life?"

I nod.

She takes in the trees. "So you'd come here with your father?"

"Yeah. Every few weeks or so. Until he . . . went away."

She looks at me. "He never told you . . . anything?"

"No. Nothing. And then he was gone. Made me believe he'd turned, then perished in the sun."

"That must've been hard."

I pull a blade of grass from the ground. "It was lonely. A part of me refused to let go. For the longest time, I pretended he just went away somewhere." I smile sadly. "I used to walk the streets in the daytime hoping to . . . no, never mind."

"No, what?" She angles her body to face me. "Really."

"It's ridiculous, but I used to think he hadn't died. That he had made it somewhere safe, some place far away. And that he would send me a message to tell me he was okay." I pull another blade of grass. "Thought he'd send it by a remote-controlled plane. Yeah, I know, it was silly. But I was a little boy, alone for the first time in my life. All I could do was cling on to fantasy."

"Well, you were right," she says lightheartedly. "He *did* just go away."

I don't say anything.

"I'm sorry," she says softly, putting her hand on mine. "I didn't mean to make light of what happened."

"Nah, don't worry about it." I give her a quick smile to let her know everything is okay.

"I actually know what it feels like," she says after a minute. "He did it to me, too." She stares into the distance, her eyes moistening. "It was the suddenness of it. No good-bye. No explanation. One day here, the next day . . . gone. Like I didn't even matter."

I twirl the blades of grass around my finger, snap them. "That's what I don't get. I mean, we know why he left me. It was to go to the Institute and protect you." I turn to her. "But Sissy, why did he leave you? And why only months before the Heper Hunt was to begin?"

She leans forward, arms on her thighs. "I can't figure it out," she says.

"No one can. Not even the chief advisor."

She nods. "And you know what really bothers me as well? Why did your father leave the Mission only weeks before we were to arrive? I know he was having it bad with Krugman, but still. Why not hold out in that cabin for just a little longer?" She exhales in frustration. "Something must have happened for him to jet off so quickly."

I clear my throat. And when I speak, it's with a quiet, broken voice. "Maybe it's obvious."

"What is?"

"Something caused him to suddenly leave the Institute. And something later caused him to leave the Mission."

"Yeah?"

"Maybe it's not something . . . but someone."

Her eyes turn to mine.

"It's pretty obvious if you think about it," I say. "Each time, he moves just before a certain someone is due to arrive." I go on, ignoring Sissy's shaking head. "Me, Sissy. Before I'm due to arrive at the Institute, he leaves. Before I'm supposed to arrive at the Mission, he leaves. It's like he's avoiding me, deliberately trying to make sure we never meet again."

"Gene—"

"Maybe it's me."

"We don't know that—"

"Certainly looks that way, doesn't it?"

"Gene," she says, and when I don't look up to meet her gaze she touches my chin lightly, tilts my head to her. "He loved you. You were precious to him. We can't go jumping to these conclusions."

"It adds up, though, doesn't it?"

She shakes her head, her eyes never wavering from mine. "We don't know that. There's a dozen different ways to interpret his movements. And we've got to give him the benefit of the doubt."

I stare into the distance. "I want to find him more than ever," I whisper.

"I know, Gene," she says. "I know."

For ten minutes, we watch a scrim of clouds drift across the blue sky. A gentle breeze blows, rustling the tree leaves. Sissy's stomach rumbles with hunger.

"Wish I had my daggers," she says. "What I wouldn't do for some barbequed game." Her fingers absentmindedly stroke her waist where she usually sheathed her daggers.

"We still got our guns."

She shakes her head. "No good. Dagger's the way to go. Clean, efficient."

"You really think you'd have energy to go chasing prairie dogs? And then make fire?"

She spits a seed out of her mouth. "Good point there." She spits out another seed, this time with distance.

I spit out a seed from my mouth. It sails only a couple of feet away.

"You're going to have do better than that if you want to beat me," Sissy says, a small grin on her face.

"I haven't even begun," I say, and take another bite. "Game on." I spit out a seed. Despite rising high up into the air, it falls less than halfway to Sissy's seed.

"That's just pathetic, Gene," she says, laughing. She slaps the grass. "Even *Ben* could have done better than that. When he was, like, three."

"Hey, this is my first time, okay! I haven't had years of training like you guys!"

She laughs again, in her usual deep-throated manner. "If Epap were here, he'd totally school you. Nobody was better than him. That boy could spit farther than he could throw."

We both laugh. But the mention of his name is a painful reminder of reality. Our laughter fades away, the brief moment of lightness over.

"He never had a chance, did he?" she says quietly after a minute. "*We* never had a chance. Of saving him. I think we both knew that from the get-go. We were clinging to a hope that was more fantasy than reality."

"Sometimes fantasy is all you have."

She is silent. I know what is turning in her mind, the words before she even gives voice to them. "And what about saving David?" she finally says. "Going back to the Palace to rescue him—is that fantasy, too?"

It is. I realize that now. Even if we had been able to kill Ashley June and been able to return unscathed to the Palace, the Ruler would never have released us, his promise notwithstanding.

Sissy curls her toes into the grass, turning her digits white. "The whole time we were underwater in the fountain pool, I kept thinking

175

of David. That he was in exactly the same situation, submerged in water. But how much worse off he was. Because he was alone." She turns her eyes to me. "I won't leave him there."

"Sissy," I say reluctantly. "We both know it's suicide to return to the Palace. We'll surely die."

"Then we die," she says quickly with a flash of anger. She stands up, walks a few paces away, her back to me.

I stand. Softly, I utter words I know she will be repulsed by. "Maybe we should accept what can't be changed."

"What do you mean by that?" she says without turning around.

"You and me, Sissy. We have horses. We can go anywhere. Nobody knows we're alive. Not the Palace, not the metropolis. They all think we're dead."

She pauses. I expect her to lash out with objections. But she has not spoken.

"We make our own world, Sissy. Away from everyone, everything. Go far, far, far away, never to be found again. Start afresh. Just you and me."

She stands very still. A desert breeze blows through her hair.

"But we can't go back to the Palace," I say. "Even if we were somehow able to escape from there, they'd never stop coming after us. Not the duskers, not the Originators. Once they know we're still alive, we'll be hunted forever."

And still, she does not speak.

"I'm just trying to be honest with you," I say.

"Have you, Gene?" She turns around now, and her eyes are moist. But these are not tears of sadness or resignation but something else I can't quite identify. "Have you been completely honest with me?"

Of course I have, I'm about to say, but the words choke up inside me.

She speaks, and her voice quivers with anger. "Why did you bring me? From the Palace into the metropolis? You say it was because you needed help. That's not true, is it?" Her eyes pierce into mine. "Because in the metropolis, I'm a liability. You would have been better off without me."

She folds her arms in front of her chest, then unfolds them, stuffing her hands into her pockets. She doesn't know what to do with them. They are like her emotions, her thoughts, unable to find a place to alight. "At first, I thought it was because you just wanted us to be together. Because you wanted me. But then yesterday, when you didn't take the shot, you hung me out to dry. You just about killed me."

"No, Sissy, I—"

"Stop, Gene." And she turns away, walks out of the shade and into the sunlight.

I follow after her. No words. Just my feet, taking me toward her. She spins to face me before I reach her. She's standing in the white purity of day; I'm in the shadows.

"I know why you brought me with you." Her eyes shimmer with angry, pained tears. "You need my blood. It's not *me* you want. Just my blood."

"Sissy—"

"I suspected all along. But I decided to give you the benefit of the doubt. Held out believing, hoping that you'd actually take down Ashley June and kill off my suspicions."

"Sissy, please—"

"And you know what, Gene?" Her voice hitches with a raw intensity that can only be honesty. "I would have come with you. Even if you'd told me you only wanted me for my blood, that you only needed me for Ashley June, I still would have come."

All I can do is stare into the sun. Directly into it, wanting the intense whiteness to burn holes into my corneas, wanting pain, needing the punishment.

"I'm sorry, Sissy," I finally say, my voice strangled and raspy.

She wipes her nose with her fist, her chin tilting up. "I know she gave her life up to save yours. I get it." Tears glimmer but don't overflow. "And I would have been fine with it, you wanting to do the same for her. Even if it meant I came second to her. Even then, Gene. But only if you were truthful about that." She winces. "Because what I can't live with is dishonesty. Deceit."

"You're not second, Sissy."

"Stop."

"I was there yesterday to *kill* her. Please believe me." I take a step toward Sissy, my hands spread open before me, pleading. "Yes, you're right. When we left the Palace, my initial plan was to try to re-turn her. Yes, I didn't tell you because I didn't know how to make you understand. I'm sorry. But I couldn't take it anymore after a while. The deceiving, the putting you at risk. So I changed my mind. Believe me, Sissy, it became every bit my intent to kill her. You're not second."

Her eyes search mine. "So you say. And yet still. You couldn't take the shot last night," she says, but softly, without recrimination. I was expecting more anger, reproach, not this sudden gentleness. "You had her in your crosshairs, but you couldn't pull the trigger."

I stare down at the ground, unable to look into Sissy's probing eyes.

"I don't hate you, Gene, for that. I understand. Because if it were you in her shoes, I wouldn't have been able to do it, either." She stares off into the distance, then at the horses. "But it's the dishonesty. That's what does me in." Then her next words. "I can't trust you anymore."

"Sissy," I say. I step toward her. "I'm going to prove it to you. That you're not second. Somehow, someway, I'm going to show you."

"You already had your chance," she says. "You've already shown me."

"Sissy. Please."

She turns, walks to the carriage.

"Where are you going?"

"I'm going back to the Palace for David. There're two horses. I'll take one. You take the other, go wherever you want. To the metropolis. Or with me to get David. Or head east alone. It's your choice. But as for me, I'm going back for David."

"Sissy, don't—"

"I can't desert him, I can't betray his trust." Her next words, they sting. "Loyalty is the proof of love." I know she didn't say it viciously. But her words hurt all the more for that.

She starts untethering a horse from its collars and traces. Not once does she look at me or say anything. I only know she's working quickly, will be saddled up and galloping away within a minute.

"Sissy. Come on. Let's think this through."

She doesn't stop, doesn't even lift her head to me. Her fingers work the straps, unwinding the leather with loud snaps. The horse is almost completely untethered when she stops. But not with indecision. With surprise, with confusion. Her head tilts to the side.

And that's when I hear it, too.

Hm-m-m-m. Hm-m-m-m.

Coming from just behind me.

Hm-m-m-m. Hm-m-m-m.

On the ground, still sitting in a splash of sunlight where I'd placed it.

The TextTrans. It's buzzing, shaking the blades of grass around it.

Thirty-six

FOR A FEW seconds, all we can do is stare. Then I'm jumping on the TextTrans, picking it up. It vibrates along the digits of my fingers, along my bones, jolting my whole body. But on the screen are only scrambled characters.

→   ▯▯▯∘ϗ⊥ℏ_▽_ℓ

"Is it Epap?" Sissy says, running to me.

"I can't tell." I shake the TextTrans as if that might help. "The screen's all messed up."

"Try to send something back," Sissy says.

With shaking fingers, I type EPAP, but it comes out as:

→   ▯▯<↦<▯▯

There's nothing I can do about the garbled letters. I hit SEND. And as if I've just hit the OFF button, the TextTrans dies on me. It stops vibrating. The screen powers off.

"No!" Sissy shouts. "What did you do?"

"Nothing! I just hit SEND."

"What happened?"

I smack the back of the TextTrans. "It was probably just a glitch. Inside circuits dried up in the sunlight, then sent a phantom message in error."

"Or it could've been Epap."

Before I can reply, the TextTrans comes alive again in my hand, vibrating hard and furious. I almost drop it.

"Gene!"

"I know, I know." Faces pressed together, we read the screen. And again, I almost drop the TextTrans.

> → Guys? Is that you, Sissy? Gene?

Sissy and I stare at each other. With thumbs that suddenly seem too big and cumbersome and slow, I type out a reply.

> → Who is this?

We wait for what seems like an eternity. Then:

> → E<↦><☐☐

Sissy and I glance at each other, eyes hopeful. I type: Resend.

The TextTrans hums, and this time when we read the screen Sissy lets out a cry.

> → Epap.

I start typing furiously.

> → Where are you?

> → Not su_☐☐. In buil☐☐ing

> → You okay?

→ No. Broke☐ leg.

→ RU in Convention Center?

→ No. Tall bu☐ℓding. Tallest one aro_nd.

→ Large atrium inside?

→ Y. lots of glass. And sun.

→ Good. Coming now.

→ K. hu_ry.

"He's in the Domain Building," I say to Sissy. "Makes sense. Lots of sun inside. A good place to hide."

Sissy taps her mouth with a curled knuckle, forehead furrowed. She glances at the TextTrans. "How can we be sure it's Epap?" she says. "What if it's someone pretending to be him?"

I stare down at the TextTrans, my body chilling over despite the sunshine beating down on me. Sissy's right. On the other end might be someone who has just finished devouring Epap, and has now lucked upon a way of luring two more unsuspecting hepers.

"The Domain Building's sun-proofed," I say. "No dusker would hide in there to lure us. Not in the daytime. It's got to be Epap."

But Sissy's not satisfied. "Daytime will be nighttime in a few short hours." She rubs the back of her neck. "If we're going back into the metropolis with night fast approaching, we need to be sure it's him." She grabs the TextTrans out of my hands.

→ I'm coming, Epap. And on your birthday, too.

She stares intently at the screen. "His birthday's eight months away."

The TextTrans buzzes. We read the characters before the TextTrans blanks out completely. It will be the last characters to ever appear on the TextTrans finally gone kaput.

→ ◫⃗◫⊣∠↦∘∢⊥ℏ

Thirty-seven

I HEAD OVER to the carriage. I'm reattaching her horse to the traces when Sissy catches up with me. She stands on the other side of the horse.

"What are you doing?" she says.

"What *we* are doing." I pull the leather strap through the latches, hard enough to cause the horse to snort with complaint. "We're going back for Epap. Together."

"You don't—" she begins to say.

"It's already late afternoon. We don't have much time. We certainly don't have time to argue. I'm coming with you. We're both doing this."

She stares at me silently. She starts shaking her head. "Gene—"

"By the time we get to the Domain Building, dusk will be almost upon us. We need to slip in and out quickly. Find Epap, then get the hell out." I reattach the horse collar, fastening it securely. "There's going to be no room for error. No room to get your bearings, to find your way. I know the Domain Building. You need me."

Sissy doesn't say anything, but I feel her eyes scrutinizing my every move. I slide between the two horses, double-check the axle. The carriage is ready. Sissy is still staring at me. I walk to the nearest tree. "Getting fruit for Epap," I tell Sissy over my shoulder. I pluck a few of the larger dangling fruit, cradle them in the nook of my arm.

I throw the fruit through the window into the carriage. As I walk around to the front, I see no sign of Sissy. She's not inside the carriage, nor is she standing by the horses. I scan the trees.

"Up here," she says from the driver's seat. She's sitting on one side of the bench, leaving room for me to sit next to her. Our eyes meet and she holds my gaze. I hop on, sit beside her.

I grab the reins, slap them down. The carriage takes off, slowly, then faster as the horses break into a gallop. The ground blurs beneath us, green to brown. With every bounce, Sissy and I bump against each other. She slides closer to me, leaning against me. I press back slightly. Wind blows hard against our faces. We don't speak as we push toward the distant skyscrapers. Back into the hornet's nest. But Sissy is next to me, Sissy is with me, and there's nowhere else I'd rather be.

Thirty-eight

IN THE HEART of the metropolis once again. The horses trot nervously along, hoofs stamping loudly on the hard concrete, their ears flicking. Everything feels too close: the shuttered store fronts, cafés, delicatessens, the towering skyscrapers flanking us like enclosing fingers. Absent is the sense of emptiness and desolation that had always attended my daytime visits. Now there is only the sense of millions hanging behind paper-thin walls of the steeled skyscrapers.

By the time I pull the horses over and tether them to a pole in front of the Domain Building, the sun has dropped more than half-way to the horizon. Shadows creep across the street as if clawing us. There is less than an hour of sunlight remaining. We walk to the front entrance, a set of wide revolving doors. Unlocked, like everything else in the daytime.

"That's a lot of floors to cover," Sissy says, her head tilting back as she looks upward.

"Sixty-four to be exact. But Epap said he was hiding in sunlight. We'll only need to search the atrium and the top floor—those are the only two areas where sunlight can penetrate."

"What else is in that building?"

"A bunch of government bureaus. Laboratories and conference

rooms and lecture halls. We avoid them, okay? Our approach is simple: search the atrium, then, if we have to, get in the glass elevator, head up to the top floor. We'll be covered in sunlight the whole way up. And back down, of course, when we leave."

"With Epap, right?"

"With Epap."

Sissy nods. She takes out the TextTrans one last time. Nothing. She puts it back into her pocket, biting her lip. "You can leave now if you want, Gene. I can find my way around on my own." She places her hand on my forearm. "There's no telling what'll happen once it's dark. This might be your last chance to get out of the metropolis alive."

"That's not an option." I take out the two guns from the backpack, hand her one, tuck the other into my waist. "We both live or we both die, but we do it together. Understand?"

She holds my gaze for a moment. Then nods. We push through the revolving doors, and then we're inside.

It is exactly as I remember it. The only slight difference is the lighting. Because it is later in the day than when my father and I usually ventured into the Domain Building, the sunlight is more diffused. Instead of the sharp noon light that would gush down the sixty-four-story atrium and set the lobby afire with spinning flares of light, an orange haze burnishes the inside.

Sissy stands amazed, briefly forgetful of the circumstances that brought us here.

"They designed this building to be the securest in the whole metropolis," I tell her, gazing upward. "That's why this glass atrium is so huge. And the top floor is all glass—all the top-secret documents are kept there. With so much sunlight, there's no way a dusker can break in during the day hours."

"Well, day hours are about to end. Let's get a move on."

I nod. But as she turns around, I grab her arm. "Wait."

"What is it?"

Something in the air. My head tilts down with concentration. Something off-kilter. My sixth sense, almost as reliable as any of my other senses, is ringing with alarm.

"Gene?"

Instead, I shake it off. "Stay in the sunlight," I say.

"What is it?"

"Don't know. Just stay in the sunlight at all times. Don't be tempted into the dark for even a second. And let's be quiet. Don't call out for him too loudly."

Her face tenses. "Okay."

We start out on the north side in front of small delis and kiosks. In the corner, a shoe-polishing stand. Next to that, a newspaper stand. Nothing moves. Everything is devoid of movement, of life.

"Epap," I hiss as loud as I dare. "Epap!"

Silence.

"The security desk," Sissy says. "We didn't check behind the counter."

"He's not there."

"Did you check?"

I shake my head.

"I'll just take a quick look." And she walks away, her strides short and nervous.

I peer into a small café. Chrome tables and chairs stare blankly back at me. Cautiously, I check behind the counter. Nothing. No one.

Sissy's at the security desk, her head disappearing below the countertop. She's being thorough, no nook left unsearched.

Ping.

That's the sound I hear. A small electronic beep, barely audible.

Ping.

I turn around. It takes me a second to notice it.

The glass elevator. It's open now. Was it open before? I can't be sure.

"Hey, Sissy, come here." I move toward the elevator, glancing from side to side. She mumbles something in reply. I've taken this elevator many times in the past. It's the only way to reach the top floor. It travels along duo traction rails that rise all the way to the top floor. I used to love riding it as a child, the sensation of flying as the floor of the lobby dropped away and you sailed up the atrium like a bird. I'd stare out, face pressed against the glass, sometimes gazing at the floor of the lobby, everything down there diminishing, fading away.

I stand straddling the precipice of the elevator car. "Sissy, over here," I say again. I hear her shoes click against the marble floor and echo up and down the atrium. And that's when I see something odd. Inside the elevator car. A security key is inserted at the top of the operating panel. It's where my father used to insert his top-security key to gain access to the top floor. I step into the elevator to take a closer look.

"Gene!"

I turn around at the sound of her voice. She is walking toward me. No, she is running, alarm rippling across her face.

And, too late, I see why.

The doors are closing. With wicked speed.

"Gene!"

Too late, I lunge forward. The doors clap together, and before I can reach the panel and start mashing buttons in panic, or kick at the doors, the elevator ascends. With sudden force, as if I'm being catapulted into the air. Sissy falls away until she is only a dot, her cries ("Gene! Gene! Gene!") fading, diminishing.

Thirty-nine

THE ELEVATOR ZIPS past every floor. Only as it nears the top, my ears popping, does it slow down. The glass doors open. The sun, hovering over the lower skyscrapers, shines directly into my eyes, burning a rust-red tint into my eyelids.

The elevator lobby on this floor is empty. On the far side, a reception desk and a small glass sculpture of the Ruler that's been there for years. Otherwise, nothing. The glass wall across the reception area is angled, and I see ghostly reflections of the floor beyond, faint outlines of desks and chairs. Nothing moves.

I stay pressed against the back wall of the elevator. Reaching out, I start pushing the L button on the panel. Nothing happens. Push the CLOSE button. Nothing.

I look down through the glass floor. I see Sissy below, tiny as a nit, standing by the security desk.

"Push the CALL button by the elevator!" I yell down. She doesn't move. *"Sissy, push the CALL button!"* I shout again, cupping my mouth. I see her move toward the wall. But nothing happens. The doors stay open.

I punch a few buttons in frustration. Nothing.

"Epap!" I shout out to the empty floor lobby. "It's Gene. Epap! Are you there?"

Silence.

I study the panel, wondering if there might be some way I can pry it off, trip the wires behind. That's when I see the intercom. I push the orange button. "Sissy, can you hear me? Go to the security desk! I'm using the intercom. Go to the security desk!"

Below, the tiny dot that is Sissy races toward the security desk. A few seconds later, her voice crackles through, static distorting it.

"Gene!"

"Sissy, the elevator's stuck on this floor! See if you can find some external controls at the desk."

"—kay— " A crash of more static, obliterating her voice.

"Sissy, can you hear—"

"Help me."

Those words. Not from the intercom panel. Not Sissy's voice. But spoken with clarity and within close proximity. From somewhere on this floor.

"Help me!" Louder now, the fear in the voice obvious. The owner of the voice now obvious, too.

"Epap!" I shout. "It's Gene! Come here, Epap, to the elevator!"

But he keeps on shouting, yelling as if not hearing me. "Help me! Help me!" His distress crescendoing into raw panic.

Sissy's voice breaks out of the intercom. "Epap?! Oh crap, that's his voice, that's Epap—" She is shouting until she's cut off again by static.

And still Epap keeps shouting. I peer out the elevator doors, trying to see him. But the angle is all wrong. I can't see the rest of the floor unless I step out.

"Epap!" I shout. "Come here!"

But he only keeps shouting, his words overlapping with mine. "Help . . . don't, please don't, *no!!!*" he screams.

And then I'm sprinting out of the elevator, out onto the glass floor.

And as soon as I'm out, the elevator doors, as if waiting this whole time, snap shut behind me like a steel trap.

Forty

BUT THERE'S NO stopping me. I race forward, past the elevator lobby, hopelessly lulled deeper into the floor by Epap's pleading voice. I can see right through to the far side of the floor because everything is made out of glass. I sprint past the eight office suites, all identically decorated, and sparsely so: a desk, a chair, a deskscreen, and little else. No sign of Epap in any of them. Splintered flares of dusk light refract off the walls, the color of rust and blood.

I reach the far end of the floor. No Epap, just his voice drawing me in. I fly into the conference room. Still no sign of him. Only his voice sounding from the flickering TV monitor mounted on the wall. But no sooner do I raise my eyes than it suddenly turns off. And Epap's screams as well, cut off mid-shout. His voice was coming from a video recording this whole time.

I spin around in the large conference room, certain that I'm about to get jumped. But there's no one in here but me. With Epap's voice now gone, an eerie silence—the silence of watchful eyes, held breaths—clamps down on me.

Something is on this floor with me. I know it. I can sense it. Eyes watching me, gauging my every move and expression.

All the chairs are pulled under the conference table in perfect symmetry. Everything in order. Nothing under the table, the floor clearly visible through the glass top. But something is lying on top of the table. A large hypodermic needle. I walk over, touch it tentatively with my fingertips. A yellow fluid in it.

I scan the room left to right again. I'm missing something. My eyes glide along the glass walls, the floor-to-ceiling windows, past the Panic Room, outside to the adjacent skyscraper—

The Panic Room. It sits, on this top floor of the Domain Building, like a tiny black cataract in the sky. Everything else on this floor is bathed in sunlight, but tucked away in the northeast corner is this small closet-like chamber. Tinted black as death.

The Panic Room was built after the DBS (Death By Sunlight) on this floor of a high-ranking official. He had indulged in a little too much wine throughout the night and fallen asleep in his office. Dawn had caught him by surprise. Afterward, sleepholds were removed from all offices. And the Panic Room was constructed, designed to be an emergency last-resort option for anyone accidentally left behind. A button in the Panic Room's interior dropped the occupant down a shaft ten stories deep, into the dark safety of the shuttered floors below.

The Panic Room is black as night before me.

I train my eyes, trying to see through its thick black glass. The dark tint of the glass is a composite of rare glass and a compound—highly expensive and difficult to produce—that supposedly neutralizes the deadly gamma rays of sunlight. Nobody's ever dared test it out.

"Gene."

I jump at the sound. The sound of my name, breaking the silence. The sound of the voice, that voice, shattering my heart.

I thought I'd forgotten her voice. But one whispered syllable of my name and instead of becoming afraid, I feel an immediate, deep solace in her presence.

"Gene, come to me."

And I do, helplessly lulled toward the black chamber. I stop in front of the glass wall, my breath frosting on the surface. Yet still I see nothing. Then the tint of the glass lightens. Ever so gradually and slowly, until I can make out the gray outline of a body standing inside. Then more: the curve of her shoulders, the length of her hair, the shape of her eyes. Despite the pain of sunlight, she isn't wearing shades. She wants me to see her eyes.

"Stop, Ashley June."

But she continues to turn the glass from dark to a light-gray transparency, her fingers, which I can now see, moving one of many dials on some kind of remote control in her hand. She doesn't stop, not even as sunlight further illuminates the interior of the chamber and causes her to flinch with pain. She finally stops, stares into my eyes.

I thought I would feel fear. Or guilt. But what I feel instead is an emotion I never expected.

Tenderness.

I'm standing less than a meter from her, from her fangs, her claws, and I know I'm safe with her. That she can no more harm me than I could have pulled the trigger on her. It's a strange sensation, to be before such terrifying instruments yet to feel so completely at ease at the same time. Even back at the Mission, when she could have easily decapitated me with one slice of her razor claws, the death blow never came.

Our eyes meet; I see the reciprocal tenderness radiating from her eyes, flowering off her porcelain-pale skin. This unexpected kindness makes me want to whisper a thousand pleas for forgiveness for deserting her so many days ago at the Heper Institute.

I had forgotten. How my heart tugs so effortlessly and spontaneously for her. Despite everything my heart knows about her nature now, despite our separate shores. I turn my eyes away.

"Gene," she says softly into a small mike she's holding. Her voice whispers through the room's surrounding speakers. She lifts her hand and presses the palm flat against the glass. Pale, the whiteness of the midnight moon. "Gene," she whispers, this time so softly,

I don't hear the word, only see her lips mouthing my name. Her lips curling around the syllable of it, as if embracing the contours of every letter.

Slowly, I lift my hand, press it against the glass opposite from hers. I cannot feel heat, only the cold indifference of glass. And still, I cannot look into her eyes.

"Gene, please look at me," she says softly.

And at that, I meet her emerald eyes, the piercing color visible even through the glass, glowing like gems aglow.

"Don't be afraid, Gene. You're safe with me. I can barely smell you—the chamber is hermetically sealed. So don't—"

"I'm sorry," I say. My voice juddering over those two simple words.

Her slender pale arms, slimming out of a sleeveless blouse, look fragile and vulnerable although I know they contain the power to smash through this glass and rip me apart in seconds. "Did you ever get my letter?" she says. "I left it in the Umbilical."

I nod.

"I knew you would," she says, and her fingers scratch her wrist lightly, once, twice. She looks away for a second, then gazes softly back into my eyes. "I had so much more to write. I had all these things I wanted to tell you."

I lean forward until my forehead presses against the glass. "I'm sorry for deserting you. I'm sorry for never coming back. I should have tried—"

"It's okay, Gene." She presses the flat white of her hand harder against the glass. "It doesn't matter anymore."

The sun sets lower, its rays diminishing in strength, bleeding into a darker red. Already the skull of the moon is etched into the darkening parchment. Night will be upon us soon. And with that thought, the initial shock of seeing Ashley June wears off, and I glance suspiciously around me.

"That was you on the TextTrans, wasn't it?" I say. "You used that to lure me here. To trap me."

"Yes. And to *save* you. Back at the Convention Center it was me who sent the message to you. I saw you as soon as I walked onto the stage. Toting that ridiculous weapon. If I hadn't sent that message, you'd have fired your weapon. And given away your position; you'd have been devoured in five seconds flat." Tenderness on her face. "I'm always saving you, Gene. Like now. I'm about to save you. That's why I brought you here."

Her fingers turn the dial of the control in her hand, making the tint of the glass lighten even more. She is enduring the pain, wanting, for a reason I don't yet comprehend, for me to see her more clearly. She blooms into sharper focus, her beauty more intense, more savage, now. The small mole at the corner of her eye peeks through. Again, I turn my eyes away.

"And where is he?" I ask. "The person you took the TextTrans from."

Ashley June drops her hand from the glass. When she speaks, it is with timidity. "I'm sorry. He came to me in the hospital. He was somehow able to sneak into my room despite the security detail, despite the constant camera surveillance. He was going to kill me, Gene. With a loaded weapon. So when I killed him, it was out of self-defense. Partly, anyway." A spittle of saliva dots the corner of her lips. Her tongue snakes out, erases it.

I take a step backward, bump into the table. Grab at the hard edges, glad for something solid to brace my wobbly legs.

"I recognized him immediately," she says quietly, almost apologetically. "One of the dome hepers. I saw him a few nights ago up in the mountains. Saw him escape on the train. With you. So I knew he was your friend. And because of that, I tried to restrain myself, Gene." She looks down at her feet. "You have to believe me. And when I knew I could not, I made his death as quick and painless as possible. Because I knew that's what you would have wanted."

Epap. Dead. I thought I'd already made peace with his death. But this confirmation knifes me. I remember what he said to me back at the Mission, his face ridden with guilt. *I'll make good. I will*. I wish I could tell him now that he never had to make good. He didn't owe a thing to anyone. He was always laying himself on the line: back at the Mission, carrying my collapsed body along the meadows toward the train, fighting off a trio of duskers from Jacob on the train platform. And here in the metropolis, venturing alone into this vast unknown labyrinth of death, determined to complete the impossible. For Sissy, for David, for me.

I hear Sissy's words in my head. *Loyalty is the proof of love.*

"It wasn't quick," I say, my voice strained with accusation. "You made him beg. You made him plead. And you recorded his final moments, a recording you just played to lure me here. How sick can you be?"

She shakes her head vehemently. "My hospital room had a security camera and I stole the tape. I didn't want to play it, but you forced my hand. When you refused to exit the elevator, as I'd predicted you would, you left me with little choice."

"Well, I'm here now. What are you going to do? Eat me for yourself?"

"If I wanted to do that, you'd be dead now, and you know that." Her fingers curl, causing her long nails to screech against the glass. "I'm here to save you, Gene."

I shake my head, take a step toward her. "No. Ashley June, listen to me. There's a cure. Something called *the Origin*. It reverses the infection. It re-turns you back to human. I can save *you*. Not just you, but every dusker. Back at the Palace, there's a whole arsenal of Origin weapons. To restore, to re-turn everyone."

Her face darkens like the landscape blackened by clouds passing before the sun. "There is something you have to know, Gene. Let me tell you—"

"There's no time, Ashley June. Dusk is almost here."

"Yes, and whose fault is that? What took you so long to get here? I wanted to explain *everything* to you. There's so much to explain, stuff you won't even believe at first. I wanted to take you down to the fifty-ninth floor and show you things that would help

convince you of the truth." She stares at me. "You know how difficult that was, all the red tape I had to jump through to get that floor
opened? It's been locked forever. If I didn't have this whole metropolis fawning over me, if I didn't have the authorities at my every
beck and call—"

"I have no idea what you're talking about. But listen to me! I can
save you."

"You want to *save* me?" she says, her voice edged with derision.
"What if I don't want to be saved? What if I think *you* are the one
who needs to be saved?"

"What are you talking about?"

She steps forward until her face is almost pressed against the
glass. Her breath frosts, disappears. "Gene," she says, her voice at-
taining gentleness again, "there are secrets that have been hidden
for centuries."

"What secrets?"

"Have you ever felt . . . at odds with your body? That it sometimes feels like it's too small or too large or too cumbersome in all
the wrong places? Like you're a square peg trying to squeeze into a
circular world?"

I don't say anything.

She strokes the length of one long pale arm. "Remember that
time in the closet in the school gym? The spin-the-bottle game?"
She looks about the Panic Room. "That closet was about the size of
this chamber, wasn't it? Everyone else was outside the door, and it
was just you and me inside. We made out with fake passion, en-
gaged in maneuvers that meant little to us. It was just a masquer-
ade. At the time, I thought it was because we just weren't doing it
right. But now I realize it wasn't the actions. It was us. *We* weren't
right." Her eyes fall on mine, tender. "We were wrong, Gene. Something was wrong with us."

"Ashley June, you're not thinking clearly—"

She raises her hand, silencing me. "No, Gene. My thoughts have
never been clearer or sharper. I feel restored, comfortable in my

own skin for the first time in my life. I'm saved. Saved from the petty existence we once had, all the faking, the pretending." Her eyes fill with a naked wistfulness. "I can save *you*, Gene. I can finally make you real."

A cold wave sweeps over me. "You're not yourself, Ashley June. This is not you. Because the Ashley June I knew would never say something like that. She was a fighter." I take a few steps back. "I don't know you: I don't know this."

"I am Ashley June," she says, and slaps the glass. "More than ever."

"No!" I shout with such vehemence she jolts back. "I can save you! Bring you back, Ashley June!" My words tumble out quick and loud. "Don't you remember back at the mountain village? You fanged Sissy. And she turned, almost the whole way. But the cure, the Origin, brought her back. The Origin is me and her, our joined blood. And in the same way it re-turned Sissy, the Origin can re-turn you! And she's here, Sissy's right in this building!"

At the mention of Sissy's name, the atmosphere suddenly changes. The sunlight flames out, goes dark. All warmth is suddenly sucked out, and a coldness swoops in. And when Ashley June speaks, her voice has lost all emotion, volume, affection. "There's just two flaws with your plan."

"Ash—"

"First, I don't *want* to be saved," she says. "I don't *need* to be saved."

Outside, long, thin shadows of skyscrapers slice across the metropolis.

"And second," she continues. "Sissy is already dead."

Forty-one

WHEN THE ELEVATOR suddenly swallows Gene and whisks him up along the atrium wall, Sissy's initial reaction is outright anger.

He left me behind, she thinks. *To search the more dangerous floors of the building alone.*

But she catches his expression as he is thrust upward. A look of astonishment. She sees his hand pounding the elevator buttons as he is flung higher, until all she can see is the soles of his shoes.

She runs over to the panel of buttons by the elevator door. She's never ridden or operated an elevator before and is unsure which button to press, or if they need to be pressed in combination. She settles on pushing them all frantically, randomly, until the buttons become less plastic protrusions to press than punching bags on which to vent her rising fear.

"Gene!" she shouts, her head snapping back as she stares up. The elevator keeps rising, faster yet, as if it is being catapulted through the glass atrium roof.

Then the elevator stops. At the top floor where it's now a mere speck of light. She hears shouting. Coming from the elevator. It's Gene, his distant voice galaxies away.

"I can't hear you!" she yells back, but she knows her voice is as inaudible to Gene as his is to her. For a moment she thinks about finding a stairwell and running up to join Gene. But she drops that thought. Gene warned her not to enter the floors between the glass lobby and top floor. Dark floors that might be holding hundreds of duskers sleeping off the night's festivities.

And then she's hearing his voice again. Loud and jarring, screeching out of speakers at the security desk.

"Sissy, can you hear me? Go to the security desk! I'm using the intercom. Go to the security desk!"

She races over. Next to the speaker is a set of different-colored buttons. Uncertain which button to press, she settles on pushing them in sequence and yelling out Gene's name. On her fifth try, finally, she gets a reply.

His voice crackles through. "Sissy, the elevator's stuck on this floor! See if you can find some external controls at the desk."

"Okay," she says, then stares at the daunting dozens of buttons before her. She punches all of them, randomly, trying to make sense of them.

"Sissy, can you—" Gene starts to say before his voice is drowned out by static.

Then something else.

Someone else.

Sissy's fingers halt midair above the buttons. Maybe she imagined it and—

"Help me!" Epap's voice.

Immediately she's pushing the TALK button.

"Epap?! Oh crap, that's his voice, that's Epap!" She bends lower to the speaker, her lips almost touching the metal grill. "Gene, do you see him, is he okay?" She starts smacking the speaker, as if to coax out a response. "Gene! Are you with him now?"

Then a horrific scream screeches out of the speaker.

It's Epap. "Help . . . don't, please don't, *no*!!!" he screams.

That gets her moving. She doesn't care anymore; she's going to storm up the stairwell if she has to. And as she turns to run, she looks up to the elevator.

It's descending.

By the time it reaches the lobby, Sissy is already there, slapping the doors with impatience. Even before they open, she sees that the interior is empty. Gene must have gotten out to help Epap on the top floor. She leaps inside, presses the button for the top floor.

The button doesn't light up. She presses it again.

The door slams shut. But the button still hasn't lit up.

And now the elevator starts ascending. The sight of the lobby dropping away makes her feel queasy in the pit of her stomach. As if gravity has been reversed and she is falling *up* into the sky. She spins around, sees the blur of passing floors blink past her, the bold numerals painted on the doors of passing floors flashing by too quickly for her to read them.

This is all wrong. She can't shake the feeling that she is being played, an invisible hand controlling her actions like a puppet. She slaps the glass in anger, hardly believing how gullibly she walked into the trap. She has to stop the elevator somehow. Can't allow it to transport her to where it wants. There's a key above the panel of buttons. She turns it. Something clicks in the panel, and all the floor buttons light up, then go dark.

The elevator only seems to pick up speed, lurching her upward faster. Then it begins to brake. The floor numerals rushing past her on the wall slow down and become readable. 55, 56, 57, 58. Then the number 59 drops into view slowly, coming to a complete stop before her. For whatever reason, the elevator has stopped five floors short of the top floor.

Ping, she hears the elevator sound.

She pulls out the handgun from her waist. Slams in the magazine. Gets into a crouch, ready for whatever might be on the other side of the doors.

Forty-two

THE DOORS OPEN.

Sissy can't see a thing. After being in bright sunshine for hours, she finds the darkness before her an impenetrable wall. She tightens her grip on the handgun. The smallest movement, the slightest shift of gray in black, and she'll blast away. She stays in this position even as the elevator doors start to shut on her. She slides forward into the path of the closing doors. They slam up against her with surprising force and don't retreat. She holds her position, but when an alarm inside the elevator begins to screech—loud enough to awaken anyone sleeping in the building if allowed to continue—she's forced to make a decision: move out of the elevator or remain inside at its mercy.

She pauses, Then steps forward. The doors close behind her.

And now she's swallowed up in darkness. And silence.

She traces the wall for a button but can find none. The elevator is gone. There's no way of calling it back up.

"Gene!"

Nothing. Only her echo rebounding back from unseen walls. But the silence is not necessarily a bad thing. If there were any dusk-ers in here, they'd surely be roused by now. By her smell. By the sunlight that had briefly poured inside when the elevator doors were opened. But there are no howls of complaint, no clatter of nails scraping against makeshift sleepholds. Nothing. In fact, judging from the ancient fusty air, it doesn't seem as though anything has stirred in here for years, decades.

She wishes desperately for a GlowBurn stick. She'd toss it in front of her, let it illuminate the floor. But now all she can do is wait for her eyes to adjust.

Gradually, shapes emerge. She sees the edge of a table. And the hooded shade of a desk lamp. Yet still she does not move.

"Damn it," she hisses as she realizes she has little choice. She can't stay in here forever. Not with Epap's desperate pleas for help still echoing in her head. She edges forward, arms splayed out in front, the side of her hip brushing against furniture. The air is mustier than she previously thought; dust motes waft into her eyes, making them water.

She walks to the desk lamp, locates the power switch. She's surprised when a dim silvery light cones down onto the desk—she didn't think it would work. There's barely enough light to illuminate even the books directly under it, but for Sissy it's the guiding light of a thousand pyres.

The desk lamp is the first in a row of mercuric lamps placed across the length of a long table. She can't see where the table ends; it stretches into the darkness, disappearing. Cautiously, she makes her way down its length, switching on every desk lamp. Many don't work, the bulbs apparently having died from overuse or, given the amount of dust settled over everything, from nonuse. Ten meters later, she's switched on enough lamps to just make out three tiers of wrought-iron stacks around her, all filled with books.

And in the far wall, she sees a door. A door that could only lead to a stairwell. To the top floor. To Gene and Epap. She looks around, uncertain if she should proceed. Something strange about this place. Above her, she sees a metal-plated sign hanging on the wrought iron of the second tier:

ACADEMY OF HISTORICAL CONJECTURE
BUREAU OF HEPER HISTORY CREATION

Cold fingers of fear grab at her. She ignores them, focuses on the task at hand—getting to the door on the far wall. But her eyes keep flicking to that sign, then down to the volumes of books and notepads piled on the table, many of them spread open. Where they've lain undisturbed for years, or even, judging from the thick coating of dust, for decades.

She turns on another desk lamp. She's almost at the end of the table. The light spits down on a rough sketch of something. She starts moving to the door—

What was that?

Her eyes drop back down to the sketch. It's actually a map, but unlike any she's seen before. This one encompasses not just the metropolis, or even, like the Scientist's map in the journal, the larger surrounding terrain. This map captures the whole *earth*. Mountain ranges and valleys, vast deserts broken up by thickets of dense forests. A map that even illustrates the ends of the earth, cliffs dropping off into bottomless, endless chasms. She's never seen a speculative map on this scale before. She stoops lower for a closer look, but her breath unsettles the layer of dust. Motes drift into her nostrils, and she sneezes loudly, forcefully. The map shifts, revealing another map underneath.

And another, and another, and another. A whole stack of them, in fact. These maps, using different cartographies, illustrate unique and often-clashing formulations of the earth. Some depict large landmasses surrounded by even larger bodies of water. Others show tiered levels of land, each separated and held up by massive earthen columns. The maps are filled with names of continents and other places she's never read before: Hintotes Sea. Mynsento Mountains. Deroze Plains. Some landmasses are apportioned off into sections, dotted lines demarcating and separating nation from nation.

Sissy frowns, looks closer. Some of these sections are labeled— and also crossed out—with what must presumably be designations: Sevibo, India, Heyan, Malinorise, China, Cheung Chau. She stares back down the length of the table, at the ancient journals and maps and books spread under the lamps. This is a river of information, containing secrets old as history itself. And she suddenly, with an intense desire, desperately wants to read everything. Despite the danger, she needs to hear the secrets whispered in these pages, see the truths unveiled.

But there's no time. Reluctantly, she moves toward the door . . . and she steps on something. There's a crack of hard plastic under her boot. Curious, she bends down. A pair of shades. She holds it under the lamp for closer examination.

Odd.

It's a newer model, a style that came into fashion only a year ago. So out of place in this ancient setting of archaic maps and moldy papers. She runs her finger lightly over its smooth plastic surface. No dust. These shades were left behind fairly recently.

By who?

She moves to the desk, picks up the lamp, swings it around slowly. She spots something: near the far wall, on the floor, not five meters away. She walks toward it with the lamp until the cord pulls taut. She sees a . . . well, it's hard to say exactly. She should forget it, her instincts tell her, get away from here. But something draws her irresistibly toward it.

It's a small cardboard box, mildewed and foul, its lid tossed to the side. The box had been secreted, from what she can tell, in the tight floor space between two shelves. Somebody had extracted it roughly out from there, upturning the box and causing sheets of paper to spill out. What immediately catches her eye is a symbol embossed in the top corner of the nearest sheet:

Tinted silver, it glimmers in the darkness. So alluring, she can't help but run her fingers across it. Yet this crescent moon is ominous as well, seemingly capable of slicing her fingertips. It's too dark to read what's on the page except for three large words stamped diagonally across: *TO BE DESTROYED.*

Not just on that one page. But on every mildewed, crinkly sheet she flips to, those same words, that same embossed moon. Her fingers, by now, are filmed with dust. She sniffs them and is almost overcome by the pungent fusty musk. They speak of an age more antiquated than anything else on this floor. In this museum of relics and artifacts, what she holds in her hands easily predates everything by at least a few centuries.

She stares at the sheets scattered on the floor, at the half-empty box. Judging from the mess left behind (and the dropped shades), whoever had snuck in here must have had to beat a hasty retreat. And probably with some papers.

She is about to move the papers closer to the light when something causes her to look up. She stares down the length of the table, watchful. There, above the elevator door. A flash of light out of nowhere. The numbers on the floor position indicator are blinking on and off, suddenly working again. Heart pounding, Sissy watches as the numbers light up in the darkness.

48 blinking out to 47. Then 47 to 46.

The elevator is descending, moving away from her.

45, 44, 43, 42, 41, 40, 39.

And there it stops. For a few seconds. Then the 39 blinks out.

The next number lights up.

40.

The elevator is coming back up.

The papers fall from her hand. She does not notice.

41, 42. Gathering speed now. 48, 49, 50, 51.

Then slowing down—52, 53, 54, 55, 56—as the elevator nears its destination.

57, 58.

59.

Ping.

The doors open.

Forty-three

SISSY IS ALREADY dead."

It takes a moment for Ashley June's words to register. Then I'm spinning around, racing out of the conference room.

"Gene!" Ashley June cries from behind.

I ignore her plea. I tear down the corridor past empty glass offices. In the elevator lobby, I smash the buttons, glancing down the atrium to the lobby far below. Nothing. No movement, no sign of Sissy, not in the lobby, not in the elevator stopped many floors below me. Even the elevator buttons remain unlit and unresponsive.

"Sissy! If you can hear me, get out! Get out, Sissy!"

The only reply is the sound of my own echo.

When I return to the conference room, Ashley June is gazing outside. At the setting sun, touching the tops of the surrounding buildings. A red glaze fills the floor, but it is heavy and dark, the color of blood clotting. The opaque walls of the Panic Room are darker now, Ashley June having dimmed the walls in my absence.

"What have you done to Sissy? Where is she?"

"It was over the moment you stepped into this building."

"Tell me where she is!"

"She's probably in the guts of about a dozen people right now." Ashley June turns to face me. "It's too late."

I move forward, slapping the glass so forcefully that Ashley June jolts backward.

"Tell me where she is. There's still time. You don't know Sissy. That girl cheats death like no one else. I can still help her. And after I help her, we'll help you."

"It's over, Gene, she's—"

"No, she's not! I'd have heard screams and howls already."

And at that, as if I'd inadvertently flicked a switch, a wail screeches from many floor below. And another. And another.

"Now it's really over," Ashley June says. "And in a few minutes you, too, will be killed. The sun has almost set. Night is upon us. And this building is filled with people. As is every building in a thirty-block radius. Rumors of two hepers on the loose last night sent the whole metropolis into a tizzy. Half the population came out, sniffing around, hoping, if not to find you, then at least to discover a drop of you, a smidgen. The dawn siren caught most by surprise; we had to find refuge in these buildings."

She looks outside at the nearby skyscrapers. "We're not just talking about thousands of people, or even hundreds of thousands. But *millions*. Millions who are awakening now, Gene, all around us. There's no way out. Not out of this building, not out of the metropolis."

I feel blood drain from my face. I knew there were people in the buildings. But not *millions*.

"Then just kill me already!" Spit flies out of my mouth, sprays the glass. "Just kill me yourself, put an end to this." I take out the handgun from my belt. "I'll shatter the glass for you, let you out. Okay? Isn't that why you brought me here? So that you get first dibs on me? Well, here I am. Have at me." I cock the handgun, aim it at the glass chamber.

"No, Gene, no!" Ashley June cries. "I brought you here so we can be together." Her eyes glistening in the dark. "I've turned, yes. But some things still remain the same in me." She pauses, and now her voice comes out as a whisper. "I still have the same feelings. I still feel the same way about you. But more intensified now. Purer."

She points to the table behind me.

"Inject yourself. With the hypodermic needle on the table. It's filled with concentrated people fluid, more than twice what you need. Use it, and within a minute it'll all be over. All the running. All the hiding. You'll no longer be prey. You'll be like all of us. And the Hunt will at long last be over. And we can finally be together."

I raise the gun until it is pointing to the top of the Panic Room. All I need to do is pull the trigger and the glass between us will shatter.

"No, Gene!"

I close my eyes. "If everything you said is true, maybe it really is over. I'll let you end it. You can have me."

"Gene!"

The sound of a gun fired.

But not from my gun. The explosion muted, distant. From a few floors below.

From Sissy's gun.

Screams break out from below. Then, another sound—Sissy shouting, her voice filled with fright and fury.

And at that, I'm running, ignoring Ashley June's pleas, ignoring the sound of her hands slapping against glass behind me.

Forty-four

SISSY

THE ELEVATOR PINGS. There are duskers inside. She knows this with a clean, cold certainty. And in the fraction of a second before the doors open Sissy considers her options. She can duck out of sight behind one of the stacks, then take them out one by one. She can leap to the corner, use the walls to funnel the duskers toward her, erase them as they converge on her. She can try to make for the exit door, close it before they get to her.

And in the next fraction she plays out the inevitable failure of each option, all of them eventuating in her death, ranging from five to fifteen seconds away. Because as long as the duskers have darkness and space and numbers, her death is a mathematical certainty.

And so she plays the only option that remains. It is not necessarily the best option. It could, in fact, be the worst. But she doesn't have time to think it through.

She sprints right at the elevator, drawing her weapon.

Her legs cut through the air, speeding along the line of desk lamps.

And now the doors start to open. Dusk light pours through. No wider than an inch, but already she's aiming between the doors. She fires off a shot. Cocks the weapon, fires off another. Hears the far wall of the elevator shatter as a bullet smashes through it. Glass shards falling like raindrops into the atrium. She shoots again. And again, running, sprinting.

All three duskers are maniacally trying to squeeze through the still-opening doors. They want her. And they want to get away from the glass elevator—it is an oven to them, filled with the searing rays of the setting sun. Wisps of smoke curl up from their skin.

A bullet catches a dusker right in the forehead, snapping its head back. The next bullet punches a black hole into its Adam's apple. The dusker is propelled backward, knocking against another dusker. Both duskers fall out of the elevator, tumbling through the space made vacant by the shattered far wall.

Sissy empties the handgun at the last remaining dusker, but her aim, jostled by panic, is off. One shot hits a panel by the side of the elevator doors, and the floor elevator doors suddenly freeze in place. But the opening is wide enough for the last dusker to leap out, howling with pain, its eyes scrunched shut. Slip, slide, gone. Into the darkness of the floor, scurrying along the walls, finding shade, finding shadows, finding darkness.

It's weakened. Not by a bullet—Sissy knows she missed—but by the blinding dusk light. Its time inside the elevator was pure torture, hellfire scorching the marrow of its bones. But here in the darkness of this floor, it has found a haven in which to recover.

Sissy goes after it, loading a new magazine. Light is pouring through the jammed elevator doors, and she is able to see a leg dragging like a lizard's tail, banging into stacks and furniture as it scuttles away. The dusker is trapped now, caught in a corner where two bookshelves meet. It starts climbing up, frantic feet and hands gripping the shelves like rungs on a ladder, leaving trails of melted flesh dripping from shelf to shelf.

Sissy cocks her weapon, aims—

It's vanished.

She doesn't dote on her missed opportunity. Or on her now-evident folly in going after the dusker. She simply turns and sprints for the elevator. The doors are still stuck halfway open, but whatever damage her wayward bullet caused, it's apparently had no effect on the elevator itself. She watches in dismay as the elevator disappears down the wall of the atrium.

A snarl behind her, deep in the shadows of the floor. She spins, half-expecting to see the dusker coming after her. But she sees only the line of mercurial lamps shining before her. Follow them, she knows, and they'll lead her right to the door on the far wall. Her escape.

But one of the lamps on the far end blinks out. It could be coincidence—the bulb going out right at that moment. But more likely, it's the dusker darting in front of it.

Because the dusker has recovered now. Vision regained, advantage restored. Now cutting off her escape route. Sissy stops. Turns back around, races to the precipice of the atrium wall. She stares down. Sees the glass roof of the elevator descending into the atrium. Her only other escape option disappearing by the second.

A howl from behind. Sissy spins around. Two beads shine at the edge of darkness—the dusker's glowing eyes.

She doesn't hesitate. Not anymore. She steps one foot out into the atrium and drops into the void. She falls, lands with a loud smack on the descending elevator rooftop. The glass roof holds, even as she half-bounces, half-skids across its slippery surface, almost falling off the edge. She spreads out her legs, arms, holds herself flat. The atrium wall beside her rushes by, floor numbers shooting up past her, as the elevator continues to descend. She raises her arms, gun clasped tightly, and aims up. First sign of the dusker peeking its head out to look down and she will empty the gun into its skull.

And then the elevator starts slowing. Not even halfway down to the lobby, it comes to a stop. She holds her breath, fear clutching her throat.

The elevator bounces slightly under her. Bodies getting on the elevator, piling in under her.

She hears teeth gnashing, fingers scratching the glass walls with agony. It's the dusk light. Its rays might be fading and weak to her, but to them the rays are blades of razor pain. A small price to pay for the taste of heper flesh.

The elevator starts moving again. Upward.

And still, they haven't seen her.

Slowly, she turns her head. Looks down from the corners of her eyes.

There are five of them. She sees the tops of their heads, flicking from side to side in a rapid, jerky motion. One of the duskers is smashing the elevator buttons with frenzied impatience, over and over, deposits of melted flesh sticking to the buttons. They're all in anguish, their flesh already beginning to sizzle, their eyeballs burning like pots of boiling water. Any moment now, they'll do what she suspects people do when heading up a glass elevator with great impatience and anticipation. They'll look up.

But, as it turns out, they don't need to. They smell her first. The whole back wall of the elevator is gone, and her odor is pouring in unimpeded like a waterfall.

As one, with terrifying speed, they flick their heads up. Their eyes meet hers.

They're confused, shocked, slack-jawed, and in this small slice of time Sissy points the gun down—

One of them leaps through the space where the back wall used to be. Its hands slap down on top of the roof, its legs swinging up and over. As soon as its pale face crests over the roofline, like the rising moon, Sissy is ready. She fires a round right into its face.

Its head disappears in an explosion of white spray.

Yet its headless body still holds on. Legs scrabbling for purchase on the elevator roof, its arms swinging at her. Claws, black and razor sharp, miss her face by millimeters. Sissy kicks out, thumping it on the chest. The headless dusker falls down the glassy throat of the atrium, its arms still swinging, legs still kicking.

A smack from below. With such force, Sissy is bounced off the roof a few inches.

She flips herself on all fours, facing down. She aims the gun at the duskers beneath, is pulling the trigger. Then stops. If she shoots through the glass ceiling, it'll shatter and she'll fall into their very midst.

But it doesn't matter, because in the next instant a dusker leaps up. Its head crashes through the glass roof as if surfacing out of water. The whole roof shatters, splintering into a thousand pieces and raining down on the duskers below. Sissy, screaming, falls into the interior of the elevator car, now really only a horizontal platform, without ceiling, without walls, still ascending.

The force of the fall pushes her right through them. Her back *thunks* against the hard floor, dislodging the gun from her grasp. It bounces once off the floor, then falls into the atrium. Walls of white-pale flesh tower over her; she's trapped in the tangle of their legs, ankles, shins. There's no way out. She's penned in.

It's strange, the things she observes. It's not the obvious. Not the gleam of wet desire in their eyes, the dripping fangs, their cheeks wobbling wildly, smacking loudly against rows of teeth. But she instead notices the vibration of the elevator engine humming against her back, the wall on her right rushing past her as the elevator continues to ascend. The glimmers of dusk light slipping through the tiny gaps between their enclosing bodies. She is looking everywhere but at them because, she realizes with the slow-motion clarity of one knowing the end is near, she doesn't want her last vision to be of duskers.

She thinks of Ben.

And David.

Epap.

Jacob.

Gene. Her lonely Gene, her sad Gene, her unreachable Gene. Years ago, when she was only a child, she dreamed a dream. Of a boy she had never seen and did not know. She woke up and stared through the glass dome at the starry sky. For the first time, her little girl's heart felt its own emptiness. She never believed this boy was anything more than a figment of her imagination, and over the years the memory of this dream faded. Until that day about a fortnight ago when she saw his stick figure walking toward her, a wavering, trembling dark line on the desert horizon, a mirage gradually, miraculously, filling out and finding form. His bangs blowing in the wind, his teeth so white, his eyes so haunted and real.

She thinks of the dome. Her prison. Her home. By now, with dusk coming to a close, the dome has risen out of the desert ground. She imagines what it must look like now, with onyx dusk rays beaming off its glassy, globular surface. She thinks of the pond inside the dome, its surface flat and still as a mirror, of the mud huts that sit empty and uninhabited, as they will for centuries and millennia to come—

And in that last second of existence, she closes her eyes. She feels so terribly, terribly alone.

Forty-five

I RUN INTO the elevator lobby. Slam up against the glass door. Peer down the atrium. At first, I can't quite comprehend what I'm seeing. The elevator, stripped of walls and roof and reduced to a platform, is rising toward me, about twenty floors below. White-pale blobs swirling on the platform. And for just a millisecond, there is a part in the bodies and I catch a glimpse of Sissy. Her face oddly placid.

The gun fires in my hand before I'm even aware of aiming or pulling the trigger. The bullet punctures a hole into the soft, pale mass, a meter from Sissy. The bodies ripple like a flag in the wind; one body keels over and falls off the platform, down into the atrium, splattering when it hits the marble floor of the lobby. But the other bodies seem unaffected as ever.

I pull the trigger again. *Click*. The chamber is empty.

The elevator, still ascending, is now about fifteen floors below. Too far below to leap—from this height, I'll likely bounce right off the platform and down the atrium to my death. But there's no time to spare. I bend my knees, leap out. Wind gushes through my clothes; my lungs ram up my throat. I plummet, arms pirouetting, toward the ascending platform.

Forty-six

SISSY

THE DUSKERS CAVE in on Sissy. They hiss loudly, their rank breath whistling between their exposed teeth and fangs.

So dark under them, so cold.

Everything happens so quickly, afterward she will barely be able to recall what happened.

A gunshot. Then a falling blur. The shape of something smacking into the duskers from above. A sickening splat. Someone crashing to the floor. With such force, it causes the whole platform to gong and hum.

The duskers domino into one another, plummet down the atrium. Leaving only one dusker on the platform, dizzy and concussed, temporarily out of commission.

Whoever just crashed down is now bouncing toward the edge, about to fall off.

Afterward, she will not know what possessed her to reach out. But still curled on the elevator floor, she snaps out her arm at the hazy shape skidding away.

Fingers wrap around her wrist. The shape falls over the edge, still gripping her.

And now she is being pulled across the platform. To avoid sliding any farther, she hooks her feet around the ankles of the disoriented—but quickly reviving—dusker.

Her face is pulled over the precipice, and she stares down the vertigo-inducing drop of the atrium. Fallen duskers lie far below, splattered on the lobby floor. Glass shards scattered everywhere.

And Gene, his face directly below hers, his sweaty hand clasped in hers. Slipping out.

The dusker shakes its head, hissing. Its eyes turn to Sissy.

Sissy and Gene stare at each other desperately. "Help me," they both utter at the same time.

Forty-seven

HELP ME," I whisper through clenched teeth.

"Gene," Sissy says. Her eyes do the rest of the speaking. They are pleading with me. Because she can't hold me much longer.

A dark shape looms above her. It's a dusker.

"Sissy!" I shout. "Let go of me."

Still she holds on. Its shadow falls over her.

I let go of her hand. In that same moment, she flips over to face the dusker.

For a moment, I'm suspended in air, touching nothing but the emptiness of a vacuum. I begin to fall. With a shout, I grasp for something—anything—and my hand catches a thick outcropping at the bottom of the elevator floor. I scrabble for purchase until my hands meet the metal framework of the elevator and I'm able to pull my whole body up and over onto the elevator floor. Gravity presses down on me as the elevator continues to rise.

Sissy is holding the dusker by the cuff of its neck. She's the weaker creature, but not now, not after what the dusker's been through. Its skin and joints and muscles and bones have softened under the burn of sun rays, and it is now more soft putty than hard bone and muscles. Digging into some hidden reserve of energy,

Sissy slams its head into the wall that's still rushing down past us. And she holds it there, the skull that's been softened by the sun into the consistency of an unshelled boiled egg. And even though the dusker fights back, flailing its arms and trying to kick, Sissy doesn't ease up one bit. She holds its head pressed against the passing wall, and like cheese being grated, its head is shredded into oblivion.

The elevator reaches the top floor.

Ping.

Forty-eight

UTTERLY EXHAUSTED, WE crawl out of the elevator. To keep the elevator from descending and picking up more duskers from the lower floors, we pull the headless dusker across the precipice. The body will prevent the doors from fully closing. For a while, anyway. Like persistent toothless jaws, the doors will open and close on it, open and close, gnawing the gelatinous body. Eventually, they'll ground the dusker to into a soppy mush, enabling them to fully close.

I look at Sissy. Her clothes are splattered with a white-yellow creamy substance. Dusker fluid. She is staring out the window, at the disappearing sunlight, her hair bejeweled with glistening shards of glass. She looks ten years older than the day we first met at the pond. All the innocence beneath her skin has cauterized into hardness.

"Epap?" she asks.

I shake my head.

Her eyes well up, but no tears fall.

I take off my splattered shirt. Using the less filthy underside, I wipe clean the sticky fluid from her lips, cheekbones, nose. I dab her tears, gently wipe her eyelashes to remove the gooey droplets before they can dry and glue her eyes shut. The last few dying rays of dusk light fade from the sky. In the streets below, a sea of black creeps up the façades of nearby buildings, floor by floor.

We should be moving, thinking of a way to escape. But for now, all I can do is pick out the glass beads from her hair, one piece at a time.

"We were idiots," she says, her voice whittled to a whisper. "Walked right into a trap." She looks at me. "Did you get scratched anywhere? Cut, bitten?"

I don't answer, only stare outside.

"No?" she asks.

"Does it matter anymore?" I say.

"What are you saying?" She gazes at me quizzically.

"Nothing," I whisper. I wipe the gooey mess off her arms, dislodging something tucked into her pocket. It clatters to the ground.

"I found it on the fifty-ninth floor," she says when I pick it up. It's a pair of shades.

Just then, a chorus of screams and howls breaks out from all corners of the Domain Building. Even the floor starts trembling, like a quickening. Ashley June was right. There must be thousands in this building alone. And millions more in the adjacent buildings stirring awake.

"Let's move away," says Sissy. Her hand slips into mine, and our fingers interlace as we walk to the other end of the floor.

Sissy leads us to the conference room, the farthest point from the elevator. The dark interior of the Panic Room is empty now. Ashley June gone. The bottom of the Panic Room has given way to a dark chute that tunnels down to floors below.

"Gene," Sissy says. "We break this glass, slide down the chute. Maybe that'll buy us some time."

But I shake my head. "Then we'll have, what, fifty more floors to get through before we reach the lobby? With each floor crowded with who knows how many duskers? We're outnumbered. We're out of weapons. We won't get past one floor, much less fifty."

Across the street, a window of a facing skyscraper smashes outward. A dusker scuttles down the face of that building, over the ledges of each floor. It is joined by many more duskers, pouring through the same smashed window, three, four, a dozen duskers. They've heard the screams and wails coming from this building, have recognized the pitched heper excitement in the cries. They know we're here. They all know. Another window, a few panes down, smashes outward. And another, another, until glass is falling like rain from a few dozen different spots on that side of the building. And just like that, in another nearby skyscraper, another windowpane explodes outward. Duskers slide out, like teardrops gliding down.

"There's got to be a way out," Sissy says. "Some way to get to ground level."

"And then what?" I lay my hand on the side of her face. "We have a few minutes. Maybe five, tops. Let's just . . . let's just stop running. Go out on our terms. Pretend it's just you and me and none of them. For just these last few moments. Can we do that, Sissy?"

"We fight this, Gene. We keep going."

"Sissy—"

"No, there's always some way out. Some way to fight for another minute, another second—"

"—Sissy—"

"—we'll find a horse on the street, we can at least try—"

"—Sissy—"

"—that's what we've always done, Gene! Survive. Then we get back to the Palace, we get David—"

"Sissy." My voice soft, tender. And one last time, I whisper her name. "Sissy."

I don't need to say any more. I feel something inside her bend, then break. For the first time in her life, for the only and last time, she knows surrender. She gasps, eyes widening. This is a new emotion, an unwanted one. It is a gale of ice wind to her hot, fervent, beating heart.

Outside, duskers are now pouring down the sides of every skyscraper and sprinting along the streets toward the Domain Building. The race is on; the Hunt has begun. The spoils go to the few, the swift, the risk takers, those willing to endure the piercing-sharp effects of the last rays of dusk. The sight of so many jumping the gun convinces even the more cautious to leap out as well. The dominos are falling now. Every dusker in a ten-block radius is pushing out of skyscrapers, sweat out of pores, pus out of pimples.

"Gene," she whispers. She can barely say the next words. "Is this really the end?"

I can't say anything. I can't even nod. I can only look deep into her eyes.

We fall into each other, embracing with crushing strength. We hold tightly, as if to form a shield against the brutal and gruesome end that will surely and swiftly come.

I pull away to look into her eyes. I want to see only her, not the horrific outside.

Sissy stares uncertainly at me, then gives a shaky smile.

I return the smile. "I wish this was all a horrible nightmare. And then we wake up and everything is gone, all the buildings, all the duskers, and it's just you and me."

"And we're lying in green meadows," Sissy says, her eyes drawing close, wet and soft and glimmering, "a rainbow over us, the sun warm and sweet in the pure blue sky. Our cottage a short walk away, beside a gentle brook."

"Trees, too. Fruit trees."

"And milk and honey and—"

"—sunshine." I lean forward and our lips touch with tenderness, an antidote to the violence that is to come. Regret and sadness rise up in me, and then we're kissing hungrily, lips pressing with desperation, as if to make up for the kisses we should already have shared, as if to compress all the thousands of denied kisses from the years that now will never come.

The sun disappears, its wilting rays suddenly cut off. The world plunges into darkness.

And now the walls and floor begin to vibrate with more force. Sissy and I pull apart. The duskers—the thousands of them—have reached the Domain Building and are now slithering up its glass walls. They skid across the glass like leeches, gaining traction on one another's smeared flesh. As they climb higher, their slimy yellow-pale bodies further darken the building's interior.

They reach the top floor in less than a minute. Panting with exertion, rib cages jutting out of membranous skin. Mushed against the glass, they gawk at us with eyes agog, the squeak of slipping, sliding skin on glass deafening. Many are thumping their fists against the windows in an attempt to break through, even slamming their foreheads into the glass. But on the slippery wall they lack the traction necessary to deliver a sufficiently forceful blow.

Loud thumps suddenly explode from inside the Panic Room. Duskers have flown up the chute from the floors below and into the tight confines of the Panic Room. There's no time or room for them to spin around; another flurry of bodies follow quickly behind, ramming them until more than a dozen bodies are crammed into that tight space. And still more press in from below. No wonder Ashley June booked out of there. I hear the squish of flesh, the breaking of bones. Arms, hands, faces, legs, mashed up against the glass, too packed to move even a finger. Nothing moves in there except one blinking eye.

Cold enshrouds us. Bestial wails assail us from every direction.

"Look at me, Gene." Sissy's eyes are warm and steady, her fingers interlacing with mine with crushing force. "Don't look anywhere else. Just at me."

Wet, squishy sounds. From under the glass floor, beneath my feet, a sea of pale bodies. Like raw fatty meat stored in clear plastic bags, their flattened faces glare at us, lips misshapen and pinched white. Oodles of saliva shine wetly between narrow creases and folds of bodies.

Metal beams groan, the shatter of glass drawing closer.

"This is it, Sissy." I wish I didn't have to shout. Not now. Not to Sissy. And the only thing I want to say to her is, *Forgive me for letting you down, forgive me, forgive me.*

She nods before I can say more, as if she can hear the thoughts in my head, as if she understands. And her eyes suddenly seem more alive than ever, full of daring. She says something I can't hear.

"What?" I shout.

And a small smile touches her lips, full of sadness, full of release. She leans in and shouts into my ear words never uttered to me.

"I love you."

Forty-nine

I DON'T WANT to die. I don't want her to die.

I don't want *us* to die.

And suddenly, I know how we live.

Fifty

I RACE OVER to the table, pulling Sissy along with me.

"Gene?"

There's no time to explain what I'm doing. In the dark, it takes me a second to locate it on the table. There. I grab it—the hypodermic needle Ashley June left for me to use. I thrust the needle into the crook of my arm, depress the needle halfway down.

"Do you trust me, Sissy?" I say.

"What are you—"

I pull her shirt sleeve up, inject her. She doesn't resist or flinch, only stares at me. I push the remaining fluid into her bloodstream.

And it hits me right then. A spasm of cold wetness shudders through my viscera, a cold blast that suddenly, on a dime, turns boiling hot. My bones, cells, the electrons within those cells, all set aflame. My legs turn to ash as I slump down onto the tabletop. My body slides to the ground.

Sissy kneels next to me. "Gene? What's happening to you?"

Lying on the floor, I feel the sway of the Domain Building, its oscillations keening wider and wider. I hear their howls ratcheting up in volume, so many of thousands of them, their screams mirroring the frenzy in my own head.

"Gene?"

Hard to speak. But the pain subsides for just a moment. "I injected us with concentrated dusker serum. We'll turn really quickly, in under a minute."

"What? Say that again?"

"We're going to turn. Human to dusker."

Her eyes widen with horror. *"What the hell have you done?"*

"No, Sissy, listen. This is the only way we survive."

She stares down at her arm. At the spot I injected her, right above the branding. Her eyes huge with disbelief. "You've turned me into a . . . *dusker?*"

"No, listen, Sissy." I clutch her arm, hold on desperately like it's a rope over a canyon. "This is the only way we survive. Once we turn, we become *them*. We won't smell. We won't stick out. We'll blend in seamlessly. Don't you get it? We won't be prey. When they break in, they won't be able to find us. We can get the hell out of here."

"But Gene," she says. "We become *them*. I'd rather die—"

"No. Listen." I lean in closer. "Once we're somewhere safe, we ingest each other's blood. We'll re-turn. We'll become human again."

"How can you be so sure—"

"We're the Origin. We're the cure!"

"I know that! But you still shouldn't have—"

"I don't want to die, Sissy!"

"And I don't want to live if it means becoming one of them!"

Now I grab both her arms. "This is the only way David has a chance to survive." Something in her eyes relents at the mention of his name. "We get out of here alive, we book for the Palace. We get him out of that tank. Think of him, Sissy!" An idea comes to mind. "Once we get back to the Palace, we find the Origin weapons and use them on each other. We'll re-turn much faster that way."

Her chest rises and falls, uncertainty swimming in her eyes.

"We can do this, Sissy. We won't forget who we are."

Her eyebrows knit close together, a deep vertical line creasing between them. Her hands suddenly clench. "Gene, it's beginning!"

she cries as her body arches upward, her back bending and locking in place. I reach for her, wrapping myself around her, ease her down to the floor. Her arms start to thrash, smacking me across the face, as cold-hot sweat gushes out of her pores like lava ice. Then she calms, in the eye of the storm I entered a few seconds ago.

And which I am now leaving. The internal burning comes even hotter now, scorching my bones but somehow freezing the marrow. My vision goes white, then red, the colors reversing themselves like a photograph negative. Acid for blood, hot coals for organs, boiling soup for brains.

Never forget, I start to say. But the words are mush on my burning tongue, and my tongue is swollen and unwieldy. Then a cloud blooms in my vision, terrible and horrific, a thousand petals of black that burst into pollens of poison. *I'm turning, it's overtaking me, it's a mistake!* And then my body goes limp, and—

Fifty-one

Iт is over. The turning is over.

So suddenly. It doesn't feel like a slow disintegration. But rather, a quick correcting, like a separated shoulder popped into place. Instantly righted.

I thought I'd feel a foreignness about this new turned body. As if, within my own skin, I've been converted into an alien. But instead, for the first time in my life, I feel a settlement.

Like a knuckle cracked. Like an invisible blockage in my nasal passage suddenly, finally cleared. Like a film of mucus between my heart and soul wiped away.

The smells come to me, rich and vibrant and luxurious, in 3-D, in 5-D, textured threads flowing through my nostrils and felt by the tendrils of every olfactory nerve. Identifying, sequencing, separating, splitting, savoring. My whole life, I had only scratched the surface of the olfactory nirvana that swirled in the world, fumbling with cheap, blunt knockoffs. But what I smell now I could luxuriate in for hours here in the dark.

Except it is not dark. Not anymore. When I open my eyes, the night has become day. The darkness bleached into a crystalline clarity, not a single pocket of black. If anything, the outside light, already muted from the covering of bodies cloaked over the building, is too bright, the glare causing me to squint.

In wondrous clarity, in a way I have never really viewed her, I see Sissy. Still in the eye of the storm of transformation, she's backing away from me. I don't know why she looks terrified of me. But the lines of her face are cleaner, her hair and skin purer.

And I smell heper.

It wallops my senses like an overpowering deluge of opiate wonders. Wave upon wave flung onto me, centering and energizing me to a degree that makes adrenaline seem like a sedative. A desire is carving out a large vacuum in me that. Must. Be. Filled. It consumes everything, makes sexual lust seem like a mild itch in comparison.

Saliva flows out of my mouth. For the first time, the torrent that gushes out is true and genuine and unstoppable.

Sissy. Heper smells roaring off her, drawing me to this flesh, this bone, this blood.

It moves, backing away. Fear and suspicion growing in its eyes.

With a sudden burst of speed that surprises even me, I leap atop it.

The smell. Oh, the intoxicating fragrances rippling off its skin in waves, saturating my senses. It struggles under me, its quivering body beckoning me. I feel an irresistible need, a desire, a *must* to plunge into it, and devour and drink.

"Gene!" it shouts.

I stop. Shake my head.

It's Sissy.

I throw myself away from her, fearing what I will do next. With shock, I realize I've thrown myself up to the ceiling, am suspended upside down. I slide away from her, trying to get away, away from the soft melt of her skin, the alluring fragrances flowing off it.

It flops over, but not in defense. It starts to shake, shift, spasm.

I can't hold back any longer. I give in, dropping to the floor, my body twisting midair. Claws rip out of my fingertips; fangs jut out of my mouth.

On all fours, I pounce toward it.

It smacks me in the side of the head, and I go pirouetting into the ceiling. I land awkwardly, body smacking against the table. When I spin around, readying to pounce again, she's staring me down, crouched like a cat about to spring.

She snarls. Fangs gleam.

All heper smells cut off like a spigot turned. She's no longer heper; she's turned. Only the *drip-drip* of residual heper sweat and oily secretions on her skin. And on my own skin, which I smell now. I lick my arm, lapping at heper sweat. A burst of flavor exploding on my tongue. I lick again, the length and thrust of my tongue surprising me.

The people around us are shouting. Their voices are loud and excited but are no longer the high-pitched wails that once lashed my eardrums. Or perhaps it's my ears that have changed and I'm merely hearing the same sounds differently.

Sissy is licking all over her body, her thick red tongue lapping across her arms, fingers. I go to her, the virginal female heper fragrance smeared on her skin even more tantalizing and intoxicating than the male heper residues on my skin.

I lick her exposed shoulder. She shrugs me off halfheartedly, too distracted in her own licking. I lick, lick, on her neck, behind her ear, lick, lick places she is unable to reach.

She smacks me on the back of the head. I hiss at her, fury burning in my eyeballs. Then I smell her armpits, the residue of heper oils emanating from those twin coves. An electricity animates my every nerve. I must have at them.

The glass ceiling suddenly cracks with a splintering intensity. Hundreds of people, having scaled the walls, have gathered above us, and their cumulative weight is too much for the glass roof.

At the sight of the large cracks quickly spreading into a web of smaller gashes, a vestigial fear kicks in, clearing my head for a moment. They're going to come crashing through any second now. And though Sissy and I may be two of them, it will be only a fine distinction to them. They'll smell the residual heper smells on us. They will rip us to shreds.

I grab Sissy, pull her away from the conference room. She gets it. We bound down the hallways, even as the roof caves in. People falling to the floor all around us, already picking themselves up, chasing after us, smelling the heper scent still on our skin.

"Sissy, this way!" I say, the feel of her name on my tongue cumbersome and slightly ridiculous. It is already feeling odd, this labeling of a person with a personal designation.

We race into the floor lobby on all fours. Even in the midst of this pandemonium, I feel a strange exhilaration. The speed, the dexterity of my body, everything connected and working in fluid, animalistic coordination. Clunky kinks worked out, a grace and a power surging through my flowing movements.

"Gene!" Sissy shouts, glancing back.

A flood of people is racing toward us, on the ceiling, the walls, the floor. Ramming through glass walls, smashing aside furniture.

But we have velocity, too, now. We are nimble and agile and strong, too, now. We turn the corner with too much speed, but our arms and legs skate under us with instinctual coordination, claws scraping across the marble flooring. We skid ninety degrees, fishtailing slightly, then leap toward the elevator doors. We crash right through, flying right into the very throat of the atrium. As we knew they would be, the walls of this deep vertical well are covered with people climbing up, smeared with melted flesh, like thickly spread peanut butter. We take this all in with analytical eyes, even as we're suspended in the raw drop of the atrium. There's no fear, only a pulsating exhilaration. We fall at an angle, the wall within arm's reach.

We're not the only ones who jumped. The chasing horde is leaping after us, a waterfall of bodies.

Falling right beside me, Sissy links her arm with mine. "Now," she says.

And together, we reach into the thick layer of climbing people, grabbing bodies, kicking down on limbs and heads, doing whatever we can to slow down. Everything is a blur as we skim along, and then we're slicing into this thick layer of sticky bodies, slowing down. Eventually, only a few floors above the main lobby floor, we come to a stop.

We leave the building with relative ease after that. We're not the enemy, not the prey, not anymore. All residual heper oils and secretions have rubbed off and been smeared onto other bodies. And from head to toe, we're covered with the tar of their melted flesh. We've gained what I have sought my whole life: perfect anonymity. We skirt along the perimeter of the lobby, avoiding the crash of bodies still falling from above, sidestepping around the rush of people surging into the Domain from the streets.

Outside, the night sky is thankfully darkening. Visibility improves with every passing minute. Everything is wonderfully clear, sharp, and in focus. Sissy and I race with exuberant abandon side by side, avoiding the crowds. Twenty blocks out, the swell of crowds shrinks to a trickle. We continue another ten blocks, running against traffic, until it is only the two of us.

We help each other wipe off the sludge in our hair, our ears, under our claws. If she's disgusted, she's not showing it. In fact, she's not showing any expression at all. Her face is smooth, bereft of any emotion, covered with a sheen of equanimity. I can't take my eyes off the purity of it.

"We re-turn now," she says mechanically, as if reading from a script. "We drink each other's blood. Then we head to the Palace. For David."

I don't move. She doesn't move.

I stare down at my paws on the ground. "It's better if we re-turn after we get to the Palace. If we stay this way, we won't need a horse. We can sprint to the Palace in less than two hours. And we won't have to worry about being detected, hunted down. Plus, we can use the Origin weapons there to re-turn ourselves much more quickly."

She pauses, hesitating. We look at each other. Blink, once, twice.

I know this look. It's the look of a person with a new toy or gadget, wanting to test it out.

And just like that, we're off. We slice between buildings, along the empty streets, two blurs sprinting on all fours. Within minutes, we've hit the fuzzy borders of the metropolis, the concrete pavements ceding to the sun-baked desert terrain. Under the night sky, everything is possessed with pure, hard lines, a cleansing translucency to everything.

So incredible, the feeling. The wind rushing against the face, the sense of power exploding in the bunched muscles of my legs, my two arms reaching forward, grabbing earth, thrusting it beneath my flying body, soaring through the night air. The smells of the desert channeling in from miles around, my nose a sensory periscope that gathers information so much deeper, richer, than sight, touch, taste, and hearing combined.

And again, that undeniable sensation of feeling finally, completely, at home in my body. A rightness about this, a pang satiated, a destination reached.

Next to me, Sissy sprints, eyes half-closed against the wind, her nose twitching, flaring. She howls with delight, her voice joining mine. She is a marvel of beauty and grace and power, her legs launching her body into a beautiful gliding trajectory, her body long and sleek as it sails through the night air, gravity a side thought.

About twenty minutes into the run, halfway to the Palace, we pause. Lift our noses into the air. We now smell them: hepers in the Palace, their odor thick and luxurious. At first, their fragrance is only vague and generalized. But then something happens. The floodgates open, and the aroma—compelling in itself already—*explodes* into the night sky, reaching even the stars. It sweeps over us seductively in dozens of individualized fragrances. Wet, bloody scents, crystal clear, flowing across the desert plains, blown by the wind, staining crimson every grain of sand. It is almost too much, overpowering. With so much heper blood suddenly released, it can only mean one thing. They've entered the catacombs. They're hunting the hepers. They're bloodletting the hepers.

Sissy and I look at each other. The smallest suggestion of guilt flares in her eyes over the quickly forgotten and barely remembered. A tiny rupture of shame.

And just like that, all commitment to some previous agenda vanishes, replaced by an all-consuming desire. We take off, our legs pounding even faster now. Long chains of drool dangle out from the corners of our mouths, trailing like ribbons.

A couple of minutes later, we stop. Not from fatigue. But because the ground is rumbling, a deep-seated quaking. We look behind us. The shaking is coming from the metropolis. People are now leaving it in droves, racing toward the Palace. We know why: The explosion of heper odor from the Palace, blown by a fierce gust of wind, has reached the metropolis. Has filled its streets and buildings with a pungent musk. Causing the millions of citizens to simultaneously cock their heads toward the Palace. In wonderment. For this is a fragrance never before imagined, of a quantity and variety never before even fantasized, comprised of *hundreds* of hepers. And now, the whole metropolis is sprinting toward the Palace, the young and old, male and female, a 5 *million* strong horde. For heper blood, heper flesh, so much of it.

I feel no fear. I'm not the prey. I'm the hunter, *a* hunter, one of millions. I'm just like everyone else and the thought fills me with a strange gladness. I belong. For the first time in my life, I don't feel *other*; I feel together. Not apart, but a part. Joined with everyone, with the millions behind me, with the whole world. And so when I kick out my legs and start racing for the Palace, what fuels my excitement is not only the prospect of what lies ahead but also the deep joy of belonging. The kind of elation you feel when the last puzzle piece—so oddly shaped—is finally fitted in to complete the picture, beautiful after all.

The wind gusts hard against us. So many succulent heper odors, I almost miss the one other distinctive non-heper smell in the desert plains. A fresh trail, only minutes ahead of us. Ashley June's.

Fifty-two

ASHLEY JUNE

ONE WEEK AFTER her operation, Ashley June's family went out without her. She was still bedridden and feverish, and the pain below her waist had barely subsided. They were running low on fruit, her father told her, and she needed all the nourishment she could get.

They would be gone for only a few hours, they promised.

But they were not gone for only a few hours. They never came back. She waited all day, and the next, and the next after that. But they never returned. It was the last time she ever saw her brother or her mother.

But it was not the last time she saw her father.

That happened years later, a decade after she'd long assumed him perished. After she'd spent all that time learning to survive on her own, forging a life of her own.

It was at the Heper Institute. When she along with all the other hunters were taken down to the Introduction. He had come out of the Pit and at first she had not recognized him. The same way she had failed to recognize him nights earlier on her deskscreen when he had selected numbers for the Lottery. Amidst all the screaming and drooling and bone cracking, she could not see past the pasty skin, the bald head, the languid, soft body.

She saw the body emerge from the trapdoor in the ground. An arm propping open the cover, head emerging, eyes peering out. Then he came out.

There was nothing of the straight, angular posture she most remembered of her father. This heper was slow, with a soft potbelly that spoke of surrender. But it was his eyes that had changed the most, that droop weighed down with sadness. His eyes never met hers as he studied the pens and pencils laid as bait in front of her. But it was then that she recognized him.

She screamed. A horrific scream that shook her bones and unmoored her organs.

The other hunters around her erupted with screams of their own, but theirs were filled with hunger and desire and hunger-lust, not ice and fear and horror.

And she saw everything unfolding with a maddening slowness. Gaunt Man pulling out a dagger, hacking through his restraints. She screamed yet again. But her father did not look, did not pay any attention to her or to any of the other screams echoing off the walls of the Introduction.

And when the end came, she tried to block off all her senses. Shut her eyes behind her shades to blind herself. Screamed as loud as she could to erase all other sound. But nothing could be done about the blood that splashed across her face, because her hands were restrained, her arms tethered to a pole. The droplets of her father's blood were still warm. All she could do was scream again, but even that didn't seem enough, her mouth was too small an outlet for the horror exploding within. And when she felt a tongue—Gaunt Man's—licking the blood off her face, up and down, the texture of his tongue rough and coarse and wet and sticky, she screamed even louder. But their screams around her were louder yet.

Two days later, she was back in the Introduction. And as before, she was screaming. But this time, it was with fear, not horror. And this time, she wasn't tethered to a pole but was racing across the arena, gunning for the entrance to the Pit, three duskers hot on her heels. Blood dripped from a self-inflicted gash across her palm. The scent of it enticed the pursuing duskers, drove them batty. She ran thinking of Gene, many floors above her, hoping she'd created the diversion necessary for him to get away.

Run, Gene, run! *she yelled in her head.* Now's your chance to get out!

And she ran, too, the soles of her feet shredded away, her lungs singed with exhaustion. And although every step increased the distance between her and Gene, she also believed these steps were somehow bringing them back together at some distant point in the future, that she was merely running along the circumference of time. They would meet again. Gene would come for her. Theirs was a story only beginning.

She slid, then fell into the Pit, pulling down with her the pole that held the Pit door open. She hit the ground hard, the solid limestone rattling her spine. Above her, the door slammed down, sealing the darkness inside. Scrabbling, scratching sounds, claws on metal. And then curved slivers of light rimming through. The three duskers, they were wedging in their fingers and claws, trying to pry the lid off. Ashley June shot up and turned the lock-wheel until there was a click and she knew the entrance was sealed.

She found candles, matches. The interior was larger than she'd expected, the size of a small bedroom. On shelves lining the far wall sat a riffraff of containers and canisters, stacked cans of food, bottles of water in various stages of emptiness. Rough bedding lay against the nearest wall, blankets folded neatly on the ground, the pillow still depressed in the center. Candles, long extinguished, sat on small ledges that jutted out of the limestone walls. Melted wax lay pooled and hardened, some of it lining down the walls, eerily artery-like, as if these walls pulsed with life.

It was only then she felt the blood. Soaking through the back of her shirt. Her hand trembled as she reached beneath the fabric. She felt three long gashes. Running deep and wet and parallel to one another, across her spine.

One of the duskers had slashed her.

The gashes meant nothing, she told herself. She wasn't infected, the claws were clean of saliva. She was fine, she was fine, she was fine. This was what she told herself for hours even as the adrenaline gave way to sharp pain, even as a fever erupted from deep within her bones. Only when she collapsed to the floor, cradling her legs, her body slick with ice-hot sweat, did she finally accept the undeniable.

She was turning.

Gritting her teeth, she forced herself to her knees. She would not succumb to this. She would fight the turning. There had to be something inside the Pit that might help her. She began to search. For something, anything. The Pit was a tight, confined space and it didn't take long before she found something. But it was not what she was expecting.

Under the pillow, she found a dozen or so snippets of paper, folded many times into tight squares. There were words written on them. Not her father's handwriting—someone else's. She frowned, not recognizing it.

Whoever wrote them must have passed these notes to her father from the outside. But how? The Pit door was too tightly sealed to allow even paper to slide through the rim. The more she thought about it, the more she realized the notes must have been secretly passed during the Introduction—that initiation procedure when her father was lured out of the Pit by the offer of food and morsels and water and other necessities. Whoever wrote these notes must have secreted them in the bottles and cans that held these items.

She read the notes. Most were short, clipped messages of obscure meaning.

Tobias, it's me, Joseph. I'm here.

Can't believe you survived.

I'm sorry about what happened to your family. But know that your daughter is alive.

The Origin is fine.

The Hunt is proceeding according to plan.

Hang in there, we'll get you after this is all over, too dangerous now.

But it was the very last sheet that most caught her attention. It was the longest of all the notes, a letter really.

Tobias,

I screwed up. I ventured back to the Domain Building yesterday and was—miraculously—able to break into the 59th floor. I couldn't believe it. After so many failed attempts . . . But I had to hurry, had only a few minutes before the doors locked on me again.

I stumbled upon something. Almost literally. A stack of old documents in an old box. These documents—we're talking *ancient* here. Not sure what's in them. They're written in archaic script—almost like hieroglyphics, really—it'll take me weeks, months to transcribe them.

But I heard someone coming and in my haste to leave I left documents scattered about and I dropped my shades. Didn't realize it until hours later. If found, those shades will be linked to me; and the missing documents are bound to create a stir. I can't chance the attention, which could lead them to the Originators. The risk is too great.

So I must disappear. Before any link can be made, before I might be seized. I just need to *poof*. Quickly, immediately. I haven't even been able to tell the Originators at the Palace what happened.

It kills me to have to leave you. And even more to leave Sissy. Obviously, without even a good-bye. The same way I had to leave Gene—suddenly and without explanation. Not a day goes by that I wish it could have been done differently. I would rather die than hurt him again.

And so . . . I must simply . . . vanish.

But the Hunt plan is still in play. The fixed Lottery, the boat, the arrangement to house Gene in the library, the sunbeams leading to the map—everything is in place. And although I wish I could be here for them when the Hunt begins, it's too risky to stay. And so I will return to the Mission and await their arrival. For a reunion I've been dreaming about for a decade now. I'll inform the Mission eldership about the Origin plan (if I trust them—please let it not be Krugman who's in charge now, remember that cad?).

Up in the mountains, to pass time, I'll keep working on the green-liquid weapon. After so many years, I think I'm almost there. And I'll start transcribing those ancient documents I found on the 59th floor. I think they hold some important information, though I'm not sure exactly what. So hang tight. I will return for you. I don't know when, but all in due time. I won't forget you, friend. I will return for you. Stay strong. Burn this note, as I know you have all the others.

Ashley June read this last letter, over and over. Even in her deteriorating state, she could not stop reading it, mulling over it. Even as her fever intensified, even as sweat poured down her body, she read. One sentence in particular leaped out at her. I would rather die than hurt him again. *Those words branded themselves into her mind.* I would rather die than hurt him again. I would rather die than hurt him again.

But when the turning clamped down on her with a vicious finality, twisting her body in agonizing spasms and seizures, her mind fastened on a different phrase. Up in the mountains . . . Up in the mountains . . . Up in the mountains . . .

That was where Gene would be.

The next night, after the turning was completed, Ashley June emerged from the Pit. She snarled at the people around her, smacking them aside with a glorious newfound strength. They sniffed her, could not understand. Where had the heper odor gone? When they realized she was just as they were and that she had just pulled a cruel prank on them, they poured into the Pit.

They demolished everything down there in their yearning to taste anything heper. Nothing survived. Everything was licked and ripped to shreds. Even the notes were torn asunder. All except one: the letter—that she had folded and tucked into her back pocket. But she found she didn't even need to look at that letter to know the only words that mattered. Just four words.

Up in the mountains.

Fifty-three

SOMETHING HAPPENS. INSIDE the Palace. We sense it miles before we reach the gigantic disc-shaped building. The wind, once saturated with heper blood, suddenly loses its pungency. Only the slightest of scents remain. Sissy and I pause. The heper massacre is over. All heper bodies have been devoured, flesh eaten, blood drunk.

Sissy shakes her head, and long trails of saliva loop around her head. She seems conflicted. Without the heavy influence of heper odor overloading her senses, older priorities are being reclaimed. She's thinking about David. She's thinking about re-turning. She's thinking about the Origin weapons.

I'm thinking about David, too. But not necessarily in the same way Sissy is.

Behind us, the rumble of the millions increases. More of them, and closer now. Sissy and I push forward. A mile from the wall, we see movement along the ramparts, dots of people racing about. We hear their excited voices, chaotic and exuberant.

Once we reach the walls of the Palace, Sissy and I don't slow down but leap up the walls, scaling the ancient marble easily. We race along the parapet walk, observing the chaos below. Staffers are running across the courtyard, most of them naked, hair disheveled, eyes keening and hungry. But despite the electricity in the air, it is plainly leftover excitement. We're joining the party late, the apex long passed, the aftermath cooldown already begun. The carnage is over.

But instead of slowing down, a renewed energy surges through Sissy. She stares up at the obelisk, considering, then bursts forward. She leaps down to a lower level, tears along the roof of a covered parapet walk before jumping to the courtyard. She's barely landed before she's springing forward, charging down a corridor as if possessed. She doesn't look back, certainly doesn't wait for me. It's all I can do to simply keep her in sight as I bound after her.

As we tear down the corridors, we pass groups of people dashing to and fro. I'd once thought the sight of these naked bodies, gleaming with a sickly anemia, was repulsive. And I never understood their wont for nakedness during the hunt. But now I know. It's the excitement, the raw energy that pulsates through the system. I grab my shirt and rip it into ribbons in seconds. I shout into the sky.

Sissy stops and looks at me, cocking her head. A wariness in her eyes as she takes in my naked upper torso. For a second—less, maybe just a tenth of a second—I feel shame. Because she hasn't given in, not yet, not completely. I know it from her clothes, still wrapped around her, untorn. She's still resisting. She's not on the prowl for hepers. She's here to rescue them, one of them, anyway.

"What is it?" I say.

"Help me find it."

"It's up in the obelisk tower. In the Ruler's chamber."

Her eyes turn suspicious. "What are you talking about? Help me find the Originators' science lab. Where the dart guns are stored, the ones loaded with Origin blood." She stares down a corridor, then down the other. "It all looks the same to me," she hisses.

Forget sight. Eyes aren't going to help us. I lift my nose into the air, sniff deeply. There. The faintest trail. Of metal unlike any other in the Palace. And an even slighter hint of gun oil.

Sissy sees me raise my nose and realizes what I'm doing. A sec-

248

ond later, she catches the scent as well. Her body stiffens, then she's flying down the corridor, her feet kicking out behind her.

We find the door leading into the laboratory. It is smashed inward, but the hinges and lock have held. Along the edges of the cratered door, a draft from the laboratory flows through tiny cracks. That is how we were able to detect the artillery and weapon scents.

Sissy wastes no time. She backs up, then flings her body at the door. Again. And again. I join her, and on the seventh try we bust through the door.

The laboratory is empty. Not an Originator in sight. A pity, that. "Over here," Sissy says, and rushes over to a dart gun lying on a laboratory bench. Next to the guns is a row of darts, filled with the Originator serum.

Though I can't smell the blood through the sealed darts, I'm suddenly drooling uncontrollably.

"Gene." Her voice has changed, a hint of threat in her tone. She picks up the dart gun, loads it. "We re-turn you first. Then me. Then we go up the obelisk, find David." Her voice hard, guarded. Suspicious.

But I'm braced, ready for it. "No, wait."

She lifts the gun higher, at my chest. "No time to wait."

"You don't understand. If we re-turn here, we'll clod along at a snail's pace. We'll never make it to the obelisk, much less climb to the top where the Ruler's Suite is. Truth? We won't get fifty meters before we're detected and hunted down."

She pauses, considering. She's conflicted. Her battle is not only with me but also with herself. She doesn't want to re-turn. Not back to that unwieldy, cumbersome heper form.

"We have to hurry," I say, urging her. Then the lie. "The sooner we get to the Ruler's Suite, the sooner we rescue David."

That settles her mind. She throws the dart gun strap over her head, pulls it taut so that the dart gun is secured against her back. Throws her hair over it like a hood. "As soon as we get to the top of the obelisk, we re-turn," she says.

"Fine," I say. On the way out, I grab a double-barreled shotgun from the weapons aisle. We'll likely have to blast through the door to the Ruler's Suite. I loop the shotgun around my head, strapping it against my back, grabbing a few shells on the way out. And two prototype Origin grenades for good measure. Then I'm leaping through the doorway, following Sissy.

Fifty-four

With our enhanced sense of direction, Sissy and I are able to find the entranceway to the obelisk in no time. We tear up a spiral staircase that coils along the inside wall of the tower. A darkened vertical shaft runs up the center of the obelisk like a black spine. I know what it is. It's the column through which enclaves are transported.

What would have taken us a good ten minutes to climb if we were hindered by the cumbersome coordination and pathetic endurance of a heper is over in less than two. At the top is the door to the Ruler's Suite. It's locked. Judging by the fresh scratch marks and the dents pinged into the door, many have already tried to get in, futilely.

Sissy takes a running start, slamming into the door hard. It rattles, but the hinges remain secure. The door is self-locking and triple-barreled. We could be smashing our bodies against the door for the next hour with nothing to show for it.

I pull the shotgun over my head. "Stand back," I warn. I point the barrel at the doorknob.

The flash of light turns my vision into a white sheen. The sting like a thousand razor blades exploding in my eyeballs. I collapse to my knees, try to blink away the pain. Sissy, bumbling forward, arms outstretched, pushes past me. I hear the sound of the door being ripped apart. Forcing my eyes open, I stagger in after her.

Inside the Ruler's Suite, I stumble into a metal contraption. It's the restraint apparatus upon which the Ruler had tied himself two days ago. Eyes still clenched shut, I touch along its width and height. It's empty. Only the remote control used to open and close the glass partition dangles from the frame.

It takes almost a minute before I regain my vision. There's no one else here. The suite feels so different from before. Instead of a claustrophobic confinement, it's airy and spacious, the sensation akin to floating in the sky. The windows, shuttered against daylight the last time, are open now and span the entire circumference of the suite. They offer a panoramic view that lets me see a hundred miles in every direction from an unblocked, elevated vantage point.

I gaze outside. Rushing toward us, from the direction of the metropolis, is a one-mile-tall, five-mile-wide wall of dust. It's the horde of naked millions of citizens coming in at breakneck velocity. At their speed, they'll be here in less than five minutes.

Around us, glowing like lanterns, are the five tanks. They're still filled with the green liquid. When I first saw the tanks two days ago, they were dark and opaque, illuminating little of what lay within. Now they are bright and clear and I see everything in them.

Drool drips down my fangs, splatters against my chest. I try to swallow before more saliva spills out, but there's too much, too fast.

Sissy hasn't seen the tanks yet. She's preoccupied, bent over an opened enclave on the floor. Sniffing, licking the interior. I trot over to her. A heper was devoured in here, every ounce of flesh ingested, the glass licked clean twenty times over. I smell the chief advisor, what little odor of him is left, anyway. In the corner of the enclave is his tablet. I pick it up. The screen, layered with sticky saliva, tells it all. He was trying to make his getaway. He had pre-programmed this enclave to head to the underground train station. And that's not the only thing he's activated—he also remotely started the train engines.

"Over there," Sissy says, head lifting. Her voice flat and hoarse, emotion ripped out. She walks to a tank on the far side of the suite, her paws silent on the marble floor. The heper inside the tank is drifting submerged in the fluid. Eyes closed, arms drifting upward as if surrendering, its hair waving back and forth languorously. The heper boy. David. The only sign that it's still alive is the oxygen mask placed over its mouth. It looks so different from how I remember it. Sapped now, its youthful aura gone, replaced by a sadness and agony that permeate off it.

I hear a click of metal. Sissy has pulled the dart gun off her back, jacked back the trigger. She points the gun at me, her eyes fixed warily on the drool splattering down my bare chest.

"We re-turn now," she says. "You first."

"No, wait." The words sloshing in my mouth, drowning in my saliva.

Her head snaps. "No. Now." Her words coming out lispy, mired in wet bands of saliva in her mouth. "I dart you. Then I'll turn the gun around, dart myself."

The floor starts to tremble, the walls shake. I gaze outside quickly. They're almost upon us, the millions from the metropolis.

"Wait," I say, lifting my arms. "Just wait."

The dart gun trembles. Because she's feeling it, too. The conflict. The equivocation.

"I'm going to shoot you now," she says. "Don't move."

"Wait."

She stares into my eyes, past the drab, unreadable expression of my face. And in my eyes she sees something I'm trying to hide, and it is the very thing she's trying to deny.

We don't want to be re-turned. We don't want to be squeezed into the confines of heper nature again.

Hands trembling, the smallest flash of fear breaking through the plane of her face, she raises the dart gun, points it at my neck. "Never forget who you are," she says, and starts pulling the trigger.

A flash of movement. From behind her. A mere blur, a flash of white, whorls of flaming red.

Ashley June, a bullet of ferocity and velocity, smacks into Sissy's side. Sissy goes flying, the dart gun skittering across the floor. Ashley June pounces, her body looping right across the suite, landing on the dart gun. She spins around, the gun pointing at Sissy.

Fifty-five

ASHLEY JUNE IS a pyre of savage beauty. The dusk sun has descended into her hair, and the stars become imprisoned in her eyes. I'm seeing her not through the scope of a sniper rifle or the tinted glass of the Panic Room. Nor, most of all, through heper eyes. But in the flesh, in dusker flesh, with dusker eyes. And it is as if I'm seeing her for the first time. And when her gaze falls on me, my lungs grow hot because I have forgotten to breathe.

"You," she says. A huskiness scraping her monotone voice. Her face shines with the alabaster white glow of a corona. "You did it. You turned. I knew you would." Her tongue licks out. "It feels perfect, doesn't it?"

"What have you done?" Sissy says. "What have you unleashed here?"

Ashley June's face flicks back to Sissy. "I did what anyone would have done in my position. What *you* would have done." She turns to me again. "I used my knowledge to my advantage. I stole in here, hunted down as many hepers as I could. It was easy. They were all in the basement, like food served up on a platter. Then all the Palace staffers wanted in on it, started hunting down the remaining hepers. It was an all-out binge. Better than advertised."

A pained wistfulness flares in her eyes. "It was supposed to be just me and you, Gene. To celebrate your turning. How awesome would that have been. All that heper blood and flesh and bone you missed out on . . ." She stares outside, at the approaching masses of people. "And now look, you're just like those latecomers. Not a heper left. Except one."

My eyes swing to the tanks, to David floating, eyes still closed.

"Not that one," she says.

"Then who—"

"Her," she says, keeping the muzzle pointed at Sissy. "Once we re-turn her."

"Stop. You don't understand," Sissy says. "We can help you. We can re-turn—"

"Sorry, but we've already had this conversation."

"You don't get it," Sissy continues. "We'll dart ourselves with this Origin serum and—"

"—it'll turn us back to heper?" Ashley June finishes. "Do you really want that? Be honest now: do you *really* want that?" Ashley June scratches her wrist. "Because by now you've realized how much more comfortable you feel. Everything simply flows better, doesn't it? Feet and hands gliding and sliding in synch instead of crashing about like uncoordinated appendages."

Sissy steps toward Ashley June. "Give me the dart gun."

But Ashley June only shakes her head, raises the gun. "Everything that has fallen apart is coming back together. Everything is being restored. Everything is going to be perfect. Except there's one last thing to do." The temperature in the room suddenly plummets.

Ashley June, keeping the muzzle pointed at Sissy, places the stock of the gun firmly against her shoulder.

Sissy falls into a crouch, lips pulled back, fangs jutting out.

Ashley June hisses, her finger tightening around the trigger.

Sissy kicks out with her legs, bounds toward Ashley June. Closing the distance by half, Sissy leaps at Ashley June. Fangs bared, claws unsheathed.

Ashley June pulls the trigger. A *twang,* no louder than a rubber band stretched and released, so innocuous, I think the dart gun has misfired.

Sissy spins sideways in the air, then falls to the ground, arms and legs splaying about. She stands up on her legs and blinks, quickly, rapidly. A dart is jutting out the base of her neck, right in the tender dip between collarbones. She pulls it out, throws it against the wall. "Nothing's happening," she says, scratching her wrist. "It didn't work. You—" And then she is suddenly collapsing to the floor. Reduced to a quivering heap of flesh.

I start to move toward Sissy.

"Don't," Ashley June says. She cocks the dart gun. Fires again at Sissy, hits her in the thigh.

"What are you doing?" I say in a loud voice.

"Giving her what she wants. She wanted to become a heper again, didn't she? So I'm just helping her."

With the two Origin darts injected into her, Sissy is re-turning rapidly. Her head snaps back. Her hands smack against the ground in quick, jerky pats. An anguished groan escapes her mouth.

"Why are you doing this?" I shout.

Ashley June turns to me. Her eyes, a shattering softness in them. "Because I know *everything*. The whole truth. And it's not what you think. It's not what you think at all."

"What are you talking about?"

"Sometimes the truth doesn't set you free. Sometimes it haunts you. Sometimes you wish you never found out."

A horrific yell issues from Sissy. Her back severely bent, concaving her stiffening body. I start moving toward her. And that's when I smell it. A whiff of the decadently delicious. The fragrance of heper, blooming and ripening by the second.

"Shissy!" I say. Her designation odd on my tongue, slushing out, snared in saliva. I turn to Ashley June. "She's re-turning." My jaw starts vibrating uncontrollably.

Ashley June wipes drool from her lips. "That's the idea."

Heper fragrance is flowing out of the pores of Sissy's skin, an irresistible velvet seduction. She moans in pain, but all I can think of is the flow of her bloodstream, swishing and pulsating so very near.

I fight my impulses. Take two steps away from her, every centimeter a tug against the grain of my craving. To lick her, to taste her.

To eat and drink it.

I smash my hand against the window. It cracks, first in a single line, then, as I pound it again and again, into an expanding web.

"Don't fight it," Ashley June says. "You will understand later when I explain. But she has to die." She lifts the dart gun at Sissy, readying to fire off the last dart.

"Stop!" I shout. The odor, so much thicker, so much more luxurious, now. I curl my claws into the marble floor, trying to hold myself in place.

"Better that she dies," Ashley June says. "Better for us. For everyone. You will come to understand. Go on," she says to me, flicking her chin in Sissy's direction. "You get first dibs, poor baby." Tilting her head, she howls with pleasure. And her voice is joined by another, a harmonizing howl that takes me a second to realize is coming from my own mouth. Ashley June shudders; I shudder.

A heper. Right in front of us. Virginal and tasty and irresistible.

"Don't fight it," Ashley June says. "Don't resist it."

My tongue, red and thick, laps out. I can almost lick up the odor in the air, it is so thick and tantalizing. The flesh of the heper quivers suggestively, and I am about to leap at it, on the soft, wondrous flesh, on the lava of blood that is mine with the slightest prick of my fangs. The desire so pure, so overwhelming, even the succumbing to it will be an exquisite pleasure in itself.

"Gene!" Its face is twisted in an effluence of emotion. Fear humming off it, sweat dripping off its chin, a tornado of ungainly excitements tiding off its body.

I hunch my body down, preparing to pounce. I can almost feel the warm melt of supple flesh on my lips, its blood gushing into my mouth, its body squirming under my paws.

"Gene." It's spoken again. Its voice is calmer, though still tinged with fear. But there's a different look in its eyes. Not fear. Not panic. Something different. It holds me in place, glues my hands and feet to the ground. "Gene," it says again, and this time all fear is erased from its voice and its eyes are filled with strength and softness both.

I stop, head cocking to the side. And then I see. A brief moment of clarity of a different kind. Of a watermark imprinted on my mind, my heart.

It's Sissy.

And then I am remembering; then I am reseeing her. Who she is, what she means to me.

There's only one way out of this.

I pull the strap of the shotgun over my head, touch its long, cold length. And press the muzzle against the bottom of my chin.

"*No!*" shouts Ashley June. "*What are you doing?*"

"I can't, I can't," I say, and even now my saliva is running down my chin and sliding down the long shaft of the gun.

"Don't!" Ashley June says, her hands white against the cold steel of the dart gun.

"Then shoot me!" I shout to Ashley June. "Shoot me with the Origin dart."

"No—"

"Do it!" I shout. "Do it or I shoot myself."

"You don't understand. She has to die!"

"No! It's you who don't understand. Both Sissy and I have to live. We're the Origin. We're the cure!"

Ashley June lowers the dart gun. "You and this heper girl— you're not the cure. You're the *contagion*. What your father discovered wasn't 'the cure.' It was a *virus*."

"What are you talking about?"

Everything starts to shake around us. The masses have arrived, and they haven't slowed down, not even as they reach the outer fortress walls. They buffet against the walls, over and over, until the walls, unable to withstand their collective might, collapse. Pale bodies race across the grounds, blanketing the Palace in a sheet of membranous white.

Sissy. Her heper flesh shuddering, ripples of fat and muscles moving irresistibly up and down her body. Only a few more seconds before I will have lost complete control.

"Shoot me!" I yell. "Shoot me with the dart!"

"No!"

Muzzle still pressed into my chin, I start pulling the trigger.

"Gene!"

I don't know what causes me to look up. The urgency in Ashley June's voice or the oddity of hearing her speak my designation. But when our eyes meet, a strange resignation settles upon her. As if she's just realized something. Slowly, and very deliberately, she places the dart gun on the floor.

Then her legs crouch, and her back arches as she prepares to launch herself at Sissy. Everything about Ashley June's body is tense, like a drawn bow. Her eyes, though, as she gazes at me. Softer than I've ever seen them, with a strange quality, almost a sadness, blazing in them.

"Look to the moon," she says. "The truth is in the moon."

And then she springs toward Sissy, a blur of action, her eyes rolling back, her clawed paws slashing forward.

I see them both as in a photograph, this moment frozen. Ashley June silhouetted against the window, her hair flaming behind her, descending on Sissy; and Sissy trying to rise, pushing off the floor with her sweaty arms.

I pull the trigger and the shotgun explodes.

Fifty-six

THE BLAST CATCHES Ashley June with enough force to send her flying into the window. The glass craters under the impact of her body, bulges out like a cracked eyeball, but does not break.

"Don't," I say.

But she does. Ashley June picks herself up, her legs buckling. Her body riddled with holes, her eyes clenched in excruciating pain, she's blinded by the flash. She had not known to shut her eyes against the blast as I had. She sniffs the air, her nostrils flaring. Trying to locate Sissy.

"Don't."

Ashley June keeps moving. Right toward Sissy.

I fire another round. A warning shot, into the window. It blasts a huge hole, one body length in diameter, right next to Ashley June. Wind gusts through. Whistling, it blows through Ashley June's hair, and the strands seem to reach out to me like bloodstained, pleading arms.

"Don't."

She crouches down to leap at Sissy.

I shoot again.

The blast pummels Ashley June almost right out of the hole in the window. She is only able to stop from falling outside by spreading her arms and catching herself on the ragged rim. Her eyeballs have disintegrated; viscous white liquid leaks out from the corners of her shut eyelids. Like tears.

"Please," I say.

She leaps, once more, and I pull the trigger for the last time.

The blast swallows up my hellish scream.

She's flung outside into the open sky. For a long moment, she hangs suspended in the great wide emptiness of the night. She looks so alone. And then she falls. Shards of glass sparkle around her, twinkling, blinking, then are no more.

Fifty-seven

I PUT MY mind on lockdown. Refuse to think, to acknowledge the horror of what I have done. There is only what must be done next, and quickly, before the heper odors, still thickening, overcome me. The dart gun.

I scuttle across the floor to where Ashley June laid it down. My neck is cracking, head flickering from side to side, drool seemingly pouring out from my *pores* now. Desire revolting against my will, beginning to get the upper hand. With trembling hands, I turn the dart gun around until the muzzle is pressed against my leg. I pull the trigger. A sharp sting on my thigh.

Ice flames sweep over me.

I don't even remember collapsing to the ground. When I come to, Sissy is leaning over me, cradling my head in her lap. Five seconds might have passed, or five hours—it feels like both, it feels like neither.

"Gene," Sissy says, "it's okay now. You're okay now." She strokes my sweat-dampened hair away from my forehead. Everything is dark. Everything is night again.

I turn over and cough, heave out a stream of chunky putrid yellow. I'm vanquished, strength obliterated. My legs, thin and stilt-like, sticking out of a body that already feels clumsy and distended. Gravity, so heavy on me.

The suite is shaking. The whole obelisk seems to be canting. They're in. They're in the obelisk, racing around the spiral staircase.

"We have to hurry, Gene."

I nod, and she helps me up to my feet. I avoid looking outside, at the masses pouring into the Palace, at the gaping hole in the window through which Ashley June had been shot.

"Sissy," I say hoarsely, and her name on my tongue again feels as natural as it is comforting. "The enclave. We use it to escape. It's programmed to head to the train."

She nods.

Screams wail up the spiral staircase inside the obelisk. Harsh, grating, predatory.

"Hurry," I say. I stumble over to the enclave, fish out the tablet. The controls are self-explanatory, thankfully user-friendly. Just get in, press GO.

But Sissy is staggering to the other end of the suite, her legs wobbly and uncertain.

"Sissy!"

The screams from the staircase intensify. They smell us.

Sissy runs back, cocking the shotgun.

"Forget shooting them! There's too many. Just get in!"

But she's only remembering what I have forgotten. She aims high at one of the tanks, fires away. The glass shatters, a partial break, but the thick liquid gushing out widens the break further, until the whole tank collapses in a spill of glass and green liquid.

David slides out, his body runny as the tank liquid.

Sissy grabs him before he hits the ground. But he slips out of her arms, slick as oil, and I'm already there, catching him before he hits the floor. I flinch back in horror at the touch of his skin. It's ice-cold, flaccid, folds of wet skin layered on top of each other.

Sissy is pulling off the oxygen mask. David's congealed skin around his mouth is pried off with the mask, a soggy, stringy pulp offering no resistance.

"David," Sissy says, her voice somewhere between a gasp and a cry.

I grab her arm. "Let's go, Sissy."

But she doesn't. Not even as screams—hundreds of them—reverberate up the obelisk. She's hunched over David, pounding his chest.

Then, in the midst of the cacophony of screams, comes the most beautiful, miraculous of sounds. A cough.

From David.

Thick, soupy phlegm rises halfway out of his mouth before falling back in.

"David!" Sissy yells, then turns him over to his side, starts thumping his back. "Cough it out, David!" She flings her eyes up at me in panic. "He's choking on his own vomit."

The mob of duskers less than twenty seconds from bursting into the suite.

But there's a way to slow them down.

"Get him into the enclave!" I shout. "Now, Sissy!"

"Not until he stops choking!"

I sprint to the doorway, unclipping the Origin grenades I'd taken earlier. Flip open the switch, depress the button. A *beep-beep-beep* immediately sounds, getting faster and louder. I throw a grenade down the stairway. I hear it clang, bounce. Then nothing, as if swallowed up harmlessly by the soup of bodies. Dark shadows now race along the curved walls, heads, bodies, claws.

A flash, a loud bang.

Followed by cries of pain. They're blinded by the concussive explosion of light. And for a few, there is a different kind of pain. The pain of being punctured by Origin shrapnel deep into their bodies, of being rapidly re-turned by the Origin serum.

I toss the other—and last—grenade down the stairs. Go for broke, hold nothing back. Another flash, more screams. I spin around. No time to waste inspecting my handiwork.

Sissy hasn't moved. She's still pounding David's back, and large gobs of vomit are spewing out of his lungs. White-green-yellow bile that's rotted and gestated new bacterial life-forms, gushing out of his mouth. The stink of it horrendous. Eyes still closed, arms limp, legs splayed out lifelessly before him. If you told me this was only postmortem spasmodic vomiting, I'd believe it.

I yell at Sissy, "We have to get into the enclave now—"

Screams erupt again from the stairs. These are human screams, the shrieking holler of a newborn. The grenades worked. The shrapnel have re-turned duskers to hepers. A few of them, anyway, their skin embedded with Origin shrapnel, bodies bent over in pain, as they are transformed back to hepers. Only to be quickly devoured.

We have to move. I pick up David and cradle him to my chest, his head hanging limply as if in surrender. *No more, no more, just leave me.*

A dusker flies through the doorway, its feet scrabbling for traction on the marble floor made slick by David's vomit. Its feet slide out from under it as it goes crashing against the wall.

More time. We need more time.

I set David down, leap toward the contraption the Ruler had used to confine himself. There—dangling from a cord, the remote control for the glass partition. I press the button as even more duskers streak into the suite, slipping and sliding, their claws skittering under them as they also slam against the far wall.

The glass partition drops down from the ceiling, quick and incisive as a guillotine. The duskers, realizing, clatter onto their feet, flash toward us. But the partition closes, clicking shut a second before they smack hard into it. It holds without cracking. They shake their heads as if to flick away the fresh pain in their concussed skulls, then back up to take another running leap. Their brutish bodies bludgeon the glass with even more force, the *thump-thump-thump* ringing in my ears. The glass bends and shimmers like a sheet of metal but holds. The duskers back up for another run when they are sideswiped by a torrent of bodies flooding through the doorway. Fast and swift, the bodies gush in, filling that half of the Ruler's chamber to overflowing. Their bodies press up and squeak against the glass as their levels rise, a pale, coagulated sea.

Not that Sissy and I are spectating. On the other side of the glass wall, we're sliding David into the enclave, being as careful as we can with his battered body, even in our haste. For a second, Sissy and I stare at the remaining space in the enclave, then at each other. It's going to be tight. But we'll manage. Somehow.

The duskers continue to pour into the other half of the suite. The glass will break soon. If not from the cumulative pressure of the dozens, now hundreds, of duskers, then surely from the sheer pitch of their strangled screams.

Sissy jumps into the enclave, cradles David in her arms. I squeeze into the remaining space, my head to their feet, lying in the opposite direction. The tablet in my hands. I check the screen one last time, then hit GO.

The enclave's glass lid slides shut. We start to descend, quickly, the rectangle of gray light above us getting smaller, then altogether disappearing as it closes up. We're in complete darkness as we travel down the black spine of the obelisk. Screams dart randomly at us, from unseen duskers on the other side of the column as they race up the spiraling staircase. The enclave shakes from side to side as if the whole transportation system is collapsing. We drop, suddenly, almost a free fall, and all I can do is clasp Sissy's feet in my hands, press her toes against my cheek.

And then gravity crushes me like a giant hand. We take a whip-lashing sharp turn, moving horizontally now, the back of my head banging against the glass wall, then slamming forward again as we take another vicious turn.

A minute later, we're inundated by hot spotlights. We try to stay calm, knowing this will soon be over. Then we're off again, tearing through the dark.

And finally, the enclave slows down. Ahead, a sliver of light beams through, like a tear in a curtain, widening. Until it is large enough for the enclave to trundle through. Gray light washes over us. The enclave comes to a complete stop, and we bang on the lid, hands frantically slamming on the glass with claustrophobia-fueled intensity. The enclave lid slides open. We fall out. It takes a moment for our oxygen-starved brains to realize where we are. But when we do, Sissy and I, without a second's delay, pick David up. And start running for the train.

Fifty-eight

W E CLIMB INTO the nearest car, the last on the long chain. David still hasn't opened his eyes or said a word. But he's breathing, quick, shallow inhales with even shallower exhales. Dark circles ring under his eyes.

The configuration of the tablet screen has changed. The tablet must have some kind of internal positioning system that sensed the proximity of the train and automatically switched over to that database. More buttons appear on the screen, red circles, blue squares, green ovals. But there's only one button that matters, and it is the black rectangle MISSION. I press it. Something loud clacks under the long line of train cars. The lead engine car, already revved, lurches forward. We're moving.

And it is like before, and it is vastly different from before.

It is the emptiness that is most different. Instead of train cars packed with Mission village girls, the train is now hauntingly empty, bereft of any internal movement or sound. Even in our otherwise empty car, Sissy and I sit perfectly still, the only movement being Sissy's hand stroking David's hair.

And it is strangely quiet. No sound but the faint rattle of the moving train. No screams, no wails, nothing from above or around or behind us. The train picks up speed and the doors to each car automatically close, yet still no other sound pierces the darkness of the tunnel.

Sissy takes my hand in hers. We grasp tightly, not with fear, for there's none left in us. It's all been wrung out.

Five miles from the Palace, we emerge out of the tunnel. The train will be in view of the Palace for only a few minutes before disappearing behind low-slung hills. We stare in silence at the Palace, so small in the distance, as it is overrun like a crumb swarmed by ants. Only the initial wave of the millions-strong horde had earlier reached the Palace. But now the slower yet immensely larger and denser waves pour over it. The obelisk tower begins to wobble, then sway. Just before we round the hills and the Palace is cut off from view, the obelisk tower topples like a matchstick snapped.

Fifty-nine

For half the night, the world is ours alone. The train cuts through a desert that is as expansive and empty as the starlit skies above. The duskers do not give chase as we thought they would. Not initially. Perhaps the pandemonium at the Palace is too distracting and they have not detected the faint scent trailing us. Even hours later, the silver-glazed landscape is a motionless vacuum.

But in the hour when the moon begins to dim and the sky lightens to gray, we hear it. A rasping sound, like the rib cage of night rattling across the desert plains. The train by that point, especially with so little cargo, is traveling at a fast clip, so the sound of the duskers' approach gains on us only gradually.

The rasp festers into a deep rumble, and an hour later we see the first sign of not only their approach but also their sheer size. A wall of dust, almost as tall as that which rose out of the metropolis hours ago, lifts darkly from the land. Disjointed shouts cannonball out of the dark haze. Sissy and I sit against the bars of the train car and gaze dispassionately at the chasing winds. It is not that we are unafraid. We aren't.

It's only that trapped here in our only vehicle of escape there is little we can do. If they come, they come. If they reach us, they eat us. It's that simple. They'll cling to the caged walls, the swiftest few at first, then by the hundreds. Their aggregate mass will derail the train, and then their cumulative weight will crumple the cages inward. And then they will have at us, and perhaps by then we will be mercifully already dead, our bodies crushed under their weight. But there is nothing to do to avoid this end, or to delay it, or even to expedite it. If they come, they come. And so we lean back against the bars, my arm over Sissy's shoulders, holding hands, David's head cradled in Sissy's lap. We don't speak.

An hour passes and their approach has grown thunderous. Many thousands are racing on the tracks themselves, and the train car glides along less smoothly, juddering from side to side. They are drawing close.

Dawn catches everyone by surprise. As if we have forgotten the natural and unbreakable sequence of time, the inevitability of the moon's death and the sun's rise. Only when the dark sky becomes glazed over with a pearly gray do Sissy and I stand up, pillowing David's head with my shoes.

The front edge of the horde is about a mile away. But they've stopped gaining on us. The duskers' disintegration in those first timid dawn rays is barely perceptible at first, their pace dropping off only a notch. Muscles less robust, lungs just a little less stout. But as the darkness cedes to gray, and the gray to violet, their bodies begin to drastically wilt, their energy flagging even more. Still they press forward, our odor egging them on, the sight of the fleeing train taunting them.

The moon fades; the awakening sun burns crimson the edges of the horizon.

And when the rim of the sun breaks through and splashes its rays over the land, there is a collective scream from the moiling masses. The sky rips open. More light, the color of blood, gushes out. A critical threshold is suddenly, viciously passed; they begin to melt. Within the half hour, a lake, a mile wide, yellow and sticky, shapes itself in the desert, at first chunky and moving, then, a half hour later, liquid and still.

Sissy and I lie down on the floor of the train car. She places her head on my shoulder, wraps herself against my side. The rising sun casts long shadows of the bars slantways across our bodies.

I feel something wet trail down my chest. Sissy's tears. She doesn't shake or sob, but the tears continue to flow for many minutes. Later, after her tears have dried under the sun, I will see the residue of salt crusted on my chest, thick and jagged like a scar.

We gaze up, through the bars of the train, at the sky. A fatigue that feels heavy as death settles on us. By the time the sky deepens into the pure cobalt blue of the afternoon, we have been asleep for hours. The train cuts through the vast desert, unseen and unwitnessed, toward the eastern mountains etched in the far distance.

Sixty

ON THE THIRD day of the journey, David dies.

He held out longer than we expected. But his death still shakes us hard, Sissy especially. We had done what little we could on the train, cupping him with our bodies during the cold nights, or wringing our damp clothes for a few drops of water into his parched mouth. But it is not enough. The cruel irony, that his death, after days and nights submerged in a watery prison, would be caused by dehydration.

In those first few days on the train, Sissy hummed to him the same lullabies she sang when he was a baby. She brushed his hair back, over and over, the way she used to comfort him whenever he sobbed as a toddler, after he'd stubbed his toe, or scraped his knee.

He never really came to. There were only a few moments of lucidity, when his eyes opened but for a few seconds. He'd stare with unresponsive and glazed eyes, at the desert, and, later, at the brown blur of forests. But never at us. Then he'd close his eyes and not open them again for hours.

Nightmares raged behind those closed eyelids. He shouted, random, nonsensical words. Sometimes he whimpered. Or begged. Sissy could only cradle his head during those fraught moments, her face racked with grief, her hand trying to stroke away his dreams, away her guilt. When he flailed his arms, lashing out into the night, she did not dodge out of the way but let his hand smack into her face. Her penance to pay.

He spoke to us but once. On the morning of the third day. We were leaning against each other, bracing against the cold wind of the lower mountains. David was lying across our laps, his head in the crook of Sissy's elbow. The dawn sun was lilting orange rays on our skin, and the whole world was lent a softness, despite the cold.

David's eyes opened, and for the first time he met my gaze, then Sissy's. His eyes were weak but clear.

"You came back for me," he whispered.

Then he closed his eyes, his eyelids falling heavily and with a sigh. A single tear fell down his face.

His eyes never opened again.

Sixty-one

WE KNOW WE are nearing the Mission. There are telltale signs. Splotches of encrusted yellow dotting the rails, like desiccated bird droppings, then larger sheets dangling off nearby tree branches like hung laundry. The remains of the duskers who'd attacked the Mission nights ago. The train slows; an hour later we round a bend in the mountain, and the bridge to the Mission, still lowered, comes into view.

It is daytime and our earlier fear, that we might arrive in the dark hours of night, hand-delivered into the lap of whatever hardy duskers might still be roving about, is put to rest. So, too, is the apprehension over the duskers. None have survived.

The cobblestone streets are empty. Everywhere we look, windows and doors to the empty cottages have been smashed apart and left gaping like stunned eyes and shocked mouths. Sunbeams shaft into them. We enter the nearest one, and go from room to room, piling on layer after layer of clothing over our shivering rib cages and concaved stomachs.

Even the Vastnarium, where we feared some duskers might be holding out, is empty. The back wall has been smashed down and ground to powder, probably from the outward pressure of a panicked horde seeking shelter from the sun. Inside, layers of desiccated yellow, a foot high on the floor, an inch thick off the walls.

Evidence of their mass demise is everywhere in the Mission: on the meadows, at the farm, along the fortress wall, everywhere there are desiccated crusts of yellow. And there is not a human bone to be found anywhere, not a strand of human hair, not a stain of human blood. Everything devoured, licked up, wiped from existence.

Death has run roughshod through this blighted village, no respecter of species. Nothing moves in this village; nothing sounds. No shuffling girls, no morning chimes, no singing choirs, no midnight screams. There is only the sound of cold wind fluting between the ribs of this ghost-town carcass.

At the laundry deck by the stream, we cup our shaking hands into the ice-cold water, drink in gulp after gulp. We raid the kitchen, gorging ourselves on the nibbles of food we find scattered amidst the carnage. Pickles in cast-off jars, cucumbers snapped in half, trampled-on loaves of bread. We can't get enough; if it's edible, it's in our mouths.

Afterward, still unable to stop shivering, we sit before the fireplace of a nearby cottage. The fire is soothing; the combination of food, water, warmth, and a comfortable sofa conspire to lull us toward sleep. But Sissy's hand in mine tightens with realization.

"David," she says. "We can't leave him out there like that."

We head back outside, trudge to the train station, shovels in hand. He is in exactly the same position we left him, lying in the empty train car, only seemingly lonelier. A stab of guilt digs and twists in both of us. We'd wanted to carry him with us when we first arrived, but we were too weak at the time. Now, we dig a grave. Sissy chooses a spot next to the train tracks, in the vicinity where Jacob had leaped out of the train, where he had met his unspeakable demise. The boys would have liked this, to be buried next to each other, if not in fact, then at least in spirit.

After we shovel the last pile of dirt, we stand silently. Thin wind whistles through the bare branches of the forest.

Sissy's lips tremble. "I'm sorry, David. I'm sorry. I'm sorry. I'm sorry, I'm so, so sorry."

And she turns to me, buries her face into my jacket, and screams right into my heart.

Sixty-two

WE WALK ALONG the fortress wall, scanning the landscape. Nightfall has begun, and the bleeding dusk skies sag under the weight of fresh darkness.

"How long," Sissy asks, "before they come?"

We stare down the steep mountain slope, past the rocky outcropping, and into the dense forest canopy. The Vast stretches beneath us in the far distance, a threadbare, endless carpet.

"A lot of them perished in the desert," I say. "Maybe over a million. But there are millions more. And they will come. Give them three consecutive days of heavy rain and cloud cover and they'll make it here more or less intact. It depends on the weather." I stare somberly at the darkening horizon. "And even if it doesn't rain for weeks, if we have sunshine every day, still they will come. They'll build more dome boats, or repair the broken ones. Or they'll build a dome train. Whatever the case, we don't have more than a fortnight."

We walk down the length of the fortress wall, our minds preoccupied. "We find two working hang gliders," Sissy says after a while. "Clair mentioned there might be some operable ones. Then we fly east." She stares a long time, her face turned away from me, eastward. When she speaks, her voice is filled with self-recrimination.

"You were right, Gene. We should have all listened. Back when we had a chance. We should have all kept heading east with you. If I hadn't been so obtuse, we'd all still be alive."

"Don't say that."

"But it's true."

"Maybe it's not."

She turns to look at me. "What do you mean, Gene?"

"We don't know what's east, do we?" I say. "We don't know anything."

"We know enough. We know your father wanted us to go there."

I stuff my hands into my coat pockets. "And what do we really know about him?" And now it's my turn to look east, into the gaping black nothingness. "We don't know why he abandoned the Origin plan. We don't know why he left here mere weeks before we were to arrive." I shake my head. "What caused him to abandon his dream? And desert me for good this time?"

Sissy stares at the cottages across the meadows, crouched in the shadows. "It was something here. Had to be. Something spooked him. Something changed him." Her eyes light on the isolated shadow of a building set close to the forest edge. The laboratory where he spent all his time. When we were last here, we searched it from top to bottom, but it never gave up any of its secrets.

But she only keeps staring at it, her eyebrows knit together in deep thought.

"What happened to him?" I ask. "How could he change so drastically?"

The questions unfurl above us like rising smoke, unanswered.

It doesn't take much time to find the operable hang gliders. Sissy comes up with a methodology that is as efficient as it is effective: inspect the hang gliders for dust. Any hang glider relatively free of dust must have been used fairly recently by Clair. Using a few GlowBurns we find scattered about, we work up and down the corridor, inspecting the hang gliders—virtually all covered in thick layers of dust—hung on the walls. After less than half an hour, we find two hang gliders relatively free of dust. We leave them by the door where tomorrow we'll give them a closer inspection under sunlight.

Blackness blots the night sky. An abrasive wind sweeps across the mountain face, freezing the evening dew on the meadows to glitters of ice. We squint our eyes against the bitter gust, staring despondently at the distance between us and the cottages.

"Let's go to Krugman's office," I suggest. "We can bunk down there. Use the fireplace."

The office is unrecognizable. A constant wind blows through the smashed windows. The upturned furniture is pressed up against the wall, as if pushed there by the wind. We know that is not the case. It was the rush of duskers into this office that destroyed everything— and everyone—in it. Even the heavy oak desk is flipped upside down, three of its four legs snapped off like twigs.

Sissy walks to the desk. She stares at the deep claw marks gashed into the oak, at the white, splintered wood poking out at all angles like broken bones breaking skin. A semi-encrusted yellow substance is puddled in one of the smashed drawers. The remains of a melted dusker. Sissy grabs her arms as if to ward off a sudden cold.

"What's the matter?" I ask.

She only shakes her head. But something is clearly bothering her. Her shoulders are too bunched, her face too shaded gray.

"No, really. What is it?"

She draws a deep breath. "When are we going to talk about it?"

I sweep my eyes over her, trying to understand. "What is 'it'?"

She looks at me uncertainly. "We should have talked earlier. But . . . the moment never seemed right. Not on the train, not with David . . ." Her voice trails off, and the sentence hangs unfinished, as if waiting for me to complete it.

"What are you talking about?"

A silence descends between us. Her eyes are on mine, and when

I look up our gazes meet and hold. And then I know. What she's trying, reluctantly, to bring up. A topic conveniently pushed aside the past few days by fight, flight, and fatigue, but which is now no longer avoidable.

"You know what, don't you?" she says, her eyes almost pleading for this to be true.

I nod slowly, reluctantly. My next words, softer than a whisper, uttered like a forced confession. "Why it felt so natural. When we turned, why it felt so natural—so much better, actually—to be a dusker."

She walks over to me, arms snaked across her chest. "Why, Gene?"

I pull her gently into me.

"I don't know," I say.

Sixty-three

WE DON'T SLEEP in Krugman's office that night. The carnage inside it, the ghost of Krugman gliding between its walls, the cold wind funneling in, makes the walk back to the cottages preferable. We sleep in the fabric and design cottage. We bed down in front of the fireplace, exhausted. I close my eyes, trying to stir up the energy to make a fire. Sissy, next to me, still sitting, her body tense.

"How many GlowBurns do you have?" she asks.

"Only one left," I say. "Why?"

She shakes her head.

"Sissy. What is it?"

"Nothing. Just difficult to fall asleep without some kind of weapon on hand."

"No one's coming tonight. Or tomorrow night. Or for several nights after that. We're safe tonight." I put my hand on her back to reassure her. Her body is tense.

"I know," she says. "But still."

"We'll go get some GlowBurns tomorrow. From the lab, okay? There's plenty of them in there. Let's just go to sleep now. We're safe."

She doesn't say anything, only stares out the window.

Less than ten seconds later, I plunge helplessly into a deep sleep.

I awaken. Perhaps hours have passed. My body stiff and sore. The room so cold, my frosty breath plumes above me. Next to me, the bedding is now empty. I touch the slight indentation in the sheets. Cold. Not a hint of heat.

Outside, it's freezing. My ears start to ache, and I pull the blanket tighter around my head like a shawl.

"Sissy?" I say into the still air. Not loudly, although there is no one else around. Although there is no reason to be afraid. Although we are alone up here in the mountains for miles and miles.

"Sissy?"

The only answer is the crack of cold in the night air. I snap into operation the last remaining GlowBurn and hold it in front of me. Along the cobblestone streets, empty cottages flank me, dark and silent. When I reach the edge of the village, I see, gashing across the meadows, her trail in a thin layer of snow. It leads away from the village toward the darkened forest. To the laboratory where, on edge and unable to sleep, Sissy must have gone to get some Glow-Burns.

I hurry along even as the light from the GlowBurn starts to fade, my boots crunching on the frozen grass and light powdering of snow. I am fifty meters from the laboratory, ten meters, one meter from the opened door, and now as the GlowBurn blinks out I am looking into the laboratory, now I am walking through the doorway, now I am inside the dark, windowless building.

Sissy is slouched over a workbench. All energy drained from her body. A weak, diffused green light pools about her, silhouetting her form. She is trembling with—is it sadness, is it shock or fear?—I do not know. The only thing I know is that something has ruptured inside her, and that she is changed, irretrievably.

"Sissy."

She doesn't startle at the sound of my voice. She'd heard my approach on the meadows. But she doesn't turn to me, only continues to shiver. Even when I reach her from behind, touching her on the shoulder, she doesn't move. Her skin is ice-cold to the touch.

On the workbench in front of her is an opened trunk. I did not see it the last time we were here, when we'd turned this laboratory inside out for a clue we hoped my father had left for us. Someone else had entered this laboratory in the interim, someone who'd somehow been able to find this hidden trunk, and who had gone through its contents.

Which now lie spilled onto this bench, hundreds of sheets of paper. They are mildewed and musty, only one crinkle from disintegrating into a fine powder. At the top of each page is a silver-tinted insignia. Of a crescent moon.

I skim through these sheets, not understanding the formulas, the official memorandums, the maps, the equations, the diagrams, the correspondence. The typescript on these pages archaic and indecipherable. A heavy musk of age wafts up from these pages, sour with the passing of countless centuries.

"Sissy? What are these papers? Where did this trunk come from?"

She points to the corner of the laboratory. I can just make out a cratered bowl of darkness in the floor. Where boards have been dug up, flung aside with the strength of five humans. Or one dusker.

She puts her hand on another stack of papers immediately before her. These are Mission paperwork, administrative forms, bookkeeping riffraff. At first, I don't understand. But then she turns them over and on the backside of each sheet is my father's handwriting. I rifle through a few pages. And quickly realize what I'm reading: my father's transcriptions of the ancient documents. It was his attempt to make legible the illegible. But he'd only transcribed the incomprehensible into the unimaginable.

Sissy turns to me now. The glowing green light marbles her face. I will forever remember the look in her eyes as she settles them on mine, how they seem saturated with brokenness, how a single trail of tears falls from each eye.

"I know the truth now," she whispers, her voice freighted with horror.

———

Transcription of Documents labeled 369–384
Excerpts of official correspondence between the Ruler and
the Commander Scientist. Year of correspondence: unknown.

From: the Commander Scientist
To: His Most Eminent Highness, the Ruler
Date: October 18
Subject: HEPER development

Your Highness,

*The HEPER project (**Hush-hush Exploration for Provisional Energy Resources**) progresses well. Thus far, all preliminary tests performed on mice corpses have produced the desired results. Injection of the HEPER virus into dead mice has turned their dead flesh into edible, palatable food for living mice. Said dead mice have been consumed by live mice within the expected time frame.*

———

From: the Commander Scientist
To: His Most Eminent Highness, the Ruler
Date: January 5
Subject: Please reconsider

Your Highness,

*I must beg for your reconsideration, Your Highness. As I tried
to emphasize in our previous three correspondences, we are
simply not ready to move on to people corpses as test subjects.*

*If you will recall, the purpose of the HEPER project was to create
a virus that would, to put it bluntly, transmogrify corpses of people
into edible flesh. After the catastrophic drought and subsequent
famine of the last decade killed more than half of our population,
we in the scientific community are pleased to follow Your Highness's decree to create an alternate meat source. This top-secret
project, initiated by Your Highness, has thus far proven to be a
roaring success. Injection of the HEPER virus into dead mice has
resulted in live mice devouring said corpses in as quickly as one
night.*

*However, it is simply premature to move on to testing the HEPER
virus on people corpses. There is far too much about the HEPER virus
that we do not know. Even with the mice corpses, we are finding
disturbing results. Just last week, when we doubled the dosage the
living mice developed a craving for the dead mice that bordered on
madness.*

I urge you to reconsider, Your Highness.

––––––––

From: the Commander Scientist
To: His Most Eminent Highness, the Ruler

Date: January 10
Subject: re: increase in HEPER dosage

Your Highness,

*With all due respect, Your Highness, your request simply cannot
be followed. You previously chose to ignore my advice when you
ordered—over my vehement objection—to start injecting people
corpses with the HEPER virus. And now, you are exacerbating this
mistake by insisting on an increase in dosage. The dosage level
administered to the corpses already exceeded what we consider to
be the maximal input. The level that Your Highness is requesting is
excessive, and will likely cause unforeseen and deleterious problems.*

*While I understand you are frustrated with our lack of progress
with people corpses, simply increasing the dosage is not the most
prudent or rational next step.*

*I must restate my objection to further HEPER injections in the
strongest of terms.*

———

From: the newly appointed Commander Scientist
To: His Most Eminent Highness, the Ruler
Date: January 18
Subject: Thank you

Your Royal Highness,

*First, allow me to express my deepest thanks for the honor you've
bestowed upon me. This promotion to Commander Scientist (and
chief of the HEPER project) is humbling. And although the
former Commander Scientist—whose recent and untimely death
we still grieve—set a bar I cannot possibly hope to reach, please be*

assured that the HEPER project will continue unimpeded. In fact, I am happy to report that tomorrow we will triple the dosage level on people corpses, as Your Highness had previously requested.

———

From: the newly appointed Commander Scientist
To: His Most Eminent Highness, the Ruler
Date: February 2
Subject: re: live subjects

Your Royal Highness,

If I may be so emboldened as to query the purpose of Your Highness's latest request? I know I am new to this post and thus lack experience, but even so, I fail to see the rationale behind your Highness's desire to inject <u>live</u> subjects with the HEPER virus. I know that the latest round of experiments with corpses has produced unsatisfactory and disappointing results, but let me assure you that injecting live subjects with the HEPER virus is highly inadvisable. In fact, it seems to go against the purpose behind the HEPER project, which, if I may be so impudent as to remind Your Highness, was to produce edible meats from <u>corpses</u> in order to replenish food supplies in the unfortunate event of a famine.

———

From: the Commander Scientist
To: His Most Eminent Highness, the Ruler
Date: February 8
Subject: re: increase dosage

Your Royal Highness,

We have been observing subject FY013 over the past few nights. The injection of the HEPER virus has had little effect upon him *except, apparently, to blind him. He cannot see. He stumbles about with arms outstretched, constantly bumping into things. Also, he has lost his ability to sleep. Now, he simply faints, collapsing to the floor and lying there for hours. Yet other than those minor changes, there is little else. Again, if I may state, I do not understand the purpose behind injecting <u>live</u> subjects with the HEPER virus. And I am at a loss why Your Highness now wants to further increase the dosage to FY013.*

———

From: the Commander Scientist
To: His Most Eminent Highness, the Ruler
Date: February 11
Subject: re: need another test subject

Your Highness,

Unexpected events have unfolded over the past two nights with relation to subject FY013. After we, at Your Highness's behest, injected him with the increased dosage of the HEPER virus, the subject began to exhibit rather peculiar symptoms. Of note: (1) stubs of hair began to show on his limbs and underarms; (2) his incisor teeth begun to go blunt; (3) he developed an apparently unquenchable thirst (one cup of water per day); and (4), most oddly, he seemed to gain a resistance to infrared and ultraviolet light. Also of note, he has begun to give off a particularly fragrant odor.

He has also, unfortunately, died. We request at this point another subject, a live one, to continue testing. Please do send said subject at your earliest convenience.

In addition, there will be a short delay—perhaps only one or two nights—as we will need to do some repairs. Some laboratory equipment was recently damaged, along with windows and doors, and the sooner they are fixed, the sooner we can resume testing. But please do send us one (or two! or three!) live subjects as soon as you can (or sooner!).

Also, Your Highness, would you let me know that you've received this e-mail. Just want to be sure you got it! ☺

————

From: the Commander Scientist
To: His Most Eminent Highness, the Ruler
Date: February 12
Subject: URGENT!

Your Highness,

Per our last correspondence, when might we be expecting you to send us more live subjects?

————

From: the Commander Scientist
To: His Most Eminent Highness, the Ruler
Date: February 13
Subject: URGENT!

Dearest Royal Highness,

Can you send over some more test subjects ASAP?

————

From: the Commander Scientist
To: His Most Eminent Highness, the Ruler
Date: February 15
Subject: young female test subjects

Dear Royal Highness,

Another round of testing completed. We've never used females as test subjects and were initially surprised when you sent us one as the subject. The result, however, was quite enthralling. We would like to conduct more tests on young female subjects. Can you send over more subjects, please, as soon as you can? Young females preferred.

———

From: the Commander Scientist
To: His Most Eminent Highness, the Ruler
Date: February 17
Subject: need more subjects

Dear Highness,

Testing continues at frantic and successful pace. Please send more subjects.

———

From: the Commander Scientist
To: His Most Eminent Highness, the Ruler
Date: February 19
Subject:

Dear Highness,

We have lost some staff members. Please send replacements for the following positions:

(excerpt ends).

———

OFFICIAL ORDER OF THE ROYAL HIGHNESS
THE RULER OF THE PALACE

CONFIDENTIAL

(excerpt begins, date uncertain)

. . . became quickly apparent that the HEPER project had spun out of control. So potent and immediate was the HEPER's effect, whole groups of Scientists—renowned, levelheaded, intelligent— soon turned on each other, and attempted to inject one another with the HEPER virus. Nothing could quell their desire for HEPER-transformed flesh, and for the red liquid which ran under said flesh.

The HEPER project is more than an unmitigated disaster. It has produced—and this cannot be overstated—a potentially devastating weapon. One which, if unleashed upon the population, accidentally or otherwise, would cause widespread death and violence, and, very possibly, complete extinction of our species. Though it appears the effects are easily reversible, make no mistake. The HEPER virus, in the wrong hands, can be used as a Weapon of Mighty Devastation. It must be wholly and completely eradicated.

Thus, by Royal decree, it is hereby declared that all formulas and data and results and paperwork related to the HEPER project be permanently deleted, destroyed, and/or burned. It never existed. The good citizens of the metropolis must never be told of its existence.

It is further decreed that the HEPER Bureau be established. The purpose of the HEPER Bureau is to give explanation for the existence of the hepers who managed to escape into society. The citizenry are curious and are demanding answers. Said Bureau will fabricate a false evolutionary history and science behind the existence of the hepers. No expense will be spared to ensure the denizens of the metropolis are forever kept from the truth behind the genesis of the hepers. To that end, the HEPER Bureau will be given unlimited resources in the years, decades, centuries, and even millennia to come.

It is also ordered that the Commander Scientist and his colleagues be injected with the HEPER virus and then detained in the catacombs of the Palace. Their fate shall be later determined by the Ruler.

In addition, it is (excerpt ends).

Sixty-four

For almost a half hour, I read my father's transcribed pages. I turn the sheets slowly at first, uncertain of what I am reading, their meaning still veiled. But as I follow the flow of my father's hauntingly familiar handwriting, passing over the occasional ink blot where his pen, as if paused in stunned disbelief, had bled into paper, I eventually, page by page, piece it all together.

These papers are obscene.

I pull away from the workbench, away from the stack of papers still only half-read. I stare outside. Nothing is the same; everything has changed.

"Back at the Domain Building," Sissy says, her whispered words drained of life. "On the fifty-ninth floor. I saw documents just like these. Old, moldy papers, falling apart, each with this crescent moon insignia. They were in an opened box half-empty. Somebody had broken into that floor, discovered the box."

I stare at the pages, their crescent moons glinting. "It was my father who broke in," I say. "Those were his shades you found."

Sissy nods, sadly. "These are the papers. He stole them and brought them back to the Mission. Translated them here. And afterward, hid them himself, their contents too unbearable."

I glance at the cratered hole in the corner of the room. "Ashley June," I whisper. "She was here. She found the papers, dug them up."

Sissy steps toward the workbench. "Look to the moon," she whispers, her finger trailing the moon insignia on a page. "The truth is in the moon."

I remember those words. Ashley June's words. And I remember something else she had said, how she had uttered them like a warning.

Sometimes the truth doesn't set you free. Sometimes it haunts you. Sometimes you wish you never found out.

And I realize that I can't talk. Not about this, like it is something that can be discussed, analyzed, grappled with, brought under control with mere words. And suddenly I'm bursting out the door, needing to be away from the laboratory, needing to be outside, needing to have nothing between me and the stars and the moon.

"Gene!"

And still I keep running, as if pain in my legs and lungs might erase the truths learned, the knowledge acquired, the innocence lost. And even as I sprint as fast as I can, choking back tears, I feel it: the encumbered body. So different from the soaring grace with which I'd sprinted across the Vast as a dusker, the harmony between my moving limbs, the segueing of brute power with grace. Now, my human body jiggles upon my frame ungainly and burdensome.

"Gene! Wait!"

The lake looms ahead of me, the destination I never consciously set upon but toward which my eager feet now move ever swifter. The wind howls, whipping around the nape of my neck, nipping at my exposed ankles. And then I'm running down the slight bank, leaping over driftwood logs. My feet smash through the smooth surface of the lake.

The cold cuts me like glass. But before I can wade any deeper, Sissy grabs my arm.

"Gene!—"

I pull my arm away. But she holds on and the sudden shift in equilibrium causes both of us to tumble into the water. My hand smacks into sharp rock sitting on the shallow floor; blood spills out from my cut palm. We surface gasping and dripping, all air sucked out of our lungs. The cold is a thousand needles pricking into me.

"I should have turned years ago!" I shout, slapping at the water. "Why didn't I just turn! Why the needless fight, why the struggle, night after night, month after month, year after year!" My body is freezing, but my eyes are hot cauldrons of fury. "Why, Sissy? Why the daily struggle to survive when we've been nothing but mutants? When we've been nothing but aberrations?"

"Gene—"

"We're the ones at odds with the universe! We should have just turned!" Hot tears gush out of my eyes, burning twin trails down my face. "When I was five, when I was six, seven, eight, when I was thirteen. I should have just turned! And this living hell would have ended! I've been one cut, one drop of saliva, from turning—turning back to normal, to the real me, the natural me. Not this!" I pound my chest, slap my face. "Not what I've always thought was true! Not this freak show that I am!"

And she looks at me, her lips trembling, and she doesn't know what to say. Something in her face crumbles, and strange gasps and cries tumble out of her twisted mouth. Because she knows it's true. We're outcasts, aberrations. We're germs, and this world of purity has no place for us.

"My *damn* father!" I yell, staring up at the stars, my anger unbridling. "You should have let me turn! Instead of using me as your test mouse, you should have—"

"He didn't know, Gene!"

"He must have known! He found the formula for the Origin, he must have known its backstory." I look at Sissy, my chest heaving. "He knew. He knew we're food."

I see her wilt a little. She shivers, her eyes blinking faster. But then something happens. Resistance, insistence flash in her eyes. "He didn't know," she maintains in a low-pitched voice. "Not in the beginning, anyway, not all those years he was with us at the dome. The way he treated us, it was like we were special. Like we were the originals, and *they* were the anomalies."

She glances back in the direction of the laboratory. "I don't think he had an inkling until he returned to the Mission. Until he transcribed all those old documents. On to *Mission* paper, did you notice that? It was here, after he left the dome, only after he transcribed those documents, that he realized."

"How would you know what he thought—"

"*Never forget who you are.*" She looks me square in the eyes. "He'd never have said that if he thought we were . . ."

"Freaks?"

"That's not how I would put it."

"Well, you better get used to the idea. Because that's what we are." A film of tears, acidic, stings my eyes. It is all coming to me now. Maybe Sissy is right; maybe my father discovered the truth only after he returned to the Mission. I can only imagine the horror of his realization in the darkness and isolation of his laboratory. The truth so devastating, so repulsive, he had to remove himself altogether from the Mission, live alone like a hermit in the woods. Away from the foul, the diseased, the impure, away from the colony of *hepers*.

She brushes aside wet hair strands dangling into her eyes. "I don't feel that way. I don't feel like a freak at all."

Her words enrage me. I unleash on her. "Good for you, Sissy! Keep on trying to delude yourself! But you know what? Bad as this is, it gets worse. Because you and me? We're not just freaks, we're not just *hepers*. We're something more. Something worse. You might think we're this wonderful Origin. But you know what we are? We're a dirty bomb. We're a walking incubator of death and disease. The cure my father thought he discovered? He'd only rediscovered the lost formula for a deadly virus. We're not the cure, we're the *contagion*. We're not salvation, we're a scourge. That's what Ashley June was trying to tell me. We are the lethal bomb that will cause the extinction of all people."

Sissy's fingers, unclenched and half-submerged in the water, tremble by her side, rippling the lake's surface. Stars reflected in the lake, once perfectly mirrored dots, warp into dissolution.

I turn my face away from her, gaze at the lake, at the trees, the mountain peak, the silhouettes of distant cottages. "That's why he abandoned us. Why he flew off east. We became an abomination to him."

"Don't say that," she says. Slowly, she pushes her shoulders back. "He instructed us to fly east to meet up with him. He wanted to see us again. Don't you remember what Clair told us at the Mission? She said, *This is what your father wanted. For you to fly east. There are machinations at work you can't even begin to imagine, Gene. You and Sissy have to fly east.*"

"He said that only to get *us* away from *them*!" I laugh, a maniacal, bitter cackle. Now I understand the truth, the terrible, horrific truth. "If the Hunt really worked—if it actually brought us both out to the mountains—he now needed a plan that would entice us away. Far, far away." I slap at the water, see the cut in my hand vomiting out blood. "That way, if the bomb detonated, it'd be safely removed from the population. The precious, pure, original population—the dusker population."

Sissy trembles—whether it's from fear or the cold I don't know—her already-ashen face paling even more. "He wouldn't feel that kind of loyalty to the duskers. Not after—"

"It wasn't loyalty to *them*! It was loyalty to his own precious principles. Because my father was never about destruction, never about genocide. He was about salvation! Remember what the chief advisor said? That my father preached there was no higher purpose than to heal the sick, to purify the impure. That there was no calling more noble than to save the duskers? Except now there was nothing for my father to save, nothing to heal. Except himself. That's the brutal irony of it. He imagined himself a savior—until he realized he was holding not a cure but a dirty bomb. Which he had to hurl away as far as possible."

Sissy recoils, her face flinching. She is resisting, needlessly prolonging the inevitable.

Something warm snakes down my hand. Blood pouring out from the gash. "See this?" I say, holding my bloodstained palm to Sissy. "See this blood? It's a plague, Sissy. It's infection. It's death. It's disgusting! It's *abominable*!"

Sissy shakes her head, eyes wide. All fight is going out of her. Her strength is failing her now, and the wall of denial is collapsing all around her like a house of cards. Her eyes blink furiously, her legs buckling.

"Look at this blood in me, in you—"

She screams.

It is a long, agonizing wail that echoes off the mountains and ends only when she falls to her knees. Her head slumps against her chest. She starts quaking. Her sodden clothes wrapped tightly against her pale whittled frame, bunching in folds.

She's so different from the girl I first met at the dome. Gone is the mischievous light in her eyes, the square way she took me in, the warmth and strength emanating from her bronzed flesh. The boys constantly roving about her, her arms seemingly always around their shoulders, protecting, guiding. The way she smiled, eyes closed with sheer delight, head tilting back, sunlight splashing on her cheekbones. The way she sang. The way she kissed me. Her belief in loyalty, that it is the proof of love.

All of these qualities that charm me the most about her, that make my heart ache for her: they are nothing but the side effects of a once-extinct virus, by-products of a food experiment gone horribly awry.

I see none of those qualities now. Not on this blighted creature, her wet-black hair pressed against sallow cheeks and a wispy neck, bent over as if winded. Sapped of color, embossed cruelly into a canvas of mercury and silver.

She trembles; she quivers. She is on the verge, her body about to spasm uncontrollably, her eyes about to flood over with tears. My strong, brave Sissy. About to be broken at last.

Then something stirs in me. Something fundamental shifts, tectonic plates within. I speak. With a sudden and furious tenderness.

"Sissy."

She looks up at me. For a moment, she hesitates, as if unsure she's reading my face right, hearing my tone properly. And then I am wading toward her, and gently I lift her up, putting my arms around her.

Quiet again, only our chattering teeth breaking the silence. Then even that sound subsides as we draw tighter into each other, our faces pressing against each other for warmth. The moon lights up the whole lake, reflects off the snowcapped mountain peak. And now it is silent. Everything is still. Even our bodies have stopped shivering. The lake flattens out, becomes a mirror of the eternal skies above. We are alone in the whole wide world.

"What now?" Sissy whispers, her lips moving against my neck.

I pull her into me, hold her tightly.

"Let's go home," I say.

Sixty-five

HOME.

Home is not the empty cottages we walk past, nor the room where we take off our wet clothes and stand shivering before the fireplace. It is not the Mission still flush with food and drink and clothes.

Home is not the metropolis. Because we could make it our home. If we wanted to. If we wanted to turn, it'd be easy enough. Gather up the sun-caked crusts of their melted flesh, boil it down into a liquid, which we'd pour into an open wound, at night, once we got close enough to the metropolis. If we wanted to.

But Sissy doesn't want to.

"I am what I am," Sissy says. She pulls away slightly to look me in the eyes. Firelight dances in her irises. "I could never become them. Don't ask me to, Gene. I was born this way. I will die this way. I'm at home in my body."

I nod, pull the duvet tighter over our shoulders. The fireplace is full with flickering fronds. Shadows dance on the walls.

"And you?" she asks. "What about you?"

I pause. Not because of hesitation or indecisiveness. But only because I want to take in this moment, because it feels like something new is about to begin, that nothing will ever be the same.

"They lied to us," I say. "To the Mission elders, the villagers. For generations. Kept us from the truth because had we known, we'd all have chosen to turn to duskers. And if that happened, we'd have stopped propagating the heper species. And the only way to replenish the supply of hepers would have vanished. Forever." My voice hardens. "They fed us lies to feed themselves."

I lean forward, stare into the fire. "They killed everyone we care about. David. Epap. And Jacob. They killed my father, the man I knew him to be, anyway, the man I adored; that man they killed. How can I, how could I, possibly become one of *them*?"

Her hand reaches for mine under the duvet.

"They think of us as cattle," I say. "They think of us as far beneath them, worthless. But when I think about everyone we care about, I don't see that. I think about Epap, how he so selflessly gave himself trying to save us. Or Jacob, throwing himself out of the train before he turned. Or you, Sissy, running headlong into their midst of *millions* for David's sake."

A pained nostalgia flares in her glimmering eyes: She is remembering her boys, the years in the dome, the sunshine, the passing seasons, their shared life together. Their nights around the fire, the singing, the laughter. The tears.

"This is what we are," I say, and now my hand is clasping hers so tightly I think she might flinch. But she only squeezes back all the stronger. "We are human. We live life to the hilt. We laugh, we smile, we love, we get our hearts broken. We hold back nothing. We live glorious lives, Sissy. For each other. If these qualities are aberrations, mutations, well, so be it. I choose them over 'normal.' I choose them over the stale, colorless, selfish existence they live."

I turn to face her; the duvet slips off our shoulders, falls to the floor. Cold air slides around our bodies. But it doesn't matter. We have enough heat, just the two of us, together. I take her face in my hands, her beautiful, strong face that is a marvel to me. My vision goes hazy, and I blink away the tears, wanting nothing to blur my vision of her.

And the words, when I say them, are the purest, sweetest, truest, strongest words I have ever spoken.

"I choose you, Sissy. You're my home."

Sixty-six

W<small>E BURN THE</small> whole damn village down. We start with the cottages that store vats of oil and gasoline. After that, it's like a chain reaction, one wooden cottage catching fire after the next, combustible as a pile of tinder. Until the whole Mission is ablaze, sending up huge flames that lick the brightening sky.

We watch from the fortress wall. The enormous fire flings flickering light and shadow across the craggy face of the mountain. An easterly wind picks up, and I nod at Sissy. She straps herself into the hang glider she'd spent the previous day learning to fly. I follow suit, knapsacks dangling off a bar on each side of me, packed with as much food and essentials as we were able to squeeze into them. I check my pocket again, making sure that pushed securely into it is a piece of paper. I'd found it yesterday in the laboratory, among all the other papers. A letter. Creased with many folds, with my father's handwriting.

Ashes and embers fall on us like snow.

She looks at me, her eyes shining bright, her skin radiant.

"I'm ready," she says. We both are. We've done enough eating, drinking, and sleeping over the past few days to fuel us for the long haul.

I look beyond the fortress wall, to the dawn sky. I stare long and hard, the way my father did on this wall countless times. I think of his letter I'd found, now secured in my pocket, on paper so tattered and creased and small, Sissy and I had missed it for days. The letter was not addressed to me but to a mysterious person named "Tobias." But the letter spoke of me. *I would rather die than hurt him again.* My father's words about me, words I will never forget.

I imagine my father standing here not so long ago, all alone on these fortress walls, a broken man. Perhaps his eyes roamed one last time along the line of trees below, both wanting and fearing the sight of Sissy and me emerging from the forest, survivors of the Heper Hunt. And perhaps he had wept silent, lonely tears as he ran down the ramp and sailed off into the eastern skies on his hang glider.

How heavy my father's heart must have been. He had sacrificed everything: his wife, his daughter, and now, he believed, his son. And for nothing. The guilt, the disappointment, he carried it alone. I can see his heart breaking as he flew, the pieces breaking off like shards and falling. Until there was nothing left. I can see him undoing his straps. I can see him plummeting to the earth. I can see his hang glider, now unmanned and lighter, blown upward into the skies light as a feather. *I would rather die than hurt him again.*

"You're thinking of your father," Sissy says gently.

"I am."

She smiles, just a half smile. "Maybe."

"Maybe what?" I say softly.

"Maybe it's not what we think. Maybe he wasn't sending us afar to simply perish. Maybe . . ."

"Yes?"

"Maybe he just wanted to give us a new start. In the only place he knew we would be free. Far away. A new beginning." She stares eastward, and when she turns to look at me again her eyes are fresh and sparkling. "Benefit of the doubt," she says, smiling fully now.

Not long ago, not far from where we now stand, Clair had told me something about my father. I remember this now. It hadn't really registered at the time, but her words now resonate within. My father, she'd told me, after he'd returned to the Mission, would sometimes fly all the way to the metropolis. He did so in the hopes of catching a mere glimpse. Of me. *Even if it had to be from afar,* she'd said, *way up in the skies.*

For years, I had roamed the streets of the metropolis, gazing upward, hoping, with childish yearning, to catch sight of a remote-controlled plane. Hoping for some kind of message from my father. Anything. But, heartbroken, I'd given up after only a year or two. But my father *had* come. Only he was too late; by that time, except for occasional forays to the fruit orchard, I rarely went out in the daytime. He flew over the empty metropolis the same way I'd once walked its empty streets. Searching but not finding. I had given up too soon. And my father had come too late. We missed each other.

"A new beginning," I say. I stare at the horizon, brimming with the dawn's glow. "Yes. I'd like to think that."

She nods, her eyes clear and bright, her hair blowing in the wind. She makes a final adjustment on a strap. "Are you ready?"

I nod, my eyes damp. "I am. I really am ready now." My heart is thumping, pumping. Then, because I can't help myself, I untie my straps. Sissy's eyes widen with pleasant surprise as I walk up to her. We kiss long and hard, and when we finish we smile at each other, our foreheads still touching.

"East," she says.

I nod. "Follow the Nede River on the other side of the mountain."

We kiss one more time, softer this time. Then she is running along the fortress wall, kicking hard and fast. She leaps through the gap in the wall, and I watch as she expertly catches the current and soars securely upward. As she breaks eastward, her hand lifts up into the air for a second, her fist pumping.

I smile. One last time, I look at the Mission. Then I am running down the fortress, leaping through the gap, sailing through the skies. Within minutes, I've closed the distance between us. We'll hold this formation. For how long we don't know. All we know is that so long as the wind is behind us and our hang gliders hold together we'll keep flying east.

East. Toward that very spot where the sun is rising now, peeking over the distant horizon, radiating streams of orange and red and crimson. And should we find nothing, should we find no one, should the Nede River disappear, merging into the mythical sea, we will yet keep flying for as long as the wind continues to push us east. We will fly uncountable hundreds, even thousands, of miles, to the other side of the sea, to the other side of the earth where no dusker would ever dare to even imagine exists. And only then will we land.

And there we will make our home. We'll build from the ground up. From the two shall spring forth a civilization. Our children, and their children, and their children yet, until our people are more numerous than the stars in the sky, and the grains of sand in the desert. And our weaknesses we shall turn into strengths. Our abnormalities shall be hewn into battering rams. Our resistance to sunlight, our instinct to explore, our ability to swim, to love, our intelligence, our will to survive, our emotions, our loyalty. From these aberrations shall arise a people more dominant than the original species.

We will take what we have learned from them and make it ours. We will incorporate their technologies into our civilization time line, catalysts to our own human progress. Architecture, computers, weaponry, science, all inserted at the right junctures in our advance, seamlessly and organically woven into our history like it was our invention all along. We will take their vocabulary, their language, make it our own, make it subservient to us. To mock them, we will use the very same names of the nations and continents and seas on which they fashioned their lies about us.

And when, centuries later, millennia later, we have conquered every land and every continent and even the seas that flow between, when our population is great, we will come for them. We will come for them. We will find them, and they will be nothing to us. Nothing.

They, with their vulnerability to sunlight and aversion to long-distance travel, will still be penned in by the same provincial Vast. And we will pummel them. We will *pummel* them, they will wilt like candles in a blaze. We will drive them into the ground, scattering them into isolated pockets of the world where they will be holed in dark caves, forced to retreat into dark closets in shuttered rooms by day. Forced to retreat into mountain castles where they will learn what it is to be alone, to be isolated, to be an aberration. Until they are reduced to insignificant footnotes in the annals of not even history, but of folklore. All memory of them erased, they will be mocked in the pages of fiction, reduced to mere stock stereotypes, caricatured as pale and effete loners.

In front, flying smoothly, Sissy turns her head around, gives me a quick wave. I wave back. The dawn light is splashing all around us now, flaring off our hang gliders into overlapping kaleidoscopes of color. So many hues and tints, as if we have flown right into a firestorm of intersecting rainbows.

I unzip my jacket and take out a stack of papers. I release the pages one at a time, then all at once. They flutter in the wind like the manic flapping wings of an injured bird, the multitudes of silver crescent moons blinking and flickering. They drift downward, silently, almost peacefully, into the Nede River, where they will sink and disappear forever.

I think of the land we will make our home. We will not call it the Land of Milk and Honey, Fruit and Sunshine. That was my father's land, but this new land shall be mine and Sissy's. It will be a reversal of the world we now know. I gaze at the Nede beneath us, thin as a silver arrow pointing the way forward. It will be the last thing we see of this land.

The name of our new home will be the reversal of the Nede.

We shall call it Eden.

ACKNOWLEDGMENTS

My heartfelt gratitude to Rose Hilliard, my editor, for her wisdom and guidance in shaping each book of The Hunt trilogy. I am also indebted to Catherine Drayton, my agent, for her continued advocacy and counsel.

I would also like to thank my parents, for their support, and my two brothers, who inspire me to reach higher and farther. My sons, John and Chris, continue to surprise and astonish and bless me, and I am thankful and humbled to be their father. And most of all, my deepest thanks and love to Ching-Lee.